T0158167

CHILDREN
OF VALLEJO

Collected Stories of a Lifetime

C.W. SPOONER

iUniverse, Inc.
Bloomington

Children of Vallejo
Collected Stories of a Lifetime

iUniverse books may be ordered through booksellers or by contacting:

iUniverse
1663 Liberty Drive
Bloomington, IN 47403
www.iuniverse.com
1-800-Authors (1-800-288-4677)

ISBN: 978-1-4759-3800-5 (sc)
ISBN: 978-1-4759-3801-2 (ebk)

Library of Congress Control Number: 2012912545

Printed in the United States of America

iUniverse rev. date: 07/25/2012

CONTENTS

BOOK 1

The best place at the best possible time . . .

BOOK 2

Sliding headfirst into adulthood . . .

For all the Children of Vallejo, especially those who grew up with me in Steffan Manor. Without you, there would be no stories to tell.

Also by the author:

'68—A Novel

VALLEJO REMEMBERED

Vallejo, California, sits at the north end of San Francisco Bay where the Napa River empties into the Carquinez Strait. For nearly all of its existence, Vallejo was a blue collar, lunch pail town, home to Mare Island Naval Shipyard, the first shipyard established on the West Coast. The city was founded in 1850 and the shipyard in 1854, but it doesn't matter which came first. They grew to be one and the same, their destinies inextricably linked. If you lived in Vallejo, it is likely you either worked on "the yard" or you made your living providing services to those who did.

During World War II, the ranks of civilian workers on the yard grew to more than forty-six thousand, and the work went on twenty-four hours a day, seven days a week. The workers who flocked to the government payroll were farmers fleeing the dust bowl states, blacks escaping poverty in the rural south, and people of every conceivable ethnic composition. Their overwhelming numbers put a strain on the local housing market and the federal government responded by building housing tracts that dotted the hills around the city. The tracts had names like Federal Terrace, Carquinez Heights and Chabot Terrace, and though they were called apartments, they looked for all the world like military barracks.

The people lived and worked together, and their children went to school and played together on the playgrounds and in the recreation centers. Kids grew up tough in the federal projects, tough and hungry to achieve. Many went on to be successful in business and politics, sports and the professions, but they never forgot where they came from. They never forgot what it was like to grow up in a hard place and fight to keep what was theirs. If a true melting pot existed in America, it was there in the tenements of federal housing.

Through it all, the shipyard prospered as one of the Navy's major repair depots for the Pacific Fleet, and it earned its stripes as a shipbuilding facility. More than five hundred naval vessels were built there, including the USS *California*, the only U.S. battleship built on the West Coast. On November 20, 1919, when the *California* slid down the shipway into the muddy Mare Island Strait, the brake lines could not hold and she continued across the channel and onto the mud flats on the city side. She would find herself settled in the mud once again, on December 7, 1941, at Pearl Harbor. But the *California* would rise to fight in battles all across the Pacific, a history followed with great pride by all those who touched her at Mare Island.

When ships put into Mare Island for repair, their crews headed for town and some well-deserved liberty. Waiting for them there was an amazing enterprise zone. Georgia Street, the main street of town, ran east from the waterfront, and the west end of Georgia and several adjacent streets became known as Lower Georgia. Here the sailors found a vast array of cafes and shops, bars and honky-tonks, flophouses and brothels, all eagerly waiting to serve them. Lower Georgia became notorious throughout the Pacific Fleet as a place where anything goes. The city fathers did not interfere with commerce in this city within a city. Better to have the sailors doing business on Lower Georgia than chasing their daughters in the decent neighborhoods.

World War II came to a close and the troops came home and went to school on the G.I. Bill. Before long, the Korean War began to dominate the news and it looked as if the shipyard would be kept busy indefinitely. The prosperity of the Eisenhower years arrived and the Cold War heated up, giving the shipyard yet another boost. Mare Island built a series of nuclear submarines—seventeen in all—and sent them out to keep an eye on those pesky Soviets.

The city grew to the east, beyond Highway 40, which soon became Interstate 80. New housing tracts popped up everywhere and the shipyard workers began to buy the new two- and three-bedroom homes and move out of government housing. There was one catch: those leaving the barracks/apartments were white and those staying behind were, for the most part, black. Redlining wasn't invented in Vallejo, but it certainly flourished there. And so the former melting pot morphed into a ghetto and racial tensions at times reached the breaking point.

That was Vallejo during and after World War II. But all things considered, it was a good place to grow up. The city hummed to the rhythm of the shipyard, and every kid knew when the five o'clock whistle blew it was time to head home for dinner. The playgrounds and parks and gyms were busy with whatever sport was in season. There were miles of shoreline—from Southampton Bay, to the Carquinez Strait, and up the Napa River—to be fished for striped bass, sturgeon, and the lowly flounder. The hills to the north and east were there for hiking or hunting ground squirrels and jackrabbits, and there were a half-dozen abandoned mines to be explored—if you dared.

And if none of that was appealing, well, you could always invent your own adventure. Not a difficult task for the Children of Vallejo.

BOOK 1

The best place at the best possible time . . .

THE GOOD SAILOR

Nicholas Shane was scared, as scared as a four year-old could be. He clung tightly to his big brother Richie's leg, knowing that in a moment, Richie would finish his conversation with the teacher and Nick would be left alone in this place called nursery school.

Nick had pleaded with his father, Nicholas Shane, Sr., not to make him go. His father had explained that there was nobody at home to take care of him during the day and that nursery school was the only option.

Little Nick wanted things to be as they were before, at home playing with his toys or with one of his neighborhood friends, his mother in the kitchen making French toast or some other favorite treat. But Nick's mother Lucille was still recovering from what the adults called a stroke, and it might be months before she could come home from the convalescent hospital. Even then, there was doubt that she could take care of Nick.

Nick pleaded with his father right up to the point when Nick Sr. invoked the Good Sailor. Big Nick had served twenty years in the Navy, beginning his service during World War I. It was what he referred to as a "kid's cruise." He loved to regale friends and family with stories of his adventures in ports of call such as Singapore, Shanghai, and Vladivostok. Little Nick idolized his dad and never tired of hearing the tall tales.

When Nick Sr. wanted to teach his son one of the important lessons of life, he did so through the example of the Good Sailor.

And so Nick learned that a Good Sailor never lies. He can always be trusted to keep his word. He is hard-working, brave, and loyal to his friends. But the one Nick heard nearly every evening when it was time to pick up his toys was that a Good Sailor always cleans up his own mess. Little Nick wanted nothing more than to please his father by being a Good Sailor.

When his father told him that a Good Sailor always does his duty, and that Nick's duty was to help the family by going to nursery school, he knew the argument was over. He would have to make the best of it.

The nursery school was housed in a small building located adjacent to the grounds of Curry Elementary and Franklin Junior High schools. Sponsored by the school district, the program was a combination of day care and pre-school, and it was a godsend to the Shane family. Nick Sr. had to work long, hard days at Mare Island Naval Shipyard. Richie and their older sister Ella had to be in school and the family couldn't afford private day care. Richie was in the eighth grade at Franklin, and so his assigned duty was to drop Nick off in the morning and pick him up after school. And now, here was Nick, hanging on to his brother's leg for dear life.

"Okay, Nickie, you're all set. Enjoy your first day of school." Nick looked up to see Richie grinning at him, enjoying Nick's anxiety way too much. He wished that it was his sister Ella dropping him off. At least she wouldn't be taunting him with that silly grin. He choked back the tears that tried to come. He wouldn't give Richie the satisfaction, and he'd find a way to get even some day. His brother pulled away from his grasp and was gone.

"We still have a few minutes before I call everyone in, Nickie. Would you like to go outside on the playground?" Mrs. Benton seemed nice enough. Maybe this would be okay after all.

Nick went out onto the small, fenced yard that served as the playground. There he saw a swing set, some monkey bars, a jungle gym, and a sandbox. Several of his classmates were busy letting off early morning steam. He found a seat on the edge of the sandbox near the jungle gym and glumly drew pictures in the sand with a small stick.

Across the yard, Nick could see a group of boys gathered together. They were listening intently to another boy who appeared to be their leader. He was a head taller and heavier than any of the boys in the group. Abruptly the leader took off at a gallop across the yard and the other boys fell in behind him like a posse.

Nick glanced around the yard and wondered how long it would be until the teacher called them in. Suddenly he felt a blow to the left side of his body and found himself sprawling in the sand, flat on his back.

"Hey, stay out of the way, dummy!" The leader of the posse stood over him, the rest of the group gathered around, grinning down at him.

"I . . . I wasn't in your way, I was just . . ." Nick tried to respond but ended up stammering. He began to scramble to his feet.

"Oh yeah? Wanna make something of it?" The large boy stepped forward and pushed Nick back to the ground.

Just then, another boy stepped into the group between Nick and his tormentor. He was smaller than the posse leader and his skin was the color of dark chocolate. "Leave him alone, John. He's not doin' anything to you."

Nick was surprised to see the larger boy take a step back. "Yeah, well what's it to you?"

"Nothing," the dark boy replied. "Just leave him alone cause I said."

The boy named John sized up the situation quickly. "Come on, let's go," he said to his gang, and they galloped off across the playground.

The dark skinned boy turned and helped Nick up, brushing the sand from his clothes. "Don't worry, he'll leave you alone now. John thinks he's tough, but he's afraid of me. My name's Chester. What's yours?"

"I'm Nick," he replied.

Chester barely paused before continuing his monologue. "Is this your first day? It's okay here, you're gonna like it, and Mrs. Benton is okay too . . ."

Mrs. Benton came to the door and called them in. They sat on the floor in a circle and the teacher told them about the activities planned for that day. Nick found a place in the circle next to Chester. He was going to stay close to his protector. There were about twenty kids, boys and girls, all about Nick's age. Chester and his sister Lena were the only black children.

All through the day, Nick and Chester stayed together, in the classroom and on the playground. When it came time to spread their blankets and take a rest, they plopped down next to each other, whispering and giggling until Mrs. Benton hushed them. And Chester was right: the boy named John never bothered Nick again.

Years later, Nick would think about that day and wonder what clicked between him and Chester. On the surface, they were as different as two kids could be: one white and blue-eyed with straight brown hair, and one black and brown-eyed with short curly black hair. Their differences didn't seem to register. From that day forward, they were fast friends.

Nick's father noticed the difference immediately. There were no tears in the morning, no foot dragging while getting ready for school. In fact, it seemed that Nick couldn't wait to get there. And when he came home at night, it was with a never-ending stream of stories that all began the same way: "Chester 'n me . . ." Big Nick thought for a time that Chester was one of those imaginary friends that kids make up as a defense. But his son's enthusiasm was real and undeniable.

Spring came to Vallejo in 1947, just as it did every year, with a mix of warm sunshine and occasional showers. The wildflowers bloomed in the vacant lots and the leaves came out on the trees. Nicholas Shane, Sr., took his usual delivery of ten yards of steer manure, which he promptly spread over his garden plot that covered most of the backyard. Come Easter weekend, he would plant the first section of his vegetable garden.

All of this came under the heading of annual events. But there was something different about this particular spring. Lucille Shane had made remarkable progress. Where the doctors once told Nick Sr. that she may never walk again, at least not unassisted, they now marveled at her progress. It seemed she would make a near-complete recovery. Lucille Shane was coming home.

It was a warm May afternoon on the playground, and Nick, Chester and some other boys were playing a spirited game of tag on the jungle gym. The rule was that you could not touch the ground.

Something drew Nick's attention to the street adjacent to the schoolyard. He saw a shiny black Buick sedan pull up to the curb. It looked like his Uncle Max's car. The front passenger-side door opened and his father stepped out onto the sidewalk. Nick Sr. opened the rear door and Nick could see into the back seat.

And then, he was running as hard as he could, across the playground and into the school room, then out the front door and onto the sidewalk, and finally to his uncle's car parked at the curb. He stood for a moment and stared at his mother, sitting in back seat of the car. He went to her quickly and carefully put his arms around her neck, afraid that he might hurt her. She held him close, his head tucked under her chin, and stroked his hair gently, saying his name over and over again.

"Nick, are you okay?" It was Chester's voice. He had followed his friend to see what was going on.

Nick turned and smiled at Chester. "Yeah, I'm fine. Chester, this is my Mom. And this is my Dad. Mom and Dad, this is my best friend Chester."

Nick's parents glanced at each other and then said a polite hello to Chester. But Nick wasn't finished.

"Mom, Dad, can Chester come over to the house to play?"

His parents exchanged glances again, and mumbled together about lots to do, and they would see, maybe later. Just then, a thin black woman stepped into their circle at the curb. It was Chester's mother, come to take her children home.

"Chester, you come with me now. Excuse me folks, pardon me." She took Chester by the hand and led him away.

Nick finished the school term in June and looked forward to being at home with his mother, doing all the things he loved to do. He would start kindergarten at Steffan Manor School that fall, just a block away from home. Chester lived across town and would attend another neighborhood school. Eventually, the boys lost touch with one another.

Chester, however, would never be forgotten in the Shane family. He quickly became part of family legend. Friends and family would come to call and before long, Nick Sr. or Lucille would launch into the story about little Nick and the colored boy. How Nick thought it was perfectly acceptable that Chester was his best friend, and even invited him over to their home to play.

The adults would laugh loudly and pat Nick on the head. How cute and funny it was that Nick didn't know any better! When they thought Nick wasn't listening, they would say other things. How the colored people didn't know their place anymore. How it was bad enough that they were in the schools, now they wanted to live in white neighborhoods. They said other things too: that black people were lazy and violent, and that they could not be trusted.

Nick heard all this, but he didn't believe it. He knew his friend Chester, and Chester wasn't like that. Chester was a Good Sailor.

Suitcase Girl

C laire sat at the top of the grassy hill, her legs straddling the worn piece of cardboard, her heels dug securely into the ground to hold her back. She took a deep breath and lifted her feet onto the cardboard and now she was sliding down the hill, gaining speed every second, laughing excitedly as she hit top speed heading for the terrace at the bottom of the grade. There was no graceful way to dismount at the bottom of the hill; the cardboard simply hit the terrace and stopped, sending Claire tumbling into the grass. She bounced up and retrieved her magic carpet, quickly moving out of the way of the next slider who was now flying down the hill. And then she was running, scrambling, climbing back to the top of the hill to do it over again.

As she neared the top of the hill, Claire looked up to check the kitchen window of the apartment. Sure enough, her mother was there in the window, watching over her and her friends as they whirled in a continuous stream, up and down the hill. Each time she looked and saw her mother there, a contented little smile crossed her face. There was nothing better than knowing she was there, watching and caring, beaming love to her daughter.

Claire loved the hills around Carquinez Heights where she and her friends could roam free and invent games to fill the long, sunny days. When the rains came in January and February, followed by the warm California sun, the hills would burst into a bright green as the lush, sweet grass began to grow. Then the dry months would follow and the grass would begin to fade to a light brown—California gold

bedroom . . . and the bathroom . . . see, it's nice and big . . . and two more bedrooms down the hall." Vince could barely contain his excitement. Meanwhile, Claire was swinging in and out of the framing, thoroughly enjoying the tour.

"What do you think, Claire? Can you picture this as your bedroom?" Vince smiled at her, waiting for her reaction.

She had been to a furniture store once with her mother and she remembered a display of bedroom furniture, all in white and pink, with beautiful lamps and pictures on the wall. She allowed herself to picture the framed room with all that grand furniture carefully placed inside and the thought was too much to bear. Claire knew if she looked at her father at that moment she would burst into tears. She turned away and ran down the hall and through the kitchen, out where the future sliding doors and patio would be.

"It's wonderful," she shouted over her shoulder as she ran. She went to the stake at the far end of the property and began to pace the length of the lot, north to Georgia Street, and then east to the stake at the far end. She lost count, not because there were too many paces, but because she was praying and it was hard to pray and count at the same time. When she rejoined her parents in the garage area, they were busy with a piece of paper, her father writing down numbers and making quick calculations.

"Fran, I think we can do it. I really do!"

Claire knew what her father's words meant and she turned away quickly again and blinked back the tears. Her prayers had been answered before, but never so quickly. She could allow herself to believe it now: one day soon this would be their home.

The sun was setting beyond the hills of the city as they headed west, back toward Carquinez Heights. It had been a long day and Claire was very tired. Her eyes closed several times and her head nodded heavily on her slight shoulders. Fran saw this and put her arm around her daughter, pulling her close so that she could nap until they reached home.

Claire snuggled in and felt the warmth of her mother's body and the wonderful smell of her bath powder. She could not remember a moment in her life when she felt so safe and so loved. She relaxed against her mother's side and, just before her eyes closed again, she thought of the shelves her father planned for the garage. Claire would pack her things one more time. After that, maybe there would be a place on the new shelves for her suitcase.

FOGHORNS

T he boy was used to waking up to the sound of foghorns. There was the high-pitched *Screee,* and the baritone *BEE-oh.* It was amazing how the sound carried from way out on the bay, but he guessed that was the point. Some people said they were lonely sounds, but he never thought of them that way.

He pictured a Coast Guard ensign, stationed in the lighthouse at the entrance to the Mare Island Strait, bundled up in his pea coat and watch cap, binoculars around his neck, checking the visibility and deciding when to turn on the foghorns. He pictured a harbor pilot guiding a Navy ship through San Pablo Bay, on its way to Mare Island; or a merchant vessel loaded with sugar cane, headed for the C&H refinery at Crockett. The pilot would listen for the foghorns and direct the helmsman to turn one way or the other, away from danger. He pictured himself as that ensign or that pilot, guiding the great ships home.

The *Scree* and the *BEE-oh* weren't lonely sounds at all, because someone was out there standing watch. They made the boy feel safe.

HEROES

The house had been vacuumed, dusted, scrubbed, and polished like never before, at least not in Nick's memory. Normally his mother put very little energy into housekeeping, but this week Lucille Shane was on a mission.

Nick tried to keep a low profile and not be drawn into his mother's wake, but there was no place to hide. He had been assigned specific duties in his room, plus scrubbing and polishing chores elsewhere. He was beginning to hate the smell of Old Dutch Cleanser and Johnson's Furniture Polish.

All of this activity stemmed from the fact that his Uncle John was coming to visit. His father's younger brother had never been to their home in Vallejo, California. In fact, the brothers hadn't seen or spoken to one another in nearly a decade. Recently there had been an exchange of letters, then a tentative phone call. And now Uncle John would be coming to call for Sunday dinner.

John Shane had followed his older brother into the Navy and had decided to make a career of it. In 1949, with World War II over, the Navy wasn't a bad place to be. Now his ship was in port in San Francisco undergoing repairs. It was the perfect opportunity for the brothers to put their differences behind them.

Nick's mother was determined that everything would be perfect. The house would be in order and she would prepare a Sunday feast that John would never forget. She shopped at the commissary on Mare Island Naval Shipyard and purchased a nice lean sirloin tip roast. She would serve it with oven-roasted potatoes and vegetables picked fresh from their garden, including Nick Sr.'s prized sweet corn. To top it off, there would be German chocolate cake for dessert.

Lucille picked out the clothes that Nick and his older brother Richie would wear, and she made sure they were clean and pressed. Now as Sunday approached, she flew through the house running down a mental checklist. Had anything been overlooked? If so, she would smoke it out and make sure it was fixed.

Sunday morning came and Nick could feel the tension in the air. Uncle John would arrive from San Francisco on a Greyhound bus around 2:00 PM. Nick Sr. would take the local transit bus downtown to the station to meet him. After a stop at the Towne House for a short beer, they would catch the bus back to Steffan Manor. Dinner was planned for 4:00 PM.

Nick sat on the couch in the front room, trying to be inconspicuous lest he get roped into last minute chores. Just then his father emerged from the bedroom wearing his best sport coat and slacks. Nick was used to seeing his father in work clothes, heavy tan pants and shirts with labels that read *Big Ben Davis*. When his father dressed in a jacket and slacks, it was a serious occasion.

"Oh, Daddy, don't you look nice?" Lucille approached her husband and straightened the lapel on his jacket, even though it was perfectly straight. Nick didn't often see his mom flirt with his dad. He was a little embarrassed.

"Okay, I'm gonna take off. The bus will be here soon." Nick could tell his father was nervous.

"Just be careful, okay?" There was concern in Lucille's voice.

"Careful? What the hell, Lou? I'm just going to pick him up at the bus station." Nick Sr. was a little annoyed.

"Okay, Daddy, you know what I mean. Just be careful."

"Oh, all right."

"We'll look for you around 4:00. Do you have your watch?"

Nick's father took the watch that hung from a gold chain out of his pocket and checked the time against the clock on the bookcase. He gave Lucille a peck on the lips and headed for the bus stop at the corner of Russell and Buss streets, across from their house.

For a fleeting moment, Nick felt a tingle of excitement over his uncle's visit. It passed quickly. There wasn't much he could do now except hang around the house until it was time to take his bath and get dressed. He would take a cue from Richie and hang out in his room.

Nick was seven years old that summer, old enough to exhibit some vanity when the occasion called for it. He took a look in the bathroom mirror and found himself to be quite the handsome lad, wearing the clothes his mother had laid out for him, his hair plastered down with a generous quantity of Wildroot Cream Oil. He walked out into the living room and saw that it was nearly 4:00 PM. In the kitchen, his mother was taking the roast out of the oven. It could stand for few minutes before being carved. The table was set and there were just a few last minute things to do when John and Nick Sr. arrived.

Nick was looking out the front window when the bus arrived at their corner. He felt that twinge of excitement again, but it passed when the bus left the corner and nobody got off. He wandered back to the kitchen to tell his mom.

"They weren't on the bus, Mom. Nobody got off."

"It's okay, Nickie. I'm sure they'll be on the next one."

Lucille was a little concerned. She wasn't sure when the next bus was scheduled on a Sunday. Her concern grew as time passed and the men had still not arrived. Around 5:00 PM, she thought about calling the Towne House, but she knew her husband and she knew that would be the wrong thing to do. At 6:00 PM, she was doing her best to preserve the dinner she had prepared, covering dishes in aluminum foil, growing more anxious as the time passed.

"Mom, I'm starving. When are we going to eat?" Her son Richie was losing his patience.

"Yeah, Mom, me too." For once, Nick agreed with his older brother.

At 6:45 PM, she gave in to the pleadings from her sons. She prepared plates of food for them, all but the special sweet corn, which she was waiting to boil at the last instant. They ate quietly and quickly. They could see the strain on their mother's face and they knew better than to ask questions.

When they finished eating, Richie asked if he could go over to a friend's house. Lucille thought for a moment, and then said yes, as long as he was prepared for a phone call telling him to come home and meet his uncle.

Nick thought about asking for a piece of cake, but he held his tongue. His mother was blinking back tears now, and he felt awful for her. So bad he even cleared his dishes and put them on the counter in the kitchen.

Lucille and Nick were sitting in the front room, half-listening to the radio, when the Yellow Cab pulled up in front of the house. It was after 8:30 PM and growing dark outside. They looked at each other, then back to the street, surprised at the sight of a taxi in their neighborhood. The lights came on inside the cab and combined with the lighted sign on the roof to cast a yellow glow on their front lawn.

"Nick, stay here. Don't come outside!" His mother was emphatic. She opened the front door and went out onto the porch. Nick stood at the screen door, trying to stay out of sight. Something made him want to hide.

The rear door of the vehicle opened and Nick could see his father inside. Nick Sr. called to his wife who went to the cab and began to speak to him. He couldn't hear their conversation above the engine noise and the strange voice crackling over the two-way radio. Nick saw that the neighbors across the street had come out onto their porch to see what the commotion was about.

Nick saw his mother take his father's wallet and hand some bills to the driver. Then she took Nick Sr.'s arm and began to help him out of the cab. He made it to his feet and threw one arm over Lucille's shoulder. They had started across the front lawn, the taxi still sitting at the curb, when his father lost his balance and tumbled onto the grass, taking Lucille with him. She got to her feet quickly, but Nick Sr. rolled over on the grass, laughing out loud. The cab driver came over then to lend a hand, and together, he and Lucille helped his father up the steps and into the house.

More neighbors were coming out of their houses, unable to turn away from the spectacle. He pressed back against the wall of the living room, trying hard to stay out of sight. The smell of alcohol was thick around his father as they brought him into the house. They got him into his chair at the head of the dining room table and the cabbie took his leave to loud "thank-you's" from Nick Sr.

"Daddy, what happened? I was worried sick." Lucille fussed around her husband, dabbing at the grass stains on his pants with a napkin.

"What happened? What happened? What do you think happened, Lou?" Nick could hear the anger in his father's voice. "It was the same old shit. The same crap I've heard from him for years. How I left the family and left the farm and everybody else had to work their ass off. How it broke my old man's heart. As if that cold sonofabitch had a heart. He never showed it to me, that's for damn sure."

"But, Daddy, I thought you two were going to get past all that."

"Like hell! Not with that little bastard John. He wouldn't quit, Lou. I told him to quit, but he wouldn't quit. Same old shit, all over again."

"But what happened? Where is John?"

"What happened is I popped him. Right in his fat mouth. Knocked him on his ass. Then Pete Bennett stepped in. He put me in a cab and he had some guys take John back to the Greyhound station. That sonofabitch'll be on his ship in about an hour. That's where he belongs. He's the Navy's problem now."

"Oh, Daddy, no. And I worked so hard all week to make this special dinner . . ." Her voice tailed off, as though she knew immediately she had said the wrong thing. It was dead quiet for a minute, like the calm in the eye of a hurricane.

"Special dinner, eh? Special dinner? And just where is this special dinner?"

"Daddy, the kids were hungry. I finally had to give them their dinner. It was nearly seven o'clock."

"So, you couldn't wait to carve that damn roast. Couldn't wait! A man works hard all week and his family can't wait to sit down to Sunday dinner. Now that's a fine piece of work."

"I can fix you a plate in a minute, Daddy. I'll heat it up for you. It's a fine roast, it really is." Lucille started for the kitchen, but Nick Sr. grabbed her wrist in his iron grip.

"Don't walk away from me when I'm talking to you. I don't want any of your damn roast."

"Daddy, that hurts! That's my bad arm, please . . . let go." Since recovering from a stroke, Lucille had always favored her right arm.

"You think that hurts, well it can get worse." Nick Sr.'s voice was hard and bitter.

"Ow, Daddy, please stop!"

With that, Nick couldn't take it anymore. He bolted around the corner into the dining room and charged his father sitting at the table. Swinging his fists like clubs, he pounded on his father's shoulder. "Stop it! Stop it! You're hurting her!"

Suddenly, Nick realized what he had done. He staggered back a few steps and stared in shock at his parents, who stared back at him in disbelief. Then he spun around and ran to the hall and into his bedroom, throwing himself on the bed, his face buried in the pillow.

The house was quiet for a minute, and then his father walked into Nick's room and sat down on the edge of the bed. He began to rub Nick's shoulders with his powerful hands.

"Son, I'm sorry. I'm sorry, okay? Things got out of hand."

For a moment, Nick was relieved. Then the smell of booze overwhelmed his senses and he was furious with his father all over again.

"Leave me alone," he cried. "You hurt my mom!" He swung his left arm and swatted his father's hands away.

Nick Sr. sat up straight on the bed and said nothing for several seconds. Finally he said, "Okay, if that's the way you want it." With that he rose and slowly left the room.

Nick stayed in his room, crying hot tears into his pillow. He was too young to offer understanding, or quickly forgive what seemed unforgivable. Years later, when he had the responsibility of being someone's hero—and failed just as miserably as his father had failed that night—he would come to see things in a different light. Heroes are human, and we all fail at one time or another. By then, it was too late to make amends. All Nick knew on that warm summer evening was that his life had changed. For Nick and his father, things would never be the same.

CELEBRATION

R ich sat in the car parked at the curb about a half block from the McGinnis's house. Both sides of the street were jammed with parked cars and the lights blazed inside the McGinnis place. Rich rolled down the window to let in the cold December air. He lit a cigarette and as he did, he could hear the steady murmur of voices raised in conversation and the occasional burst of laughter. *God, how can they laugh at a time like this?* It was way out there beyond his ability to understand.

The scene at the funeral home had been brutal. He'd paid his respects to Buster's parents—Daddy Mac and Momma Mac as everyone called them—plus all the aunts, uncles and cousins. He put it off as long as he could, but finally he went to the front of the room where the bronze-colored coffin sat on a raised pedestal.

Oh sweet Jesus! He nearly shouted it out loud. *What have they done to you? It doesn't even look like you. Oh God—.* He staggered slightly, as though hit with a blow to the chest. The only thing he recognized for sure was the Marine uniform. Rich stood there fighting for control, his best friend laid out in the open coffin before him.

That was bad enough, but now this! These crazy Irish are having a party!

He had to go in, he knew that. Momma Mac had made him promise that he'd stop by. He crushed the butt of his cigarette in the ashtray, jerked the rearview mirror around to straighten his tie, and braced himself for what was ahead. He slammed the car door and stood in the street for a minute, straightening his dress blue

Air Force uniform. If only he had convinced Buster to join the Air Force instead of the Marines, maybe this wouldn't have happened. But no, Branford "Buster" McGinnis had to be a Marine, to show that he was still the toughest kid on the block.

They had enlisted at the same time and then headed in different directions for basic training, Rich to Parks A.F.B. near Dublin, and Buster to Camp Pendleton near San Diego. This Christmas season would be their first time back home together. Buster was driving through the night, hurrying to get home, when his car left the highway and rolled a half dozen times. He was pronounced dead at the scene. It was an accident, a single-car accident. Case closed. That's all the explanation they would ever get. After all the crazy, reckless, stupid stunts they'd pulled—and survived—while growing up, he simply rolled his car. Rich felt the anger rising from deep in his gut. He pushed it down, jammed his uniform cap on his head and headed up the block toward the growing commotion.

He stood on the porch for a minute, screwing up the courage to go in. He knew the door was unlocked. He'd never known the McGinnis family to lock their doors. Finally, he twisted the knob and pushed the door open. The noise inside hit him like a slap in the face. The small two-story house was packed with friends and family. The living room, the dining room, the kitchen, and even the staircase were crowded. A cloud of cigarette smoke hung in the air and he could see that the dining room table was loaded with food. Rich removed his cap and tucked it under his arm, wishing immediately that he'd left it in the car. Someone handed him a glass and he heard the ice cubes rattle brightly as he took a sip of the contents. He shook his head and blinked quickly as the Irish whiskey burned his throat.

Daddy Mac saw him and came to wrap him in a great bear hug. "Oh, Richie, bless you for coming, lad. We love you, Richie, and this will always be your home. Ya know that, doncha?" Rich knew he meant it. He'd always felt at home here, as though there was a second set of parents he could turn to. He mumbled something inane in response. He never knew the right thing to say in a situation like this. Then again, he'd never faced a situation like this one. Mercifully, Daddy Mac was pulled away to another group of friends coming through the front door.

Rich pushed through the crowd into the living room where he saw Mamma Mac sitting on the couch next to the Christmas tree, its red and green lights burning brightly. Next to her, holding her hand, was Marybeth Baker, Buster's girlfriend.

"Richie Shane, God love ya!" Momma Mac rose to embrace him. "Thank ya for comin', darlin.' It means so much to Daddy Mac and me."

Rich held her tight and found he couldn't speak. He thought of the hours he'd spent in this home, the meals and the lively conversation he'd shared around their table. He fought back the tears while Buster's mother patted his back gently. Then it was Marybeth's turn to hold him and comfort him. He knew it should be the other way around, but he couldn't help himself.

Marybeth stepped back and held him at arm's length. "Richie, let's go outside on the porch for a minute. I need some air." She spoke quickly to Momma Mac and then they pushed their way through the crowd to the front door and the porch. On the way, Rich could hear someone playing the upright piano that stood at the far end of the room near the kitchen, and a clear, sweet tenor voice singing about Jack Dugan, that wild colonial boy.

The porch was a blessing after the closeness of the house. They both took a deep, cleansing breath of the cool night air.

"Can you believe it, Richie? It's a party! I can't take too much more of it, even for Momma Mac."

"I know. I wasn't ready for it either. I guess it's their way." He looked down and saw the glass in her hand. She took a quick drink and he saw her shudder. He started to tell her to go easy, but who was he to tell Buster's girl what to do.

"At least the funeral home had some dignity." She stared at her glass and then took another quick drink.

They stood silently for a time, side by side, looking out across the street to the neighbors' houses, holiday lights strung around the eaves, Christmas trees displayed in front room windows.

"I loved him, Richie. That big Irish mug. I loved him like crazy."
Her voice caught in her throat and she started to cry.

"I know, Marybeth. So did I."

"I know you did . . . and he loved you too . . ." Her words came
in bursts now between the sobs. He turned her toward him and held
her close until the crying subsided. He handed her a clean white
handkerchief from his back pocket and she blew her nose loudly.
Even with a runny nose and red eyes, she was a pretty girl, with her
curly brown hair and deep blue eyes. She and Buster were a great
couple. "We'd better go back in, Richie. Can you check with me
later? I'm gonna need a ride home."

They opened the door to the noise and the smoke and were
pulled back into the party. Rich saw his friends Mike and Jerry, both
wearing their Army uniforms, and he pushed through the crowd to
say hello.

It wasn't long before they were pulled into a larger circle and
were retelling all the classic stories from their teenage years. Mike
and Jerry had several adventures to share and they did so with gusto.
The stories went on and the laughter rose to fill the room. Someone
in the crowd said they were lucky to survive their teens. He was
right. Fresh glasses were pressed into Rich's hand and soon he felt
a steady buzz coming on. He made a conscious decision to slow it
down. He had to get Marybeth and himself home safely.

Rich felt a tug at his sleeve. It was Momma Mac. "Richie, you
got to come take Marybeth home."

Rich said a quick goodbye to his friends and followed Momma
Mac to the front porch. Waiting for them there was a very drunk
Marybeth, trying her best to stand still while the porch seemed to
sway beneath her feet. They each took an arm and helped her down
the steps, then down the street to Rich's car.

"I'm sorry, Momma Mac . . . I'm sorry . . . I'll see you tomorrow,
okay . . . I'll stay with you tomorrow . . . I just have to go now . . . I
have to get some sleep."

"It's all right, darlin' girl, and yes, you'll be with me tomorrow."

It was a reminder to Rich that they still had to face the funeral
service and then the internment, all that in the day ahead. He closed

SANDLOT

B efore there was Little League, there was sandlot ball, played at the schools and playgrounds around town run by the recreation district. Jake Catado was our sandlot coach and we all loved him. He was a college student in his early twenties and you will never meet a guy with a sunnier attitude. With Jake, it was all about having fun. He'd just roll out the bats and balls and let us play.

We'd hang around the playground on summer days, playing ping pong or paddle tennis, or just goofing off. If enough guys showed up, we'd head out to the baseball field to play over-the-line, or work-ups, or three-flies-up, all just games we made up.

The best part was traveling across town to play some other school. We'd all pile into Jake's old Chevy sedan, about a dozen of us, and hit the road. It wouldn't be long before we'd be singing at the top of our lungs: "Ninety-nine Bottles of Beer on the Wall," or "John Jacob Jingleheimer Schmidt." We'd even sing on the field: *Good morning to you/We're all in our places/With sunshiny faces.* On the way home, we'd stop somewhere for Cokes. God, it was fun.

Then came Little League and our coaches didn't want us playing on the sandlots anymore. Now we had uniforms, and batting helmets, and rubber spikes, and official umpires, and parents, parents, parents. We were up to our eyeballs in parent involvement. You rode to the games with a knot in your stomach, afraid that you'd mess up, maybe disappoint your dad.

It made you wish you were back in Jake's old Chevy, singing "John Jacob Jingleheimer Schmidt."

MARYSVILLE

T he Shane family sat in the living room, gathered around the gleaming mahogany radio/phonograph console. Nick Sr. opened the lid that revealed the radio dial and the knobs that controlled the tuner, the bass, the treble, and the volume. He switched the radio on and found the station he was looking for. He removed a clean white handkerchief from his pocket and wiped away a smudged fingerprint that had been left on the polished wood. This was his pride and joy, his favorite piece of furniture in the entire household, the centerpiece of the living room where the family congregated to listen and enjoy being together. The high, polished cabinet contained the radio on the right-hand side and the phonograph turntable to the left. The speakers were concealed in the front by a beige cloth covering with a gold thread woven through. The lower half of the cabinet provided storage for records hidden behind doors that swung out to the left and right.

The Shanes knew several families in the neighborhood had acquired television sets, but they didn't see the point. After all, the best shows were all on radio, shows like *Burns and Allen*, *Amos 'n Andy*, *The Jack Benny Show*, and *Fibber McGee and Mollie*. Why waste good money on a television set? Now one of their favorites, *The Whistler*, was about to come on the air with its classic opening:

> *I am the Whistler*
> *And I know many things*
> *For I walk by night . . .*

The phone rang and Nick Sr. went into the dining room to take the call. Nick thought his father would be back quickly because he was notoriously a man of few words. But the conversation went on for several minutes. Finally, he came back into the room, walked to the radio and turned down the volume. A broad smile broke across his usually solemn face. "Son, you made the All Star team."

Nick was shocked. He sat there stunned while the rest of the family erupted in excited chatter. He was ten years old and in his second year of Little League play, and even though he'd had a good season, he didn't think the All Star team was a possibility. Nick considered calling his friends to see if they'd made the team as well, but he decided to wait a while. Sure enough, the phone began to ring, all of his buddies in the neighborhood checking in to confirm the news. Brent and Darin, both eleven year-olds, had made it, along with their friend Reid, a twelve year-old and the best pitcher in the league that year. Nick would have been perfectly happy if it had ended right there. He knew about the perks that came with being selected: the uniform, the All Star cap, the warm-up jacket with "Vallejo" in neat script across the front. If that was all there was to it, it would have been fine with Nick. But it was only the beginning.

Marysville was hot! Damn hot! "Hotter than the shores o' hell," as Nick's father would say. The heat seemed to bore in from all sides. Nick felt the coarse wool material of his uniform and wondered who had decided that wool was a good idea, and why couldn't they just play in their T-shirts? Just playing catch, he had broken a full sweat. It was a little past 5:00 PM and they were getting ready for a 6:00 o'clock start. Their opponent was the host team, the Marysville All Stars.

"Hey, Nick, look: it's Mr. Walton." Darin was standing next to Nick, playing catch with another teammate. He had recognized Ray Walton, a member of the Vallejo Umpires Association. Walton had been selected to umpire in this sectional tournament, a real honor. He was known by all the Vallejo players as a fine official, and probably the best balls-and-strikes man around. When you saw Ray

Walton putting on the gear, you knew you would have a good game. He stood about five feet six inches tall, but he was built like a rock, and he commanded respect from parents, coaches, and players alike. "I didn't know he was going to be here," Darin continued. Seeing a familiar, respected face took their minds off the heat for a minute or two.

They had breezed through the first round of tournament play with relative ease, winning all their games in Menlo Park. If they could do the same here in Marysville, it would mean a trip to San Bernardino for the Western Regional. The prior year, Vallejo's team had made it there and came within one win of advancing to Williamsport, Pennsylvania, for the Little League World Series. This year's team had big shoes to fill.

Nick had seen little playing time so far, just a couple of pinch-hit appearances and defensive innings when the games were safely in hand. He was perfectly happy to let his older teammates carry the load. He looked around at the gathering crowd, the grandstands beginning to fill and fans lining the low fences down the foul lines and around the outfield. His eyes searched the grandstand and located the group from Vallejo, perhaps fifty parents, family, and friends there to root them on.

Reid would be their starting pitcher tonight, which gave the Vallejo kids a boost in confidence. He had contributed strong innings in the Menlo Park tournament, earning a spot on the all-tournament team. But there, it was just a question of playing ball. Here, it was a matter of dealing with the intense heat as well. It was the curse of baseball teams from Vallejo, where the summer temperatures ranged from sixty-five to seventy-five degrees, to wind up playing in the Central Valley where the thermometer frequently registered triple digits in July. After infield practice and introductions, the Marysville team took the field. Nick saw Ray Walton trot out to third base, his assigned post for the night.

The game went quickly with neither team able to mount much offense. Reid was pitching another strong game, and after four innings the score was tied at one apiece. With two out in the top of the fifth, Brent lined a single up the middle. Darin was next up and the Marysville pitcher promptly walked him on four pitches. This brought their coach out to the mound and he waved in a left-handed pitcher who was warming up in the bullpen down the third base line. The crowd settled into a low-level buzz while the pitching change was made. It would be the last calm moment of the night.

Reid was the first hitter to face the new pitcher. He saw only two pitches, both out of the strike zone, before Ray Walton called time and headed out to the mound. Nick could see from the bench that he was demonstrating something to the pitcher, trying to explain an infraction of some sort. The Marysville coaches came out of the dugout and met Walton at the third base line. The conversation appeared to grow a little intense with the coaches obviously disagreeing with Walton. Now all four umpires joined the discussion, which went on for several minutes. Finally the conference broke up and the first base umpire stopped by the Vallejo dugout to explain the situation to the coaches.

"Walton says their kid is lifting his pivot foot off the rubber, walking into the pitch. His foot is supposed to maintain contact throughout the pivot. Says he'll have to call a balk if it happens again." Nick was close enough to overhear this conversation. The umpire continued: "Their coaches say he's been doing the same thing all year and nobody ever objected. They're not happy." With that, he headed back to first base.

Reid stepped back into the box and fouled off the next two pitches while attempting to bunt. With the count two-and-two, the pitcher wound up fired a fastball just off the plate. Nick saw Walton raise his hands and call out "balk!" He then waved Brent down to third base and Darin to second. With that, the Marysville coaches charged out of the dugout, heading for Walton, and the argument was on. The sound that came from the crowd surrounding the field was like a loud growl. Nick could see people pressed up against the screen of the backstop, their eyes blazing, their faces red, shouting in the direction of Ray Walton. He looked for his parents and his brother in the stands and found them among the Vallejo contingent, the only group of fans sitting quietly in a sea of screamers.

Just then he felt a hand on his shoulder. It was Coach Wheaton. "Nick, I want you to go down to the bullpen and get warmed up." Nick couldn't believe it. This hardly seemed like the ideal spot for a ten year-old pitcher, but he grabbed his glove and headed for the bullpen with Mickey, their backup catcher. He had only taken a few soft tosses when he saw that the game was getting back underway. He backed up to the bullpen mound and began to throw a little harder. And then he heard it, loud and clear, from the third base line: "Balk!" Walton had called it again and now he was waving Brent toward home plate with the go-ahead run, and bedlam was breaking loose all around the ballpark.

The Marysville coaches were back on the field, screaming at Walton. Others soon joined the fray and the infield area started to fill with angry adults. Mickey shouted something to him, but the noise from the crowd was so intense Nick couldn't hear. He ran in to be close to Mickey, afraid to be standing alone on the bullpen mound. Then they saw Coach Wheaton waving them into the dugout. Their coaches were gathering all the Vallejo players there until, hopefully, the storm passed. Nick saw police officers in dark navy blue uniforms appear at intervals along the fence and in the stands. Someone had obviously placed a call to report a situation potentially out of control.

Through it all, Ray Walton was standing strong. It was a balk, the run scored, and that was that. Finally, the field began to clear. The Marysville coaches made another pitching change and the unfortunate lefty headed for the dugout in tears. Nick couldn't help but feel bad for him. There are times when all pitchers are members of the same tribe; only another pitcher knows how you feel.

The side was promptly retired on a pop-up to short and the Vallejo team headed to the field for the bottom of the fifth inning. Coach Wheaton sent Nick back to the bullpen to warm up.

It may have been the intense heat, now beginning to subside, or the emotional tension that engulfed the ballpark. Or maybe, he was simply worn out. Whatever the reason, Reid seemed out of sync. He walked the first two batters he faced and he was clearly laboring. Coach Wheaton went to the mound for a brief conversation. Then he turned to the home plate umpire and signaled with his right hand. He was bringing Nick in to pitch.

Nick ran to the mound in a daze. All the infielders were gathered there, surrounding their coach. Wheaton handed him the ball and issued a short list of instructions, which Nick really didn't hear, something like *two on, no outs, just throw strikes.* Darin was standing there with the catcher's gear hanging loosely from his small frame. Normally, he would review the signs with his new pitcher, but he knew that wasn't necessary. Nick only knew one thing at age ten: reach back and throw the ball hard.

Years later, Nick would think back on that night and wish he could remember all the details, pitch by pitch, every play, every out. He thought once about trying to locate a scorebook that could help him reconstruct what happened next. The only thing he could remember was feeling like he was in a tunnel and it was just he and Darin and Darin's glove. And then, somehow, they were running for the dugout, the inning was over and they still had a one-run lead. He felt like a huge weight had fallen off his shoulders; he'd done his job. Hopefully, someone else could close out the sixth and final inning.

Vallejo went down 1-2-3 in the top of the sixth, and now they were heading out for Marysville's last at bat. Nick was surprised to find that he was heading back to mound. It seemed the coaches liked his work; it was his game to finish.

He took his warm-up pitches and settled back into that tunnel with Darin at the other end, aware of the noise all around him but with the volume turned down, muffled in some strange way. And again, all the details were absorbed into the hot summer air, as though they didn't really matter. He remembered throwing strike three to the final Marysville hitter, and he remembered celebrating with his teammates around the pitchers mound. The game was over, but for Nick, the night was just beginning.

The Vallejo coaches gathered the team around first base, waiting for the crowd to dissipate. They watched the Marysville police come onto the field and escort Ray Walton to his car in the parking lot, his progress tracked by shouts from the fans still milling around. Then they became aware of a commotion in the stands and the sound of a siren approaching the park. They could see the flashing lights of the vehicle as it entered the parking area. Nick saw his brother Rich hurry onto the field and approach the coaches for a quick, intense conversation, after which he came to collect Nick.

"Mom passed out in the stands," Rich said, his voice shaking a little. "They're taking her to the hospital. Dad is going with her. We're gonna follow in the car." He grabbed Nick's hand and led him quickly through the crowd. The ambulance was already heading out through the neighborhood and Rich had to drive hard to keep the flashing lights in sight. It was one of the scariest rides Nick could remember.

Nick and Rich sat in the emergency waiting room at the hospital for what seemed to Nick to be forever, Rich thumbing nervously through a wrinkled copy of Life magazine and Nick fidgeting in his chair, trying his best to be patient. Finally, Nick saw his father come through the broad swinging doors that led to the examining rooms. He was accompanied by a man in a white lab coat. Pinned to it was a nametag with a long, foreign-looking name that Nick couldn't pronounce. Following the name were the initials "MD." Rich and Nick jumped to their feet.

"She is going to be just fine," the doctor began. Nick could see the look of relief on his father's face. "She was somewhat dehydrated, plus the heat and the excitement. But that's all. We'll keep her here overnight to make sure, but I'm confident we can release her in the morning. You can go in and see her now."

They entered the examining room and Nick saw his mother, a mask over her nose and mouth, a tube running from her wrist to a bottle hung from a hook above the bed, and wires that connected her to a monitor pulsing in the background. Suddenly he wanted to cry and it was all he could do to fight back the tears. "It's okay, honey," she said, reaching out to take his hand. Rich and Nick stayed for a short while, until the hospital orderlies arrived to take their mother to her room.

It was very quiet in the car on the way back to the motel. The events of the day had drained them completely. The immediate fear was that Lucille Shane had suffered another stroke, a repeat of what had happened six years earlier. It was a great relief to know that it was something minor and that she would be back on her feet as soon as tomorrow. Nick looked at his sweaty wool uniform and realized he'd totally forgotten about the game.

The game on Saturday was scheduled for a 1:00 PM start, and if they thought it was hot the night before, it was nothing compared to the scorching mid-day sun. The team had gone out for a hearty breakfast and now, as they prepared for the game, one by one they were hurling that meal into a large trash can that had been pulled into their dugout. Collectively, they had no clue about how to handle the valley heat. Some said take little sips of water; some said don't drink water at all, it will make you throw up; some took salt tablets because it was supposed to help you retain fluids. The salt tablet kids seemed to be the sickest, but no one was immune.

This game against the Oroville All Stars came with a new set of controversy. The Oroville team included two boys who were nearly six feet tall and built like linebackers. There was a lot of grousing about who had checked their birth certificates, and how could twelve year-olds have evident facial hair, and so on.

Nick started at shortstop, evidently a reward for his pitching the night before. It was a big mistake. He was overmatched in the field and at the plate. One of the linebackers hit a shot directly at him that took one bounce and nearly took his head off. In fact, it only missed Nick's head because he ducked at the last instant. Brent pitched a decent game, but Vallejo lost gracefully, which meant the end of their season. There were no tears after the game. They'd had a very good run and they were glad to put Marysville in the rearview mirror. And yet, that was still not the end of it for Nick.

Dave Baronio, the *Times-Herald* sports columnist, had covered the tournament. In his article about the Friday night game, he wrote that Nick ". . . pitched as though he had ice water in his veins." This brought howls of laughter from Nick's friends and they called him "Icewater" for a short time. But the nickname didn't stick because they all knew the truth. Nick had been scared spit-less. It wasn't ice water in his veins; it was pure adrenaline.

Then of course there was the little headline on page three: "Baseball too much for Mom." It was a brief, tongue-in-cheek account of Lucille Shane's adventure. Nick saw the headline, but he just skimmed through the article. Thinking about it made him remember the scene in that examining room and the strong antiseptic smell of the hospital, sensations that would return like a bad dream whenever anyone mentioned Marysville.

In the days that followed their return to Vallejo, a steady stream of friends and family came to call at the Shane household, checking up on Lucille's condition. They would gather in the living room to hear that all was well and there were no lingering side effects. Of course, the entire story of the game and the umpiring controversy and Nick's pitching exploits had to be told over and over again.

Nick would sit on the floor in front of the Zenith console, playing 78-rpm records from his brother's collection. His father didn't mind, as long as he kept the volume down, background music for the lively conversation. Nick would play the Tommy Dorsey—Frank Sinatra recording of "Getting Sentimental Over You," or the King Cole Trio's "Sweet Lorraine," or Sinatra again with "Stardust." He would slip in Louis Armstrong's "It Takes Two to Tango," but his father would give him the look that said *keep it down, son, keep it down.*

When the conversation turned to the infamous Friday night game and people would say *why Nick, that's really something, way to go, good for you,* he would smile and say thank you. For as long as it lasted, it was fun to be known as the kid with ice water in his veins.

FRONT PAGE

I.

D arin was just finishing his bowl of Wheaties when he heard the urgent knocking on the front door. He knew it was Brent and Nick, but they were at least half an hour early and he couldn't imagine what the rush was all about. It was just another summer day with nothing much planned, maybe hanging out at the playground or playing some ball. No need to come banging on the door this early.

Darin opened the door to find his friends in a high state of agitation, tripping all over themselves to tell the story. *King is sick! He has a growth on his neck and it needs to be removed, and if it isn't, well, King could die. Gary and Lenny's parents can't afford to pay for the surgery and nobody knows what to do.* They went on, but that was the gist of the crisis.

King was a majestic collie owned by their friends Gary and Lenny Pace. Picture a larger, slightly heavier Lassie, without the meticulous grooming. Wherever Gary and Lenny went, King was there, calmly keeping an eye on the proceedings, occasionally barking his approval or a warning, a constant vigilant companion. Most of the boys in the neighborhood had pet dogs. But King was special, more like one of the guys than somebody's pet. And now King's life was in danger.

The answer came to Darin immediately. It was obvious what they needed to do. "How 'bout this—we'll mow lawns to raise money for the vet?"

Brent and Nick looked at Darin for a few seconds in silence, and then burst out in excited agreement. It was a brilliant idea, and why hadn't they thought of it, and who has mowers that we can use, and let's call all the guys and get organized. Off they went to the telephone to make the calls.

Darin Maneri was comfortable with this role among his friends. It often seemed to fall to him to be the idea man, the nominal leader of their band. It wasn't from imposing physical presence. On the contrary, Darin was small for a twelve year-old, shorter than the rest of the guys, and he'd had to listen his entire life to people telling him he was too little for this or that or the other. He reacted as could be expected, by setting out to prove them all wrong. Too small to play catcher? *Give me the damn gear!* Too small to bowl? *I'll carry the highest average around!* Too small for football? *Let's see you stop me!* And when a little leadership was required, Darin was ready for that too.

In less than an hour, all the guys were gathered in front of Darin's house. They'd never heard of a marketing plan, but they quickly came up with one that would cause professionals to nod in admiration and approval. They would break into two teams. Darin, Brent, Nick and Jamie would start on Jennings Street, where Darin lived, and work their way up over the hill. Reid, Gary, George and Jerry would start on Laurel Street, one block away. Lenny, who was younger and smaller, would shuttle back and forth between the two teams with King in tow, because when they knocked on a door and made their pitch, they wanted King sitting there, calm and dignified, tugging at the customer's heartstrings. Darin and Reid would be the spokesmen for their respective teams for obvious reasons. Reid, because he delivered papers in the neighborhood and knew nearly everyone who would open a door. Darin, because he was flat-out cute, with his curly brown hair, soulful brown eyes, and freckles sprinkled across his nose; their prospective customers would find him irresistible. Nobody had to say these things out loud. They were simply understood.

The last two items to be worked out were pricing and equipment. They decided, wisely as it turned out, to let the customers decide how much to pay for their services. Finally, they listed the tools they would need—mowers, rakes, clippers, brooms—and each team member volunteered to raid his father's tool shed. And then, having planned the work, it was time to work the plan.

Darin knew he should ask his mom for permission to use his father's tools, but he was pretty sure what the answer would be. His father was meticulous about his tools and kept them in a high state of repair and readiness. Darin made the decision: he would beg forgiveness later rather than ask permission now. His mom was busy with a sewing project, and so he opened the garage door and brought out the reel-style mower, the grass catcher, and the clippers. No power tools in those days, just honest manual labor.

The plan worked like a charm. Darin closed sales on the first two houses they called on, and Reid was having equal success over on Laurel Street. They went to work—mowing, raking, edging, and sweeping—and there was no question that the customers would get their money's worth. These were boys from working-class families who watched their fathers head off to work every morning, lunch pails in hand, to return home each night with the evidence of the day's labor imprinted on their hands and faces and their sweat-stained work clothes. These were men who found it necessary to change clothes in the garage at the end of the day so as not to track dirt into the house. These were fathers who taught by example the lesson of an honest day's work for a day's pay. Their sons would leave no blade of grass untended.

The people who answered the knock on the door, housewives mainly, were touched by what they saw—a scruffy bunch of kids asking for work to try and save their magnificent collie pal. At least one picked up the phone and called the local newspaper to report a surefire human-interest story in progress. Darin's team was finishing their third yard when a car pulled to the curb on the Jennings Street hill. A woman in a dark business suit and a man holding a large camera with a prominent flash attachment emerged from the car.

It was the first time any of them had been interviewed by a reporter and they let Darin do most of the talking. After all, the whole thing was his idea. The lady asked questions, seemed to listen intently to their answers, and took copious notes on her steno pad. She asked if they could round up everyone for a picture, and Lenny hustled off to Laurel Street to fetch Reid's team. Soon they were lined up on the lawn they had just finished, King in the middle, Lenny and Gary on either side, and the rest of them arranged as if it was a team picture. Flashbulbs popped, causing them to see white spots for a time. The reporter took all of their names, double-checked spelling, and then she and the photographer climbed back in the car and were gone.

They went back to work and when the five o'clock whistle blew on the shipyard, they finished the yards they were working on and headed back to Darin's house. They added up the take for the day and found they had about twenty dollars. It would take several days to raise the money they needed. They made plans to start early the next day and then headed for home, feeling good and tired.

Darin wiped down the clippers and the mower with an oily cloth, just as he'd seen his father do many times, leaving no trace of the day's work. He thought about getting the oilcan and giving a few squirts to mower, but decided against it. Best to let his father take care of that task. He put the tools back in the garage in their assigned places.

Darin was up early the next morning, dressed and ready for another day's work. His father was still in the kitchen finishing his breakfast when Darin sat down at the small table. The room was filled with the mingled aroma of bacon and eggs, toast and coffee, and he realized he was very hungry.

"Do you want some breakfast, honey?" His mom was busy at the stove.

"Yes, please." He glanced at his father who was intently reading the morning paper.

"Well, I see you made the front page," his father said, folding the paper and dropping it in front of Darin.

Darin stared at the paper and there above the fold was the picture from yesterday, four columns wide, with a bold headline that read "Dog's Best Friends." The caption below the picture listed all of their names, and below that, the reporter's byline—Helen Ratner—and the story of their quest to raise money for King's operation.

"Did you use my tools?" His father's voice was calm but firm.

"Yes, sir. The mower and the clippers."

It was quiet for a few seconds, then his father continued: "Make sure you clean them up before you put them away."

"Yes, sir."

His father got up to leave, and then he did an unusual thing. He put his rough hand on Darin's head and tousled his hair. He crossed the kitchen, kissed his wife goodbye and headed off to work. Darin sat quietly, slightly stunned. So he wasn't in trouble for using the tools without permission. And could it be his father was proud of him? Bacon and eggs were going to taste great this morning!

Everyone gathered at Darin's house, ready to go to work. That is all except Gary, Lenny, and King. The guys waited a few minutes, beginning to get a little impatient with the Pace brothers, when Darin's mom opened the door to say he had a phone call. Darin was back soon with some surprising news.

"That was Gary. People saw the article in the paper and they called and offered to pay for the vet. Several people. King's operation is covered. And we don't have to mow any more lawns."

They looked at each other in amazement, letting the outcome sink in. They discussed what to do with the money they had earned and decided to give it to Gary and Lenny for whatever King may need. Then there was nothing left to do but head home and put the tools away. They made plans to meet later at the school playground.

Darin's mother clipped the picture and the article from the *Times-Herald* and pasted them in a scrapbook she kept for him. It would be nice to remember those summer days when Darin and his friends set out to do something good, and succeeded beyond their expectations. The newsprint would turn yellow and slightly crinkled, but the memory remained fresh.

II.

The month of August is like a great big chocolate cake with creamy chocolate icing, cut into 31 delicious pieces, to be savored one sweet, decadent piece at a time. Or so it seemed to the boys growing up in Steffan Manor. When August rolled around, the competitive year was over: baseball was wrapped up for another season and fall sports at school would not kick in until September. August was a free month.

It was a time to go in search of adventure and it seemed the possibilities were endless. They could gather their fishing tackle and head for one of their favorite spots around the bay—Dillon's Point, or the Lighthouse, or up the Napa River to The Old Destroyer. Or, they could grab their air rifles and head up into the hills to hunt for ground squirrels or anything else that would be annoyed by the tiny copper BBs.

On this particular August day the plan was to hike out to Blue Rock Springs, then up over the ridge behind the city park, to explore the old abandoned cinnabar mines. They'd done it before and it was always great fun, well worth the five-mile hike in each direction.

They gathered at the school grounds for an early morning start. All the guys who had been part of the lawn-mowing venture were there, still flush from that victory. King had come through the surgery just fine and was recuperating nicely at home.

Two older boys had joined the group for the day, friends from the neighborhood that they admired and looked up to. Grant Richards and Mike Gibbs were high school freshmen who had grown up playing sandlot baseball with the younger boys. Then, when Little League came to town, the two of them had been part of an All Star team that fell one win short of going to Williamsport, Pennsylvania for the World Series. Beyond that shared experience, they couldn't have been more different. Mike was big and bulky and somewhat sullen, not much given to laughter and hijinks.

Grant, on the other hand, was everybody's hero, well built and handsome, with a killer smile that made the young girls' hearts flutter. He was a natural athlete and made every sport look easy. There was just something about Grant—a smooth, self-assured attitude—that drew everyone to him. Among the younger boys in Steffan Manor, Grant was The Man. Few of them knew that the self-assurance was an act, Grant's way of compensating for a troubled home life.

Darin was there too, though under protest. It was not his idea to go explore the old mines. His mother had thoroughly indoctrinated him with the dangers that existed in the abandoned caves and shafts. They could collapse at any moment. Rotted timbers could give way and fall with lethal force. Solid ground could crumble under your feet and send you falling to who-knows-what fate. Darin was along for the hike and the camaraderie, but he would not go into the mines. This, of course, caused much taunting and ridicule to be heaped on his head. The fact was that his fear of the mines was greater than his embarrassment from the goading directed his way.

They left the school pretty much on schedule, heading east on Georgia Street. Their route would take them to Maple Street, where they'd head north to Springs Road, then east again to the junction with Columbus Parkway, the winding, two-lane road that would take them up into the hills to Blue Rock Springs Park. It must have been a curious sight to motorists who passed them on the road: a ragtag troop of eleven kids with Army surplus canteens on their hips, carrying rucksacks or simple paper bags stuffed with sandwiches and snacks, sustenance for the day's activities. They strung out along the apron of the road with Grant and Mike in the lead. Behind them came the natural sub-groups of close friends: Darin and Nick and Brent; Reid and Jerry and Jamie; Gary and George, with Lenny doing his best to keep up.

Along the way, a debate broke out at the front of the column and was passed back through the ranks. Grant and Mike had gotten into a dispute over "who has the biggest." Some of the younger guys weren't sure exactly what that meant or why it mattered, but their wiser friends filled them in. The debate raged on, and finally, as they neared the park, it was decided that Grant and Mike would pick someone to act as judge. When they got to the first mine in the valley beyond the ridgeline, the judge would go into the mineshaft with the two of them, make an official inspection and render a binding decision. Brent, known to be an old soul for a twelve year-old, was chosen to be the judge. It was a popular choice. All of this added another level of anticipation to the journey.

As they reached the park, the thick morning overcast was beginning to burn away. The sun would come out and push the temperature toward eighty degrees and they would strip off their sweatshirts and tie them around their waists.

The venerable old park was built around an area known for its sulfur springs and a dense stand of giant blue gum trees. The air was thick with the mixed odors of sulfur and eucalyptus. On the west side of the road was an old wooden building that served as the clubhouse for the city golf course. The course spanned both sides of the road, and on the east side it skirted a large picnic area with tables and barbeque pits and a flat-roofed building that housed the restrooms. The parking lot was nearly full on this Friday morning and they could see groups of golfers at intervals along the fairways.

After a quick restroom break, they headed out through the picnic grounds, then along the edge of a fairway, and finally east over the ridge in back of the park. It was a good steep climb and then a quick decent into a valley that ran generally north and south, flanked by another steep ridge to the east. Along this valley, land now used only for grazing, was a series of abandoned mines, cut to the east or the west into the steep hills.

At the north end of the valley, they came to the first mine on their agenda. It was one that had intrigued them since they first explored the area, with a wide, clear entrance and a shaft that ran west into the ridge. Ten yards in, there was a deep pit about fifteen feet across; then the shaft continued as far back as they could see. They had debated spanning the pit with boards or timber of some sort, but had been unable to find material to do the job. Today, however, this mine would be the site of the contest judging where Brent would decide *who has the biggest.*

Grant, Mike, and Brent disappeared into the darkened entrance while the rest of the guys milled around and speculated on the outcome. It wasn't long before the trio emerged, Brent standing between the two older boys. Grant had his usual swagger and his high-voltage smile in place, and there was little doubt in anyone's mind: Grant had won—again. Then Brent grabbed Mike's hand and raised it as high as he could, followed by surprised gasps and whoops of laughter from the audience. Mike's dour expression never changed. Darin observed this turn of events and marveled at how Grant could make a defeat look like a victory; he may not have *the biggest*, but he was still The Man.

With the contest behind them, they set out to explore the other mines in the valley, spending just a few minutes at each site. Their real target was the mine at the south end, a spectacular wreck that was irresistible to any kid with a sense of adventure. When they finally arrived, they were not disappointed.

The entrance headed east into the hill and appeared to be just wide enough for a small ore car. After about thirty feet of narrow tunnel, it opened into a great central chamber. From there, shafts shot off in several directions. There was one that went up and to the left, and one that went down and left into a broad pit. The pit was filled with large chunks of rock and it appeared that there had been a collapse of some sort that opened the central space. High up to the right was an opening that brought air and light into the chamber; it was possible to scramble over a series of large boulders and climb out into the sunshine. Across the pit, the tightly cut tunnel continued back into the hill and there were remnants of the steel rails that had once carried cars filled with ore. No one had ever had the nerve to fully explore that tunnel. When they tried, they were overcome with the sensation that as they went in, the path behind them was closing down.

The boys spread out through this amazing underground structure and began to explore, their voices echoing loudly off the walls of the central chamber. Every few minutes, Nick or Brent would head back to the entrance to breath fresh air and check on Darin. Darin was holding to the promise he'd made to his mother: he would not go into the mine.

Nick and Brent had returned to the central chamber and were daring each other to see who would go the farthest into the eastern tunnel when suddenly Darin came charging in, his eyes as wide as saucers. He paused long enough to take in the scene—left, right, up and down—and then he sprinted for the airshaft and the sunlight above. Everyone who witnessed this event found it hilarious, and laughter bounced off the walls as Darin clawed his way to freedom.

Later, when the story was told again and again, it never failed to bring a laugh, followed by the stark realization that Darin was right to be afraid, and his mother was right to scare him out of his wits. But that was 20/20 hindsight based on what happened next.

Darin had barely reached sunlight when George came running from the shaft that went up to the left. "Gary fell! Gary fell!" The central chamber went dead still and the only voice was George's. "Gary fell! There's a hole in the floor up there. He fell into the pit!" It was silent again and then they heard a faint moaning sound from the left, down in pit.

Mike, Grant, and George scrambled down over the rocks in the pit area, down to the left out of sight from the chamber. They found Gary sprawled on his back across the rocks and broken timbers. He was barely conscious and could not respond to their questions. Grant looked up but it was too dark to see the hole Gary had fallen through. He guessed it had to be at least fifty feet up there, somewhere.

"Holy shit, this is bad." Mike looked at them with fear in his eyes. "We can't move him . . . that could make it worse. We've got to get help down here."

"Okay. Stay here . . . let me go talk to the guys." Grant left Mike and George with Gary and started back for the chamber. The one clear thought in his mind at that moment was *My old man is going to kill me.* He wanted to run, to get as far away as possible, to be anywhere but here in the middle of this disaster. As he reached the chamber, the other boys gathered around him and he saw his fear and panic mirrored in their faces. "Gary's hurt bad," he said, and several of them looked as if they were going to cry. And then it hit him: all eyes were glued on him, counting on him to take charge.

"Okay, listen . . ." he started, fighting for control. "We've got to stay cool . . . and get some help. I need a couple of guys to go back to the golf course . . . as fast as possible. Have them call an ambulance from the pro shop." Reid and Brent immediately volunteered. "And I need some sweatshirts . . . we've got to keep Gary warm until help gets here. Where's Lenny? Lenny, I need you to go and stay with your brother. Okay, let's go!" With that he grabbed Lenny and an armful of sweatshirts and headed back down into the pit while Brent and Reid set out for the golf course.

The rest of the boys headed out of the mine to wait for help to arrive. They clustered together, afraid for their friend, afraid for the trouble they were in. They waited in shock and fear, hoping that help would arrive in time.

Meanwhile, Reid and Brent were on the dead run through the hills, all the way to the golf course. There they accosted the first foursome they could find and breathlessly told their story. One of golfers happened to be a doctor, and after a little hesitation and some annoyed comments from his buddies, he agreed to head back to the mine with Brent. One of the other golfers went with Reid to the pro shop to call for an ambulance. The other two debated whether or not to play on.

Brent was back soon enough with the golfing doctor in tow, but waiting for the ambulance seemed like an eternity. News would be relayed out of the mine every few minutes. Gary was conscious and responding to questions, but there was no doubt he was seriously injured. At last, the boys waiting outside the mine saw a small caravan moving deliberately up the valley, emergency lights flashing. Two police cruisers and an ambulance arrived at the entrance to the mine. Shortly after that, a man riding a tall black stallion rode onto the scene. He was wearing shiny black riding boots and a broad-brimmed Stetson hat, and they heard someone say he was the landowner. The final arrivals were another police car and an unmarked sedan. The doors to the sedan opened and Darin recognized the reporter and the photographer from the *Times-Herald*.

The policemen who were first on the scene directed the reporter to Grant, and she began to interview him, scribbling notes at a furious pace. George soon joined them and the interview continued. Darin moved as far as he could into the background. He wanted out of this story, even though he knew that was impossible. The reporter glanced his way at one point and a look of recognition crossed her face, but Darin managed to avoid any direct contact with her.

What happened next would stay with him from that day on. The ambulance crew emerged from the mine with Gary strapped to a stretcher. Gary was blonde and fair skinned to begin with, but Darin was sure he'd never seen a human being so white. In that instant, he thought Gary was going to die and he felt his knees buckle. The attendants loaded Gary into the ambulance and worked over him for several minutes. Then they put Lenny in the front seat and carefully headed off down the valley, the emergency lights flashing ominously.

The commotion around the mine continued for several minutes with the landowner engaged in a heated discussion with the police officers. The boys heard the terms "posted property" and "trespassing" tossed back and forth. Finally, the man mounted the black horse and rode away. The officers loaded the boys into the squad cars and started the journey back to town. At least they would not have to walk home.

Darin had a long conversation with his mother that afternoon, explaining as best he could the events of the day. When she asked him point blank if he had gone into the mine, he looked her straight in the eye and said no. He spent the rest of the afternoon and evening in his room and his parents elected to give him that time alone, interrupted only when his mother brought in his dinner on a tray and placed it on his desk. He picked at the food, but found he had no appetite.

Darin awoke the next morning to the sound of his mother preparing breakfast in the kitchen. He could hear his parents conversing in soft, muffled voices. He decided to get dressed and head for the kitchen to take his medicine. His mother was turning pieces of French toast on a small griddle when he entered the room and sat down at the table. His father glanced around the newspaper briefly but did not speak. They proceeded to eat breakfast with little more than "pass the butter," or "would you like another piece?" serving as the conversation.

As his mother cleared the table, his father folded the front section of the newspaper and placed it in front of Darin. "I see you made the front page again."

"Yes, sir," he said. There above the fold was the picture of Gary on the stretcher, being carried toward the ambulance, a crowd of people gathered in the background.

"Don't go there again, son." Five words. That was it. That was all his father had to say.

"Yes, sir."

There was a goodbye kiss for his mother, but no tousled hair for Darin this time around, and his father was on his way to work. Darin picked up the paper and began to read the story under Helen Ratner's byline. When he got to the part about the two boys who ran cross-country to the golf course for help, his name was listed as one of them. His jaw dropped in disbelief. In all the confusion, Grant and George had given the wrong information to the reporter. No wonder his father had so little to say: the story made Darin sound like a hero. Now the struggle began. Should he sit his parents down and come clean? Or leave well enough alone and hope it would just fade away? Darin felt like his guts were twisting into a tight little knot.

His mother clipped the picture and the accompanying article for his scrapbook, but he never bothered to look at them again. He didn't need a picture to remember how Gary looked coming out of the mine. He didn't need a newspaper article to remind him that he'd lied to his parents. And the knot in his gut grew tighter.

III.

Helen sat at her desk in the *Times-Herald* office, an array of file folders spread open across the surface. She had covered the story of the Steffan Manor kids from the very beginning, starting with the lawn mowing venture. It was simple at the onset: one group of friends, two front-page articles, a classic good news, bad news story. But it had gone far beyond that to a series of follow-up articles.

She had checked on Gary Pace's condition and found that he was recovering, finally, from a broken arm, broken ribs and internal injuries. Her story told of Gary's dog King who would not leave his master's bedside and had to be forced out of the room periodically to take food and go outside to relieve himself. Even hardboiled veteran colleagues stopped by her desk to tell her that story brought a tear to their eye.

Then there was a flood of calls and mail asking how responsible parents could allow their sons to roam about the hills, exploring abandoned mines. She'd followed up on that one too, finding that most of the parents had been told it was a simple hike to Blue Rock Springs and back, with no mention of the old mines. It seemed that only young Darin Maneri had told his parents about the real destination.

And then another flood of calls and letters demanding to know how the property owner could allow the mines to stand open, a constant temptation for kids to fall into trouble. Helen's article on that topic caused the city to pressure the owner to take action, and he was forced to hire a crew and a bulldozer to seal the entrances, once and for all.

As she looked at her files, the picture of Gary being carried from the mine caught her eye. Standing in the background, she recognized Darin. She sensed that he had intentionally avoided her that day and she couldn't help but wonder why. He seemed like a nice kid when she interviewed him for the article about King. And wasn't he one of the guys who ran to bring help for Gary? Why had he avoided her? Her reporter's instincts told her there was yet another story here. She left word for her editor and headed out of the office, bound for the Maneris' home on Jennings Street.

Helen parked at the curb on the hill and gathered her purse and her notepad. She looked at the neat white wood-frame house with its immaculately maintained yard and thought that it typified the American middle-class family dream. As she approached the front door, she admired a terraced bed to the side of the driveway, planted with a half dozen rose bushes bursting with prize-winning blooms in red, yellow, and white. Somebody in the family had a green thumb. She knocked on the door and waited.

Darin opened the door and stood staring back at her.

"Hi, Darin. I'm Helen Ratner . . . from the *Times-Herald*. Remember me? I interviewed you when you were mowing lawns for King. Are your parents at home? I was wondering if we could chat for a while?"

Darin was quiet for several seconds. Then simply, politely he said "No," and slowly shut the door. Helen stood there for a moment, and then a smile broke across her face. *I was right! I knew it!* Then she heard a woman's voice from inside.

"Darin, was someone at the door?"

"No, Mom," came the reply.

Helen could tell the boy was still standing there, facing the closed door. She smiled again and tapped her steno pad against her open palm. This time she reached for the doorbell.

GHOST SHIP

There were lots of places to fish along the shoreline that wrapped around Vallejo, but the Old Destroyer was by far the most fun. We'd study our tide tables and look for an ebb tide between 8:00 and 9:00 in the morning. The plan was to fish a couple hours either side of high tide. We'd stop off at Parmisano & Sons fish market down on lower Georgia Street and buy several pounds of fresh sardines for bait. Then we'd get dropped off on the edge of a western subdivision and hike west on the levee that bordered the salt marsh, all the way out to the bank of the Napa River.

Sometimes the fog would be so thick you could barely see where you were going. We'd find our favorite spot on the riverbank and go to work, rigging up our poles, cutting bait, getting ready to cast into the brown, brackish water. Then the sun would start to take charge and the fog would begin to lift and slowly, about a hundred yards to the north, the Old Destroyer would appear like a vision.

No one ever explained how she got there, a Navy ship lodged against the bank. She was just there. There was a plank that ran from the bank to the deck of the ship. If the fishing got slow, we could go aboard and explore. There wasn't much to see. The superstructure was gone and only the hull remained.

Fishing was always great at the Old Destroyer. It was nothing to catch twenty fish in a day, mostly undersized striped bass. The size limit in those days was twelve inches and we'd usually catch three or four keepers to bring home and show our parents. The fun part was a running contest to see who could catch and release the most fish.

If the bite slowed down and there was no action, you'd sit and look at the old ship and wonder. Of course, you could make up your own version of her history:

> *She was the USS Shane, a proud veteran of World War I, having served in the North Atlantic protecting convoys of merchant vessels heading for North Sea ports, fighting off the German subs that preyed on merchant shipping like a pack of hungry wolves. The Shane had six confirmed kills and survived many a battle with the Germans. At the close of the war, she was reassigned to the Pacific Fleet and sailed through the Panama Canal and up the coast, all the way to Mare Island for a complete overhaul.*
>
> *With the work completed, the Shane was scheduled for a shakedown cruise, out into San Pablo Bay, then about-face and back up the Mare Island Strait and the Napa River channel, then back to the dock at the shipyard. On the way up river, a cold front moved in and the temperature hit the dew point and the fog bloomed so thick that visibility dropped to zero. The crew missed a bend in the river and steamed onto the mud flats, hard up against the riverbank. All efforts to free her failed, so the Navy stripped her down, sealed her up and left her there, a proud warrior with no war to fight, an old sailor dumped on the shore for the last time.*

No doubt there were gaping holes in that story—a little truth, a little fiction, a little scrimshaw carved to fit the occasion—but in a Navy town like Vallejo, there were a thousand stories just like it.

—⁊⁊—

Note: The Old Destroyer was actually the USS Corry (DD334), launched at Bethlehem Shipyard in San Francisco in 1921. In the aftermath of World War I, the Navy decided to reduce the size of the fleet. The Corry was decommissioned at Mare Island in 1930 and towed a few miles to a spot on the east bank of the Napa River. The rotting hull is there to this day.

GAME DAY

Nick heard the usual early morning commotion outside the door to his room, his dog George prancing and scratching, license tags jingling, excited to be let into the house after a night in the garage. He knew what would come next: his father would open the door and George would come bounding across the room, leap onto the bed and stick a cold nose in his face. Then he would settle at the end of the bed, curled up with his head resting on Nick's feet. Finally, George would exhale a long, loud sigh in preparation for a nap that would last until Nick decided it was time to get up.

Nick pulled the blanket up to cover his face just as the door was opened. George's cold nose would have to settle for a spot on his forehead. The rest of the routine played out just as it did every morning as his father was leaving for work at 6:30 AM. George settled in and sighed, and Nick was ready to fall off to sleep again when he remembered that this was the day of the All Star game. He made an effort to put it out of his mind, but to no avail. There would be no falling back to sleep this morning.

He listened carefully. Maybe it was raining. Maybe the game would be postponed and he wouldn't have to pitch tonight. Maybe he wouldn't have to prove himself all over again. It was no use. It seldom rained in Vallejo this time of year, and even if it did, it was generally a thundershower, hardly enough to cancel a baseball game. It was August 1, and it would be a typical North Bay summer day: thin overcast in the morning, giving way to sunny and windy in the afternoon, temperatures in the high seventies or low eighties. There would be no reprieve.

Nick glanced at the clock on his bedside table. It was now a little after 7:00 AM. He knew there would be an article about the game in the morning newspaper. He regretted that he'd never taught George to fetch the paper. He'd have to go get it himself. George raised his head when Nick moved to get out of bed, and then settled back to resume his nap. Nick returned with the newspaper, climbed back into bed and propped himself against the headboard. He turned to the sports section and found the article he was looking for.

The headline over Don Gleason's byline read: "Jr. Peanut All Star Game Today." Nick hated the name of the league. Somehow "Jr. Peanut League" didn't sound mature enough for thirteen year-olds. But the Peanut League had a long history in Vallejo. The senior branch was intended for fourteen and fifteen year-olds, while the junior division had been created more recently as a transitional step between Little League and Sr. Peanut League.

Little League arrived in Vallejo in the early fifties and revolutionized the game for eight to twelve year-olds, introducing a player draft, safety equipment, a book full of rules, and affiliation with a national organization. The Peanut League was a much looser, seat-of-the-pants organization, and strictly local.

The Little League diamond featured bases that were sixty feet apart, with the pitcher's mound at forty-six feet. On the Jr. Peanut League diamond, the bases were at eighty feet and the mound at fifty-two feet. The several teams in the league tended to center around the Junior High Schools in town, and the more ambitious school coaches took on summer teams as a feeder system for their Junior High programs. Each team lined up a corporate sponsor and held open tryouts. The net result was that the top players tended to load up on three or four teams. The other teams, varying each year depending on sponsors, took the remaining talent and tended to take their lumps during the season.

The traditional All Star game in both divisions of the Peanut League pitted the team that finished first in the regular season against an all-star squad selected from the rest of the teams. The result was generally a competitive game that was well covered by the local newspaper and well attended by parents and fans.

Nick read the article with great interest and pride. Gleason devoted a couple of paragraphs to his exploits during the season in which he had thrown five one-hitters. He had been something of a phenom in Little League, throwing four complete game no-hitters. Now his success on the larger diamond marked Nick as one of the top players in his age group. It was fun to read these things in the local paper, and he thought of the pride his father would feel, knowing that the men he worked with on the shipyard would see this column and comment on it.

But there was still the game to be played that evening, the demand to go out and perform against the toughest competition in his age group, to prove again that he really was a talent to be reckoned with. And he had a whole day to think about it. He knew that his father had left strict instructions with his mom: make sure that Nick rests, that he's not out running around all day with his friends, that he eats a solid meal about three hours before the game.

It would be a long day, but Nick knew he'd be ready.

Carl Andrews sat in his wheelchair facing the front door, waiting for the morning paper to arrive. It was 7:00 AM and the carrier was late—again. He resolved to wait a few minutes more and then call the *Times-Herald* office to demand an explanation.

Carl had been up since first light, a life-long habit from his days on the farm in Oklahoma. He liked his morning newspaper to be on the porch by 6:00 AM, 6:15 at the latest. Today it was especially galling because he knew there would be an article in the sports section about the All Star game that evening.

Carl and Iris Andrews had moved to Fairfield, California ten years earlier to be closer to their adult children and grandchildren. Now in their late seventies, it had been a decade of declining health that left them more and more dependent. Carl now spent most of his time in the wheelchair, able to walk only short distances. A lifetime of hard work and unfiltered cigarettes had left him with crippling arthritis and emphysema. He often commented that if he knew he would live this long, he would have taken better care of himself.

Today, however, would be a good day. It was a day he had been looking forward to for several weeks, marshaling his strength and double-checking all the arrangements. That afternoon, his daughter would drive him to Vallejo, fourteen miles away, to attend a baseball game.

One of Carl's small pleasures in life was to follow the budding baseball career of Nicholas Shane, the young pitcher for the Schefield's Chevron team in the Jr. Peanut League. Nick's family happened to live next door to his daughter Anna in Vallejo, and the two families were close friends.

All summer long, Carl had eagerly awaited the arrival of the morning newspaper, turning immediately to the sports page to check the results and write-ups of the Vallejo youth leagues. Schefield's had gone undefeated and Nick had put together an outstanding year. Carl couldn't have felt more pride if Nick was his own grandson. Today he would finally see Nick pitch.

Just then, the news carrier flashed by on his bicycle and the newspaper thumped loudly on the porch. "Mother! The paper's here!" He made sure Iris could hear him.

"Keep your shirt on, Carl. I'll get it." Iris made her way from the kitchen to the front door, mumbling to herself about old men and their demands. It would be a long, trying day, with Carl so antsy about going to Vallejo for the game. She would have to find a way to keep him occupied. She dropped the paper in his lap, still muttering to herself, and returned to the kitchen. *That dang newspaper will keep him quiet, for a while at least.*

Nick finished the last of the small steak and baked potato his mother had prepared for him. He picked at the green beans for a while, then pushed back his chair and took his plate into the kitchen.

"Did you have enough, honey?" His mother took the plate and rinsed it in the sink.

"Yeah, Mom, thanks. I'm gonna get ready now." It was 3:30 PM and he had to be at the ballpark at 4:30. Plenty of time to put on his uniform and get his gear together for the game.

"You know Grandpa Andrews is coming to the game tonight," his mother called after him.

"I know, you told me already." Nick had met the old man several times and knew he loved baseball, but was still surprised to hear how closely he had followed their season.

After several seasons of use, the Schefield's Chevron uniforms had seen better days. They were a faded Kelly green with white lettering and not pretty by any standards. But Nick and his teammates did their best to look good, choosing green turtleneck jerseys to wear under the uniform shirts, the sleeves cut off just below the elbow. They carefully split the green stirrup sox at the bottom and sewed in a small strip of elastic. Clean white sanitary sox worn under the stirrups created the high-split look they were trying for, just like Mickey Mantle's latest baseball card. All of this took a while to assemble and apply perfectly. The stirrup sox had to be the exact same height on each leg, anchored at the top of the calf by a band of adhesive tape. Sometimes it took a couple of tries to get it just right. All of this took time. Finally, at 4:15 PM, Nick was ready for the short ride to the ballpark.

The field where the game would be played was adjacent to the Auto Movies on Benicia Road and was shared with the East Vallejo Little League. The permanent fence, covered in colorful sponsors ads, was set at two hundred and eighty feet. A temporary fence at two hundred feet could be set up for the Little League games. It was fun to play games at this particular diamond with a fence to shoot for. The only drawback was the lack of a real pitcher's mound, since the field had to accommodate different sized diamonds.

Nick and his friends had tried to convince Manuel Silva, a league official, to install a mound for this one game, but Manuel had been reluctant. He was a supervisor with the city street department and had access to all the necessary equipment, materials, and city labor. They had pleaded their case and Manuel had laughed at them, all the while calculating the effort required for the project.

When his mom turned off of Benicia Road and down the short gravel drive that led to the ballpark, Nick's face broke into a grin. There in the middle of the infield, in dirt that was conspicuously darker than the surrounding clay of the diamond, was a perfectly constructed pitcher's mound. Manuel had come through.

Anna McLenden left Vallejo for the short drive to Fairfield with time to spare. She knew that being late was not an option today. It had been a long time since she had seen her father so worked up about anything, let alone a baseball game. She had promised to be there by 4:00 PM, and as it turned out, she would be a little early.

She was surprised when she turned into her parents' driveway to see her father sitting in his wheelchair on the front porch, a baseball cap pulled down tightly on his head, obviously ready to go. Lord, she said to herself, I hope he doesn't get himself too excited.

Within a few minutes, she had her parents loaded into the car, the wheelchair securely in the trunk, and they were on their way back to Vallejo. There she had a pre-game snack prepared for them, after which they would be on their way in plenty of time for the 6:00 o'clock game.

"Did you see Nick today?" Carl's tone was a little anxious.

"No, Daddy. I'm sure Lucille was keeping him in, making sure he's rested for tonight. You know how they are about that." Anna couldn't believe all this fuss over a ballgame.

"Did you see the paper this morning? Nice write-up. That's one Lucille will want to keep for the scrapbook."

Iris tried to ignore all this talk about kids' baseball. She had no intention of going to the game. It was just nice to get out of the house. She gazed out the window and enjoyed the view of the Napa River tidelands and the city of Vallejo as they came down Hunter's Hill on Highway 40.

Carl took out his gold pocket watch and checked the time. Anna caught this out of the corner of her eye.

"Lord, Daddy, stop checking your watch. We are not going to be late! I reckon you're going to work yourself into a state." She turned her attention to the road and smiled a little. It was good to see him interested in something.

Nick went into his pre-game routine as soon as his mother dropped him off at the field, which meant not doing much of anything for about an hour. He sat in the third base dugout and watched his teammates go through their warm ups: jogging, stretching, playing catch, playing pepper. He held the new ball coach Wight had given him, spitting on his hands and rubbing it up with a little dirt from the infield. He would wait until his team took the field for infield practice to head for the practice mound down the left field line and begin his warm ups.

Coach Wight had it all timed out. Nick would jog, stretch, and throw easily to their backup catcher Eddie Camp while Schefield's took infield. Then Jimmy Vaught, their starting catcher, would run down to the bullpen in full gear and Nick would begin throwing from the practice mound, gradually increasing to full velocity. Finally, he would simulate pitching to the first three or four batters in the All Star line up, mixing his pitches and changing locations with his fastball. It was a routine he had memorized over the course of the season. The only new wrinkle tonight was the time required for player introductions and the National Anthem, but that was no problem.

Coach Wight called them together in a circle, they touched gloves and shouted "Team," and ran out for infield practice. Nick and Eddie jogged down the line to the practice mound. When he began to throw, he noticed at once how good he felt. At this time of year, there were generally sore muscles, aches and pains that had to be worked out as you warmed up, but not tonight. There was no pain, not anywhere, and the ball seemed to leap from his hand. This felt too good to be true.

Jimmy came running down and Nick began to throw from the mound. Now he noticed something else: he could pick a spot, any spot, and hit it dead on. He threw from the windup, and then from the stretch, and it was the same: the velocity came effortlessly and he could spot every pitch.

Nick tried a few change-ups, then a few curves. He would use one or the other during the game to keep the hitters off balance. The curve ball was breaking sharply, and consistently around the strike zone, something he had always struggled with. He went through his routine of simulating the first four hitters, and then he was ready. He put on the light jacket he had carried down to the bullpen and noticed that he had broken a good sweat. Coach Wight walked out to meet them as they came toward the dugout.

Nick spoke first: "Coach, I . . . I feel great." He wanted to say more, to tell his coach just how great he felt, to tell him that he had never felt this good before a game, not ever. But the words wouldn't come, so he just stared up at his coach, hoping that somehow he would understand.

"He's really throwin' hard, Coach," Jimmy said. "Really hard."

"So, you're ready to go?" Bob Wight was a tall, lean man with large ears and a prominent Adam's apple. After many years of teaching middle-school kids, with their hormones raging, he'd given up trying to figure out what they were thinking.

Nick could tell from the puzzled look that he wasn't getting through. He tried again. "Yeah, Coach, I really feel great."

The field announcer interrupted their conversation, calling both teams to their dugouts for the pre-game introductions.

Carl sat in his wheelchair parked next to the grandstand on the third base side. His daughter Anna sat next to him on the first row of the bleachers where they were joined by Nick's parents, Lucille and Nick Sr. They had arrived in time to see both teams take infield practice and to see Nick trot down to the bullpen to begin his warm-ups.

Carl let his mind drift back to his days on the farm where his older brothers had taught him to play the game. His brothers played for a team sponsored by the local merchants in town and they would play doubleheaders on Sunday against teams from nearby villages. It was always a family affair, with sandwiches and snacks between games and a fine picnic meal afterward. Carl was about Nick's age when his brothers finally let him play for the team. He remembered his first uniform with "Salisaw Merchants" emblazoned across the front. It took a couple of seasons for Carl to develop as a hitter, but his fielding skills blossomed from the beginning. He played the outfield and he could run down any ball hit to his field. He was long-legged and lanky and he could fly across the outfield.

The PA system switched on and the announcer's voice interrupted Carl's daydream. The introduction of the players followed with Schefield's lining up along the third base line and the All Stars along first base. Then it was time for the National Anthem. Carl gathered his legs under him and, with concerted effort, rose and removed his cap for the anthem. He had considered remaining in his chair, but not today. Today was special. He stood as straight and as near attention as he could while the scratchy recording of the Star Spangled Banner blared from the loudspeakers.

The Schefield's team sprinted out of the dugout for the first inning. Nick stood on the new pitcher's mound and admired his friend Manuel's work. He started his warm-up pitches and found immediately that the magic he felt in the bullpen had come with him to the mound. He had never felt this sense of effortless power before and he resolved to enjoy it for as long as it lasted.

The innings went quickly. Schefield's scored early and often and by the end of the sixth inning, the score was Schefield's seven, All Stars zero. The All Stars had hit only two balls out of the infield, both for long outs, and Nick had not given up a base hit.

Nick trotted to the mound for the top of the seventh and as he took his warm-up tosses, he allowed himself to look ahead. Only three more outs and the game was theirs. He felt his heart jump a little as he thought about what a win in this game would mean to his teammates.

Dennis O'Connell led off for the All Stars and Nick walked him, missing with a fastball low and away on a three-and-one count. Now Dennis danced off first base while Nick tried to regain his focus. He went into his stretch and threw over to first a couple of times, trying to keep Dennis close. He knew Dennis could run like a deer, and though Jimmy was a good receiver, throwing wasn't his strong suit.

Dennis stole second base on the first pitch, and then stole third base on the next. On the third pitch, the hitter swung at a low fastball and rapped a ground ball toward second base. Second baseman Jim Barrett fielded the ball cleanly and threw home, trying to preserve the shutout. The throw was late and Dennis scored easily from third.

The shutout was gone, but Nick didn't care. The All Stars were down to their last three outs and he had a six-run cushion to lean on. The next two hitters went down easily and now there was just one more out to get. For the second time in the inning, Nick let his concentration lapse, and before he knew it, the count had gone to three balls, no strikes. He called his catcher out to the mound. "Jimmy, put the target in the middle of the plate. We're not gonna walk this guy." Jimmy nodded and trotted back to home plate.

Nick hit the glove on the next pitch for strike one. His next pitch was on the outside corner at the knees and the hitter fouled it off. The final pitch drifted to the inside corner and the hitter swung and missed.

The Schefield's team rushed the mound and exploded in celebration, the way you would expect when kids had been holding their emotions in check for seven innings. It took a while for Coach Wight to calm them down and remind them to give a cheer and line up to shake hands with the All Star squad.

The post-game rituals went swiftly. Coach Wight gathered the team in the third base dugout and thanked them for an outstanding season. He spoke of tentative plans for a team barbeque and said he would collect uniforms at that time. Then he handed Nick a game ball he had retrieved from the umpire. On it he had carefully printed in blue ballpoint pen:

8/1/56
Schefield's 7
All Stars 1
No Hit Game

Nick clutched the ball in the pocket of his warm-up jacket as they left the dugout. A crowd of parents waited for them as they emerged, smiling and calling congratulations to the team. Then Nick saw his father moving slowly toward him, pushing a wheelchair in which the old man he knew as Grandpa Andrews was sitting. Nick went to them and took the hand that Carl Andrews extended to him. He listened to the old man's praise for his accomplishment, all the while holding his bony hand. He looked up at one point and caught his father's eye and saw his lower lip tremble a little. This was the best part, knowing he'd made his father proud.

His friend Mike joined their circle after a few minutes to ask if Nick could come with Mike's parents for burgers and shakes at a local drive in. Nick's parents gave their permission and he said his goodbyes and headed for the parking lot with Mike. It had been a long, emotional day and Nick was suddenly very tired. Mike chattered away happily, imagining the headline and the lead paragraph for tomorrow's sports page. But Nick was quiet, still picturing his father's face, still feeling the grip of the old man's bony hand.

He thought about the power and control he'd felt during the game and wondered if it would ever come again. He knew that next spring it would start again, that there would be game days when he'd awake and listen for rain, even pray for rain, before going out to do what was expected of him. At thirteen, Nicholas Shane had learned an important baseball rule: you are only as good as the last game you pitched. He felt the game ball in the pocket of his jacket and smiled. It was a rule he could live with.

Carl Andrews gazed out the windshield as his daughter Anna guided the car up Hunter's Hill, leaving Vallejo behind. It had been a remarkable day. He could not have written a better script himself, finally getting to see Nick pitch, and then witnessing a no-hit game to boot. Now in the gathering darkness, all he could think of was a warm glass of milk and a good night's sleep. He leaned his head against the window on the passenger's side and closed his eyes for a moment.

And now he was running, sprinting across the field at full speed toward that spot where he knew the ball would land, his spikes barely making a sound against the grass. And there was the ball, over his left shoulder, racing with him toward the warning track and the fence. And now he was reaching, stretching out as far as he could, never breaking stride. And there was the ball falling softly into his glove, like a dusty white butterfly.

PARTY CRASHERS

"So, whataya wanna do?"

"I don't know. Whata you wanna do?"

"How 'bout . . . nah, that's no good. Whata you wanna do?"

Nick, Darin, and Brent stood on the corner under the streetlight, re-enacting the famous scene from the movie *Marty*, even though they hadn't seen the film. It was a warm Friday evening in September and there were lots of possibilities to consider, including some old favorites from years past.

"Wanna harass the pachucos?" Nick asked, reaching back a few years for a golden oldie.

It was an activity that involved hiding in the bushes until some older guys came through the neighborhood, guys who dressed and acted like gang members and wore the pachuco uniform: unwashed Levis with the belt loops cut off, pulled down as low as possible on their hips; thick wedge-soled shoes with metal taps nailed to the heels; shirts and leather jackets with the collars turned up and a pack of Lucky Strike in the breast pocket; and of course, long hair slicked back in a ducktail, plastered down with lots of Dixie Peach Pomade.

When the pachucos walked down the street, Nick and his friends would jump out and yell, "Hey you rotten punks," or whatever vile phrase they could come up with. The tough guys would reel around, see it was a bunch of younger boys and light out in pursuit, determined to kick some butt. There was no problem outrunning the wannabe gangsters. It was hard to run in those heavy shoes and leather jackets while holding up your pants with one hand. They usually gave up after a block or so, sometimes clutching their knees and gasping for air. It was great fun, but they knew they'd outgrown that particular game. After all, they were in Junior High School now.

"Wanna do 'death scene?'" Darin asked, tapping another old favorite.

It was a game where they waited until they saw the headlights of a car several blocks away, heading in their direction. Two guys would pretend to be beating on the third, and as the car came closer, one of the beaters would make stabbing motions toward the victim. The beaters would pretend to notice the car and race away, leaving the victim to go into his "death scene," falling to the ground, clutching his stab wounds. The objective was to get the driver to slam on his brakes and come to the victim's aid. Then the victim would jump up and sprint away. But they knew this was another game they'd outgrown. Besides, most of the drivers in the neighborhood had seen it all before.

"How 'bout the Auto Movies?" Nick asked.

That was one that never grew old. The drive-in theater out on Benicia Road was only a few miles away and they could always find a hole or a loose board in the wooden fence. Then they could let themselves in and hang out on the playground down in front of the screen, or stroll boldly up to the snack bar for some popcorn or a cold drink. As they got a little older, they discovered that if they walked through the rows of cars and saw one where the speaker was connected to the window but no heads were visible, they could sneak up and look in the window and get an eyeful. It was better than any sex education class they'd attended.

Once a girl opened her eyes, saw their faces at the window and screamed at the top of her lungs. That sent them running to their hole in the fence and out to safety, even though the boyfriend was in no position to give chase. Afterward they felt bad and hoped the poor guy hadn't had a heart attack or anything. No doubt about it, though: having the drive-in close by was a constant source of entertainment, even if you never saw a movie.

At this point, Brent took charge, because he knew exactly what he wanted to do. "Let's go by Nancy Dawkins's party."

"Are you nuts? We weren't invited. I'm not goin' there. No way." Nick and Darin wanted nothing to do with a boy-girl party, especially when they were not invited.

"We'll just cruise by," Brent reassured them. "Nobody will see us. Come on, let's go." He didn't mention his real reason for going there. Claire Ryan, a girl he was very interested in, would be at the party. Somehow this was like a magnet and he could not resist the pull. Brent kept up the pressure on Nick and Darin, and Nick at least was beginning to weaken. Nick knew that Beth Scalini would be there too. One party, two magnets: a hard combination to resist.

Brent's arguments prevailed and before long they were rounding a bend in the street, approaching Nancy's house. The lights were on in the garage and they could hear music floating on the balmy air. They stopped behind a car parked at the curb, peering around the vehicle like three poorly trained spies. From inside the garage came sporadic bursts of laughter and the sound of Fats Domino on the record player singing "Ain't That a Shame."

The headlights of an approaching car startled them and they quickly stepped away and began walking nonchalantly up the street. The car passed and they continued walking for a half block.

"Let's go back," Brent implored.

"Not me. I've had enough. I'm goin' home. I'll see you guys tomorrow." And with that, Darin took off, ignoring their pleas to hang around a while.

Brent nearly dragged Nick back to the car in front of Nancy's house. A new record was on the turntable inside. It was Elvis singing "Love Me Tender," and it was too much for Brent to bear. He thought about Claire and pictured her dancing close to him, moving slowly to the music. "Stay here," he said. "I'm going to check this out." He had his eye on the window in the door at the side of the garage.

"Are you crazy? They'll see you." Nick considered turning around and making a run for home before Brent could reach the garage, but somehow his feet were glued to the pavement. He watched Brent approach the door, look quickly in through the window, then pull his head away. He turned and looked in again. Suddenly, he spun around and came walking back toward Nick, his hands plunged deep in his pockets. The door to the garage opened and someone stepped out onto the walk. Nick recognized Steve Gray, a friend from school.

"Brent? Is that you? Come here, man. Are you alone?" Steve was walking toward Brent now, and there were other kids poking their heads out of the garage to see what was going on. "Hey, Nick, is that you? Man, am I glad to see you guys. There's like seven girls here, but only three guys showed up. Come on in and join the party. We need you."

"Nah, we can't do that," Brent said. "We weren't invited."

"I'll talk to Nancy. I'm sure it'll be okay."

This conversation was relayed back to the garage and a few minutes later, Nancy approached them with the formal invitation. "My parents said it is okay if you guys want to come in and join us." She said it with a smile that was hard to resist. Nick started to open his mouth, not really sure what he was going to say, when Brent took charge again.

"Okay, we'll go home and change clothes and be back in a few minutes." The deal was done, no way to back out now. As Brent said this, Nick saw Beth, standing by the door, looking every bit the pretty, popular cheerleader that she was. He felt his heart jump into his throat. A few seconds later, Nick and Brent were hurrying for home.

Nick's parents were sitting in the living room, listening to the radio when he came in. He quickly explained the last minute invitation to the party while they glanced at one another and stifled the smiles that were trying to break out. They gave their permission and Nick rushed off to get ready.

He went into the bathroom, ran warm water in the sink, stripped to the waist and scrubbed himself with a soapy washcloth. Then he went to work on his hair, realizing immediately that he was badly in need of a haircut. His flattop with longish sides would not cooperate, no matter how much hair cream he smeared on it.

Finally he stopped and stared into the mirror. Staring back was the face that only a mother could love, with the fuzzy hair, the nose still peeling from a summer in the sun, the freckles spread so densely across his cheeks that it looked like his face was dirty. Why would Beth Scalini even look at this face? He dropped his eyes in despair and wondered if there was a way out, a way to convince Brent to go to the party alone. Then he heard voices from the living room and he knew Brent was there, ready and eager to go.

Brent was waiting in Nick's bedroom. "Come on, man, let's go. Time is a-wastin'."

"I don't know if I'm going. Why don't you just go?"

"What? Are you kidding me? Come on, get dressed. Here, man, I'll help." He went to Nick's closet and pulled out a clean shirt and a pair of khakis. Before Nick could protest any further, he was dressed and they were out the front door and on their way to the party. When Brent was motivated, he was like a force of nature.

The Dawkins' garage had been spruced up and organized for the party, with lawnmower and tools and the like all stowed away elsewhere. There was a table loaded with snacks and a cooler with cold drinks, and on another table across the floor was the portable record player with piles of 45-rpm records arranged next to it. All the girls were congregated around the record player, selecting records to be stacked on the changer, engaged in animated conversation. The boys gathered around the snack table, talking about happenings at school and the prospects for the football team. Each group made it a point to keep an eye on the other.

The record changed and a pretty ballad came on the player. Brent wasted no time. He went directly to Claire and asked her to dance. Steve chose a partner and joined them on the floor. Nick was in awe at how easy they made it look. All he could do was try to remain focused on the conversation in progress while glancing every now and then at Beth. And there she was with her short dark hair, her laughing eyes, and the smile that came so easily and made you feel so good. Why couldn't he be like Brent and just walk over there and ask her to dance? And if she said, "No thank you," then he could simply curl up and die right there on the floor of Nancy's garage.

After a couple of songs, Brent went to the record player and began sifting through the 45's. He stacked several records on the changer and then went back to Claire. The Platters' recording of "Only You" started, the sweet black voices filling the garage. Brent and Claire moved slowly around the floor, talking and laughing, Brent's eyes focusing on her pretty face. The next record was the Platters again with "The Magic Touch," and now they were cheek to cheek and Nick could see that Brent was speaking softly into Claire's ear. The record changed again and Elvis was back to reprise "Love Me Tender." Brent had obviously stacked the deck for romance and it was working as planned. Now he and Claire moved very slowly together, their arms wrapped tightly around each other.

"Hey, look what I found!" Steve called from across the garage. He was holding a milk bottle over his head, the old fashioned kind with the bulb at the top to collect the cream, the kind that the milkman delivered to the front porch. "Let's play Spin the Bottle!"

Everyone gathered around in a circle, kneeling on the garage floor—that is except Brent and Claire who were nowhere to be seen—and the game began. After each spin, the couple would go out into the backyard for their kiss. Nick had barely settled into the circle when it was his turn to spin. He spun the bottle carefully, watched it rotate several times, then come slowly to rest. It was pointing directly at Beth.

Nick scrambled to his feet and watched Beth do the same. She smiled the tiniest of smiles in his direction and then headed for the door to the backyard. As Nick followed her, he was aware of the kids around the circle egging them on, the guys saying, "All right, go Nick!" and the girls calling, "Ooo, Beth!" And then he was in the backyard, on the Dawkins' patio, his heart pounding out of his chest, face to face with Beth Scalini.

All of this should have played out in slow motion, like the famous commercial with the couple running toward each other on the beach. It might as well have been in *super* slow motion, because what happened next he would remember for the rest of his life. It's a beautiful thing when your first real kiss is like that.

Nancy's mother came out to the garage to check on things and promptly put an end to Spin the Bottle. Shortly after that, the party came to an end. Cars were arriving at the front of the Dawkins' home, parents coming to pick up their kids. Beth was gone with a friend before Nick could plot his next move, not that he had any moves. He waited now while Brent said a long, lingering goodbye to Claire. When her father arrived, Brent opened the car door for her and even reached in to shake hands with Mr. Ryan and introduce himself. Vince Ryan sat there, slightly dumbfounded, with a look on his face that said *who the hell is Brent Barlow and why is he shaking my hand?*

Brent and Nick watched Claire and her father drive away and then started the short walk home. Brent was overflowing with excitement. He and Claire were officially going steady now, and he needed to give her a ring or a pin or something, and where could he get a ring, and maybe they could ride the bus downtown tomorrow to Newberry's or Woolworth's and he could find something nice but not too expensive, and on and on.

Nick was only half-listening, preoccupied with his thoughts of Beth. He decided not to share what had happened with Brent. He would keep Beth to himself for now. On Monday, he would have his friends talk to her friends and ask *what does Beth think of Nick Shane?* And if her friends said, *well what does Nick think of Beth,* then what? He could tell them to say *he likes her.* Or, *he likes her a lot!* Geez, what if they come back with *she thinks he's a nice guy, but . . .* Oh, man, what then? He'd have to talk to Brent about it—Mr. Smooth, Mr. Confident, Mr. Shake Hands With Her Dad. Brent will know what to do. But not now. Maybe tomorrow. Nick really needed to sleep on it.

They reached the corner of Buss and Russell and stopped for a few minutes to make plans for the next day. It seemed to Nick that it had been a very long time since they stood on this spot under the streetlight, trying to decide what to do with this warm September evening.

He was right. It was a lifetime ago.

MR. GEORGE

T he only sound was the thump, thump, thump of the basketball echoing off the walls of the deserted gym. Nick set himself at the free throw line, bounced the ball three times and let the shot go toward the basket. The ball clanked off the rim and bounded away to the left side of the court. Nick sprinted after it, then shot a short jumper that also missed. He chased the ball again and then returned to the foul line to start the process all over again. He was rusty and most of his shots missed the mark. After all, this was baseball season and he hadn't touched a basketball for a couple of months. Baseball practice had ended an hour ago and all of his teammates had long since showered and left for home. This was a Friday night and the locker room had emptied out quickly. But Nick was in no hurry. In fact, he was putting off heading for home as long as possible.

The door to the locker room swung open and Coach Wight stuck his head in. "Shane, come on. Get your shower and let's get out of here. It's Friday night!"

"Okay, Coach," Nick replied. He grabbed the basketball and headed for the door. Coach waited until he was in the locker room then hit the switch to douse the lights in the gym.

"Are you okay, Nick?"

"Yeah, Coach. I'm good."

"Well make it fast. I need to get home."

Nick showered and dressed quickly. He packed his gym clothes and baseball gear in a small duffle bag and headed for the exit, exchanging waves with Coach Wight as he left. It was a warm April evening and the sun had dropped below the horizon as he headed across the campus toward Georgia Street. Hogan Junior High was situated at the corner of Georgia and Rosewood, about a half-mile from home. Nick headed west on Georgia toward the corner of Russell Street. It was a short hike, requiring only a few minutes, but again he found himself slowing his pace, taking as much time as possible.

He was mad at himself, upset over the fact that he still cared so much. He was fourteen years old and a guy his age shouldn't care so much about a pet dog, especially a mangy little mongrel like George. But he couldn't help it. He had raised George from a pup and the little mutt had been part of the family for eight years. Now he had been missing for five days and Nick was beginning to believe that he'd never see him again.

This wasn't the first time George had taken off and been gone for a day or two, but never for this long. It was the family's practice to let George out at night to wander around the neighborhood, lifting his leg on every bush, tree, and fire hydrant. He would be gone an hour or so and then come trotting up the walk and scratch at the front door to be let in. Once or twice a year, he would stay out—AWOL as Nick's father put it—and come limping home a day or two later. Nick's friend Brent would always say, "He's just out chasin' the ladies. When he gets hungry, he'll come home." And sure enough, he always did. It never occurred to the family that perhaps George should be neutered.

George was a gift from Nick's cousin Dorothy who owned a female Doberman mix named Penny. Penny had black and tan markings and a sweet disposition, and as is often the case where there are no children in a family, she was pampered like an only child. When Penny turned up pregnant, Dorothy promised Nick the pick of the litter. The father, as it turns out, was a little terrier mutt and the family joke was that he had to stand on a box to get the job done. There were six puppies in the litter, three males and three females, and they were immediately dubbed "Doberman-Terriers," as though this was a reasonable and customary pairing. Of course,

Dorothy promptly named all six puppies: Suzy, Bubbles, Annie, Humphrey, Max and Mr. George.

George was black with white boots, a white belly, and a white tip on his tail. But his distinguishing characteristic, the one feature that separated him from his brothers and sisters, was a right ear that flopped over while the left ear perked straight up. Nick knew at first sight which puppy he would take home.

He taught George every conceivable trick—sit up, shake hands, roll over, play dead, and so on—and did so with ease. Nick attributed this to native intelligence. The fact was that George would do anything for a Hartz Mountain Dog Yummy. One day Brent's father Cal was watching Nick put George through his paces. Cal said yeah, that's nice, but he'd seen a friend's dog who would balance a treat on his nose until told to get it, then flip it up in the air and catch it on the way down, and could George do that? After they left, Nick went to work and within ten minutes, George had the new trick mastered. Anything for a Yummy!

Nick reached the corner of Russell Street and turned left toward home. Just one short block to go. He thought of the rainy day game he and George had devised and played over and over again. Nick would toss a Yummy into his bedroom at the back of the house and George would scamper after it, slipping and sliding on the waxed linoleum floor. In the meantime, Nick would head for another part of the house to hide and wait for George to come and find him. As smart as he was, George had no sense of smell, and it would take several minutes for him to find where Nick was hiding. It was a great way to fill a rainy afternoon.

Whether it was hide and seek, chasing after a tennis ball in the backyard, or trotting alongside Nick as he ran around the block, training for whatever sport was in season, there was no better companion than George, and that's the way it had been for nearly eight years.

Nick was close to home now and he began to brace himself for the worst. George had a wicker basket bed that sat in the front room at the base of the window where he could look out through the glass and monitor everything that passed on the street. He was always waiting there for Nick to come home from school in the evening and he'd race to the door for a tail-wagging greeting. Nick knew if he headed up the walk and didn't see George waiting in the window, it was over: after five days, it would be time to give up.

He reached the house near the end of the block and headed for the front door. The front window was empty. Nick opened the door and quickly headed toward his room at the back of the house. His father sat in the front room reading the newspaper, but Nick passed through without speaking. His mother was in the kitchen preparing dinner and again he passed by without a word. He entered his room and closed the door behind him, then dove onto the bed and buried his face in the pillow. He tried to tell himself that he was too old for this, that he shouldn't be crying over a mongrel dog, but that didn't stop the tears. Several minutes passed before he could compose himself. He rolled over on his back and dried his eyes. He would have to pull himself together before sitting down to dinner with his parents.

Nick heard his father's footsteps approaching the kitchen, and then his baritone voice speaking to his mother. "I don't want that dog in the house until he has a bath. Make sure Nick bathes him first thing in the morning."

"I know, Daddy, we'll tell him at dinner," his mother replied.

Nick jumped off the bed and raced for the door of his room and from there to the kitchen where his mother stood over the sink. She looked over her shoulder and smiled at him.

"He came home today, honey. Just came dragging up the front walk. He's in the garage. He's filthy dirty and he's going to need a bath . . ."

Nick didn't wait for his mother to finish. He went to the garage door and flipped on the light switch as he opened it. And there was George, curled up in his bed in the garage, too tired to do anything but thump his tail weakly as Nick came toward him. He knelt beside the bed and looked at the exhausted little mutt. His white markings were nearly covered in mud, there appeared to be dried blood near his left ear, and he smelled like an outhouse.

"God, look at you . . . you little shit . . . where have you been? . . . chasing the ladies, just like Brent said . . . I should beat the snot out of you . . . I thought you were dead . . . you're not goin' out at night like that anymore, do you hear me? . . . no more . . . I thought you were dead . . ."

Through this monologue, tears clouding his eyes, Nick was gathering George onto his lap and into his arms. His father would be angry and he'd have to change clothes and scrub down before dinner, but he didn't care. He wondered if there were any Yummies in the house.

FALLOUT

Ollie's old man decided to build a fallout shelter. He got a set of plans from somewhere—*Popular Mechanics* magazine or some government office. He spread the plans across the kitchen table and studied them for a long time. Then he was ready to go to work.

He hired a backhoe to dig the hole in the backyard and hauled in concrete for the foundation. Then he built the steps and reinforced the walls and ceiling with heavy timbers. He installed the ventilation system and built pantry shelves to hold water and canned food. Then, suddenly, he just stopped. He locked the heavy trap door and walked away.

Ollie asked why, but his old man would only say *what's the use?* Maybe it was something he read about fallout shelters being useless. Or maybe it was the newsreel footage of the H-bomb tests. Ollie's old man was very quiet and sad for a long time.

One day Ollie asked if he could open up the shelter and show his friends. His old man gave him the key and said *do whatever you want.* So Ollie and his friends turned the shelter into a clubhouse. They would take some Cokes and a bag of chips and their girlie magazines into the shelter and hang out all afternoon. They took cigars down there a couple of times, but nearly suffocated because the smoke didn't escape fast enough.

Ollie's friends thought his old man was crazy—*nuckin' futs,* as one of the guys put it—but they admired his workmanship. Everyone agreed it was the best place in the neighborhood to hang out.

WILD CHILD

I.

Nicholas Shane sat back in his seat, gazing out the window of the bus as it rolled through the tidelands and salt marshes along Highway 37. They were on their way back from San Rafael, from a baseball game against San Rafael High. Nick had finished his sack lunch: the soggy bologna sandwich, a bag of chips, a red apple and a chocolate chip cookie, all of it washed down with a small carton of milk. It had been a sunny day in late March of 1959, a small taste of the warm spring weather ahead. He could see the lights of Vallejo in the distance as the bus negotiated the gently winding road in the gathering dusk.

Nick loved the trips to Marin County to play against the high schools there—San Rafael, Tamalpais and Drake. The communities nestled against the eastern slope of the coast range, watched over by Mt. Tamalpais, were quaint and beautiful, reeking of money, both old and new. In Nick's mind, when he tried to picture heaven it looked a lot like Marin.

They were getting close to Vallejo now and Nick focused his attention on the apron of the road where the wild growth had been cut back to form a clear green strip between the roadway and the cattails that grew at the edge of the slough. Then he saw it up ahead, their target for later that night: the metal sign caught in the headlights, a white background with bold red script that spelled out "Budweiser," and in smaller block letters "King of Beers." The sign was mounted on what looked to be four-by-four posts cemented into the ground. Darin and Brent were in the seat in front of Nick. He tapped them both on the shoulder.

"There it is," he said. "Right up ahead. There!"

The bus rolled by the Budweiser sign and sped on into the night. The boys looked at each other and grinned.

The dark green '51 Chevy sedan headed west across the Napa River and out onto Highway 37, beyond the turnoff for the north gate to Mare Island. Though the car belonged to Nick's mom, Darin was at the wheel as the designated driver for the evening. It was after 1:00 AM and there was no traffic in sight. The three boys watched intently, looking for the Budweiser sign on the left apron of the road. Then suddenly, there it was, ready for the taking. Darin brought the car to a quick stop just off the pavement.

Nick and Brent jumped out and crossed the road to the sign, Brent carrying the hand saw from his dad's tool shed. Darin pulled away, heading west. He would turn around a couple of miles down the road and swing by to see if the sign was down and ready to load into the car. He would switch the lights off and on so they would know he was coming.

Brent immediately went to work with the saw on one of the four-by-four posts. The posts had been soaked in creosote and the cutting was tough. When Brent began to run out of steam, Nick took over and continued the cut.

They saw headlights approaching from the east and knew it could not be Darin. They scrambled down the bank toward the slough and lay flat on the ground until the car passed. Then it was back to work on the post.

Headlights approached again, this time from the west, winking off and on. They continued working, looking up as Darin rolled by, craning his neck to see their progress, his eyes as wide as saucers. Nick and Brent saw the look on Darin's face and laughed so hard that the sawing stopped for several seconds while Nick composed himself. It's amazing how things are so hilarious after a couple of beers.

The first post was cut through and they quickly moved to the second one. Darin rolled by again, heading west this time, the same wide-eyed look on his face, and again Nick and Brent roared with laughter. Finally, the second post snapped and the sign toppled to the ground. After a few minutes, they saw headlights approaching from the west, turned off and then on, and they got ready to load the sign into the trunk. Darin pulled off onto the apron, jumped out and headed to the rear of the car.

"Oh, my God! Look at the size of that thing! It will never fit. Just leave it and let's get out of here." Darin looked east and west, checking for traffic, his face panic stricken.

"Open the trunk, man, we can get it in there. Come on!" Nick and Brent were not about to leave their prize.

The trunk lid popped up and they shoved the sign in as best they could. It just barely fit side to side, and it was clear that it was going to hang out of the trunk by about two or three feet. They pulled the lid down and secured it with a length of rope. All the while, Darin kept up a steady stream of objections, met by continuous laughter from Nick and Brent. They jumped into the car and Darin pulled back onto the roadway, heading toward Vallejo.

"Okay, assholes, what happens if we get stopped?" Darin was beside himself.

"Hey, if we get stopped, you stay with the car. Me and Nick are making a run for it." Nick and Brent made saucer-eyed faces at each other and howled with laughter, which only added to Darin's stress level.

They had to make it home to Steffan Manor and Darin was frantically trying to choose a route with as little traffic as possible. After crossing the Napa River, he started south on Sacramento Street, but quickly decided that was too risky. They veered off through neighborhoods they'd never seen before and would never see again, avoiding the major thoroughfares—Redwood, Sonoma Boulevard, Tennessee, Broadway, Springs Road.

"I know we're gonna get stopped. We should dump that damn thing right here and now." Darin was picturing himself in a police lineup, a headline in the newspaper screaming "Local Boys Busted in Bizarre Incident."

"If you get stopped, just say, 'Sign? What sign, officer? I don't know about any sign!'" More laughter filled the car, much to Darin's chagrin.

They crossed the freeway at Georgia Street and made an immediate right on Miller. At last they reached the corner of Buss and Russell. Brent's house was situated on the corner and they unloaded the sign and hid it as best they could in a small alleyway, overgrown with shrubs and wild rose bushes, which served as an easement to the adjoining property. There was no way to conceal a sign that size—they judged it to be about four by seven feet—so Brent knew he'd have to deal with it in the morning, coming up with a plausible story to tell his father. As soon as the sign was unloaded and the car was safely parked in Nick's driveway, across the street and down the block a couple of houses, Darin headed for home.

"Hey, don't you want to stay and celebrate a successful mission?" They had a few more beers on ice.

"I got you dummies home. Now it's all yours. Good luck. You're gonna need it." And with that, Darin was gone.

Nick looked at Brent and shrugged. "So, more beer for us, right?"

The sun was up and the morning dew was rapidly burning away when Nick stepped out onto the porch to retrieve the Saturday *Times-Herald*. He knew there would be an article in the sports section recapping yesterday's game. Across the street at the house on the corner, the garage door swung open and he saw Brent emerge pushing a lawnmower. Nick sat in the front room, reading the sports section, glancing out the window every now and then to track Brent's progress.

Brent finished mowing one section, and then began a long pass that would take him close to where the Budweiser sign was stashed. Nick put down the newspaper and watched intently to see what would come next. Brent stopped the mower near the overgrown bushes that shielded the alley. He turned and walked quickly back to the house, entering by the front door. After a minute or two, he emerged with his father close behind him. They walked over to where the sign was hidden. Nick watched as a brief but very intense discussion ensued. Then Brent's father turned and marched back toward the house, his eyes straight-ahead, obviously not happy with the situation.

Nick went out onto the front porch and whistled in Brent's direction. Brent motioned for him to come over and Nick trotted across the street.

"What did you tell your dad?"

"I told him, 'hey, look, somebody left this sign here last night.'"

"And he bought it?"

"Nah, not really. He's pretty pissed. I asked him if we could put it in the shed. He didn't like that at first, but then he said to go ahead and just get it out of here."

There was an old shed in the backyard that had been built by the previous owner as a workshop. Brent's dad stored tools there, but otherwise, the space was unused. Brent and his friends turned the shed into a clubhouse over the years. They hauled in an old couch and a couple of rickety chairs and decorated the walls with pictures of their sports heroes. Gradually the sports heroes gave way to Playboy centerfolds. The Budweiser sign would be a great addition.

Nick and Brent carried the heavy metal sign into the shed and admired the way it looked propped against the wall. In the cold light of day, they were amazed that they'd been able to cram it into the trunk of a '51 Chevy.

"Are you sure your old man is okay with this?"

"Well . . ." Brent paused for a moment. "He did say that if the police come looking for a missing sign, he's bringing them straight to me."

The police never came, there was no call for a lineup, and the *Times-Herald* never mentioned a missing sign. Two years later, Brent joined the Air Force and left Vallejo for good. Eventually his parents sold the house and moved to Utah. Nick was living in Minnesota at the time and Darin was busy around town doing his own thing.

They never asked what became of the Budweiser sign.

II.

They crouched behind the rocks at the end of the sandy beach, looking out at their objective. The waters of Southampton Bay lapped quietly at the pilings that supported the old pier and they could see that the tide was still rising, approaching the high water mark. Fifty feet or so out onto the pier there was a shack that served as a bait shop and rental office, and then beyond the shack and below the raised pier were the pontoon-supported slips where the fishing boats were tied. Each boat was painted red, severely faded now, with "Costa's Resort" in white letters on each side. A few of the wooden boats had been hauled from the water and were stacked on their sides like a row of clamshells, but several remained in the water, bobbing gently on the rising tide. There was a light burning in the shack and they watched closely to see if there was any movement inside.

"I don't like it," Brent whispered. "There could be somebody in there."

"It's almost midnight," Nick replied. "There's nobody there. They don't live on the damn pier."

"What if somebody's in there?" Darin shared Brent's misgivings.

"Then we'll run like hell. It's no big thing." Nick wasn't about to let either of them back out now. They were coming if he had to drag them.

It all started when Nick and his mom had dinner one evening at Spenger's. The restaurant was located on an old ferryboat christened the *Encinal*, anchored in Southampton Bay, looking out at the Carquinez Strait. Spenger's was an old favorite, famous for its seafood, and Nick and his mom had been there many times. On this particular evening, while waiting to order, Nick happened to flip the menu over. On the back was a short history of the *Encinal* and its service on the bay as a car ferry. And then there was a paragraph about a barge anchored out in the Strait at the mouth of the bay where, allegedly, illegal prizefights had been staged in years past.

Illegal fights? That got Nick's attention. Later, as they left the restaurant, he paused in the parking lot, peering out across the bay toward the Contra Costa shore. Sure enough, there it was: a large, wooden barge anchored out where the calm waters of Southampton met the turbulent Carquinez Strait. He had recently read "The Light Of The World," a Hemingway short story that referenced a fight "out on the coast" between Stanley Ketchel, the "Michigan Assassin," and Jack Johnson, the great black heavyweight champ. He recalled bits and pieces of the dialog:

> *Steve Ketchel . . . his own father shot and killed him. Yes, by Christ, his own father. There aren't any more men like Steve Ketchel.*
>
> *Wasn't his name Stanley Ketchel?*
>
> *Oh, shut up . . . what do you know about Steve? Stanley. He was no Stanley. Steve Ketchel was the finest and most beautiful man that ever lived . . . He was the only man I ever loved.*
>
> *Didn't Jack Johnson knock him out though?*
>
> *It was a trick . . . a fluke . . . Steve knocked him down . . . Steve turned to smile at me and that black son of a bitch from hell jumped up and hit him by surprise . . .*

That was the only suggestion Nick needed. His imagination ran wild. He began to construct his own narrative: Ketchel versus Johnson, a great battle out on that barge, staged there because the State wouldn't give Johnson a license and no one was sure who had jurisdiction out on the bay. Nick could visualize the barge surrounded by vessels of every shape and size, overflowing with fight fans, shouting at the top of their lungs, wagering their paychecks on one man or the other.

No doubt about it: Nick would find a way to stand on that barge. And here they were on this mild summer night, ready to execute the mission he had planned so carefully.

"Okay, let's go."

Nick took off running toward the end of the pier and a second later, Brent and Darin followed him. Now they were on the pier, approaching the shack where the light burned inside, expecting to be jumped at any moment. Now they were past the shack, climbing down the ladder that led to the boat slips. They chose a skiff in the last slip at the end of the dock and Nick and Darin scrambled aboard. Brent untied the rope and gave a strong push with his right leg as he jumped in. Now the small boat was floating free of the dock. Nick slipped the oars into the oarlocks and began to row as quietly as he could, moving steadily out into the bay. They were on their way.

Nick leaned hard on the oars, no longer worried about the noise. To his right, he could see the sandy beach as it swung around toward Lover's Point; to his left, the long arc of the shoreline leading to Dillon's Point; looking back, Costa's Resort and the pier growing ever smaller with each stroke of the oars. It was a long hard pull out to the barge. Brent and Darin each took a turn rowing as they zigged and zagged their way across the water, not a straight line but good enough given their inexperience.

Finally, they pulled alongside the barge and tied the skiff to a wooden ladder that led up to the deck. They climbed the ladder and stood on the deck at last, grinning at each other. Mission accomplished. Well, half of it at least.

The flat wooden deck was a large rectangle, about one hundred feet wide and maybe twice as long. There was a sturdy rail that ran all around the perimeter and a small wooden shack in one corner. And that was it. Nick walked along the railing, taking in the view. To the west, he could see the double span of the Carquinez Bridge, and below it, on the south shore of the Strait, the town of Crockett and the sugar refinery with the bold C&H sign in red, white, and blue lights. To the east, the lights of Benicia burned brightly. All around them, the dark waters of the Strait lapped at the barge.

They had arrived at high tide. He tried to picture a fleet of boats, jockeying for position to view the epic fight, the crowd raucous and loud, fistfights breaking out here and there.

"Okay, so that's it. There's nothing' to see. Let's get the hell out of here." Brent broke the mood and the scene faded from Nick's mind. They headed for the ladder and the skiff to begin the journey back to shore.

It was a typical July night at Lover's Point with four or five cars parked facing the water. You could drive out onto the point, turn slightly to the left or right to keep the center aisle clear, facing out toward the Contra Costa shore or inward toward Southampton Bay. Every now and then a door would open slightly and some lovemaking debris would be dropped to the ground. Then headlights would come on, the car would back out of its space, turn and head back toward the street. Before long, another vehicle would arrive to take the vacant spot.

It isn't likely that any of the couples in the parked cars noticed the little skiff making its way across the water, angling toward the beach just north of the point. If they noticed, they didn't react. There were more important things to do.

The boys pulled the boat up onto the sand well out of reach of the tide, which was past its ebb and beginning to turn. Before long, the current out in the Carquinez Strait would be flowing hard toward San Pablo Bay. They scrambled up the path from the beach and made their way to the car where they retrieved an ice chest from the trunk. A few minutes later, they were relaxing on the beach, enjoying an ice-cold beer, toasting their successful mission to the barge.

They would leave the skiff there on the beach. When the sun rose in the morning, it would be easy to see from Costa's pier. The Costas would have no trouble recovering their property. No harm, no foul.

Many years later, Nick would learn that the great championship fight that took place on that barge was between Gentleman Jim

Corbett and Joe Choynski, twenty-seven brutal rounds, finally ending when Corbett landed a devastating body blow. It was reported that both fighters had to be carried from the barge. The fight actually started in San Anselmo on May 30, 1889, but was broken up by the police after four rounds. The battle resumed on June 5 out on the barge in Southampton Bay, surrounded by boats of every description, most of them, according to the newspaper reports, coming in from San Francisco.

It isn't often that reality trumps fantasy, but Nick had to admit that the historical accounts of the fight and the setting were even more vivid than his imagination. It was July of 1959 when Nick and his friends stood on the deck of the barge, seventy years after the Corbett-Choynski fight, and it seemed incredible that it was still there after all that time.

Yet even faced with the facts, Nick had a hard time giving up his fantasy version of the event. He could almost hear Hemingway's characters in that train station up in Michigan:

> *He was a great fighter . . .*
> *I hope to God he was . . . I hope to God they don't have*
> *fighters like that now . . . My soul belongs to Steve Ketchel.*
> *By God, he was a man.*

For Nick, it would always be the Ketchel-Johnson Barge.

III.

Brent and Darin stepped out of the car, paused for only a moment, and then started their run across the field toward the chicken coops. The coops were built in several long rows running north and south. To the right, on a slight rise, was the farmhouse, a neat one-story stucco structure with a red brick façade. On the left side of the house, there was a small porch and steps that led to a driveway where a late-model pickup truck was parked. Their mission was to grab as many eggs as possible and then beat it back to car and get out of there—fast. They were almost there, bags at the ready, making no effort to be quiet now, brush and twigs crackling underfoot. The commotion roused the chickens, just a few squawks at first, followed shortly by a full-blown cacophony. It's amazing what a racket several thousand chickens can make.

Inside the farmhouse, a middle-aged couple sat watching television.

"Do you hear that, Henry? My, what a ruckus."

"Damn kids! Happens every Halloween. They think they can come out here and grab a bunch of eggs to throw at each other."

"What are you gonna do?"

"Same as always." He walked to the side door where a loaded shotgun stood propped against the wall.

A light above the porch came on, the door opened and the man stepped out of the house, a long, narrow object in his right hand. He raised the object above his head and pulled the trigger. The boys felt their ears ring as the shotgun blast split the night sky and reverberated through the valley. They dropped their bags and began an all-out sprint for the road and the waiting car, expecting any moment to hear a second blast, this one aimed in their direction.

Brent and Darin made it to the road where Nick was waiting with the car, engine running, headlights off. They piled in shouting "Go, go, go, get the hell out of here!" Nick hit the gas and the car started to roll. There was no screeching of tires or flying gravel as he pulled out onto the highway. The '51 Chevy sedan with PowerGlide transmission wasn't built for fast starts. The car gained speed steadily, heading up the highway toward the town of Petaluma.

It was several minutes before anyone could speak. "Who the hell's idea was this, anyway?" Brent knew the answer. He was glaring at Nick. Nick swallowed hard and felt bad for his friends. It had seemed like a good idea at the time.

They cruised slowly through Petaluma, "The Egg Basket of the World," trying to attract as little attention as possible, and soon they were rolling down Lakeville Road, heading toward the intersection with Highway 37. It would take a good forty minutes or so to make it home safely to Vallejo.

The plan had been to raid the chicken ranches in the rolling hills west of Petaluma and gather as many eggs as possible. Someone had told them that the coops were built so that the eggs rolled down into a wire trough. All you had to do was run along and scoop them up. Easy pickings! Back home they would cruise through the popular spots—Patches, Scotty's, Eat 'n Run, Terry's—and pelt their friends' cars with fresh eggs. It was Halloween and this would be a great prank. Unfortunately they had nothing to show for their little adventure. They would have to settle for several dozen water balloons, if they could find a place to fill them. At least they had a Plan B.

Nick pulled into a service station out on Broadway and ordered a couple of dollars worth of regular. The attendant went through the ritual of pumping the gas, checking the oil and radiator, and washing the windshield. Meanwhile, Darin and Brent hurried off to the restroom to fill balloons with water. They emerged from the men's room carrying cardboard boxes filled with balloons, varying in size from grapefruit to cantaloupe. One box went into the trunk in reserve and the other into the back seat of the car. Now they were armed and ready to cruise.

The process was pretty straight-forward: drive through one of the popular places around town, spot some people you knew, pull up alongside and get them to roll down their windows, then bombard them with water balloons. It was good clean fun, especially if the other car was full of girls who would screech and scream when the balloons started to fly. Of course, they had to be prepared for incoming bombs, because they weren't the only ones that were armed and ready for battle, and water wasn't the only substance flying.

They were making a pass through the parking lot at Eat 'n Run when Nick saw Tony Bonetti and several friends heading in their direction. Tony was behind the wheel of his daddy's brand new Chrysler 300E, a beautiful hardtop coupe with a gold-bronze finish polished to a mirror shine. Darin and Brent immediately began grabbing balloons in anticipation of splattering Tony and his gaudy new ride. Nick, on the other hand, felt a surge of panic. Tony

"T-bone" Bonetti was big and swarthy and mean, and so were his friends. They had the reputation of being guys you just did not mess with. The big Chrysler approached and Darin and Brent were cranking down the windows, getting ready to launch.

"No no no no no, not Tony, not T-bone . . ." Nick was desperate to stop the attack.

Tony was nearly alongside now, his window rolled down, smiling and waving.

"No no no no . . . don't do it, don't do it . . ."

But it was too late. Darin and Brent fired the opening salvo. The first balloon caught Tony square in the face. The next round splattered the roof and the door of the beautiful new coupe. Tony wasn't smiling any longer. They heard him screaming expletives as Nick hit the gas and sped toward the exit.

"Whoa, here he comes!" Darin was looking out the back window. He could see Tony speeding toward the opposite exit, determined to wheel around and give chase. They were about to get their butts kicked by some guys who really knew how.

Nick had about a thirty-second head start as he sped down Georgia Street, heading east. He knew he could not outrun that big 300E. His only chance was to head off Georgia and try to lose Tony with some quick turns. He took a hard right onto Gleason, a left on Campbell, then another quick left, which took them back to Georgia. All the while, they could see headlights trailing them in hot pursuit. Nick headed east on Georgia again, then a quick right onto 14th Street. Up ahead he saw a low building with a paved parking lot in front. He flew into the lot, skidded to a stop just to the left of the building, doused the headlights and killed the engine. They slid down in the seats, their heads out of sight, and waited. A second later, Tony made a fish-tailing, tire-screeching right onto 14th and came flying up the street. Nick inched his head up as the roar of the engine passed—just in time to see the brake lights come on as the Chrysler came to a quick stop. They'd been made. The jig was up.

Nick jumped up behind the wheel, started the engine, threw it into "drive" and hit the gas. The car lurched over the parking curb and started across the open field beyond, pitching and bucking over the broken ground, heading toward the chain link fence that bordered the freeway. Suddenly, the hood dipped sharply and then rose up again as they bounced through a shallow ditch. The next sound they heard was an ear-spitting roar. It took Nick several seconds to realize what had happened: he had ripped the exhaust system from the engine manifold and it was now running completely un-muffled. He could not believe the sound that came from that old Chevy.

Back on 14th Street, Tony and his friends watched in utter disbelief. After a minute or two, the big Chrysler pulled slowly away. They were content to let the idiots out there in the field self-destruct.

Nick would not remember much about what happened next. Somehow he managed to get the car back on the pavement, over the freeway and home to Russell Street, in spite of the deafening noise and the sparks flying from the muffler as it was dragged along under the car.

When he finally pulled into the driveway and shut the engine down, Darin and Brent jumped out and made a beeline for home, leaving Nick to deal with the consequences. He walked up the front steps and opened the door as quietly as possible, hoping his mom was sound asleep.

"Nick, is that you?" His mother was calling from her bedroom.

"Yeah, Mom."

"Are you okay? What was that awful noise?"

"Nothing, Mom. We'll talk about it in the morning. Okay?"

It was quiet for a few seconds. "Okay, honey. Sleep tight. See you in the morning."

"Night, Mom."

Nick closed the door to his bedroom and leaned back hard against it. He stood there for a moment in the quiet, darkened room. *What a night,* he said to himself. *What a Halloween . . . Trick or treat.*

In the morning, Nick made up a whopper to tell his mother. *Geez, Mom, we were just driving down the street and we hit a bump or something and the whole muffler thingee fell off. Must have been worn out, rotted through . . . or something.* His mother, being sweet and gullible, bought it without question.

He told the real story to his older brother Rich who was decidedly less accepting. "You're gonna have to pay me back for the repairs, buster. And you and I need to have a little talk." Nick knew he was right. Stupid pranks were one thing. Tearing up the family car was another.

He figured he'd have to go to Tony Bonetti, hat in hand, and beg for forgiveness. Strangely enough, Tony never said a word, as though none of it ever happened. It was a bizarre ending to a Halloween Nick would never forget.

Trick or treat, indeed.

IV.

Rich poured the charcoal from the bag into the barbeque and then used the long metal tongs to stack the coals in a neat pyramid. When he was finished, he nodded to Nick who proceeded to douse the stack of coals with lighter fluid. When Nick was finished, they both stepped back a little as Rich struck a match and tossed it into the stack. The lighter fluid caught with a resounding whoosh and the flames leapt into the air.

"You know, that muffler repair—the whole exhaust system actually—was not cheap. I'm expecting you to pay me back out of your GVRD checks. Okay?" Rich was speaking calmly, deliberately, making his point clear. He was referring to Nick's part-time job with the local recreation district.

"Yeah, I know. I'll pay you back." Nick was contrite, and in full agreement with his brother.

Rich took a long drink from his can of Hamm's. Nick did the same. It was a cool evening in early November, yet the ice-cold beer still hit the spot. They watched as the charcoal pyramid began to turn gray around the edges. Rich would wait until the coals were entirely covered with gray ash before he spread them around the base of the barbeque.

"I mean . . . driving out across that field—what the hell were you thinking?"

"I don't know. I guess I just panicked."

"And what about the chicken farmer with a shotgun? Geez, Nick!"

Nick had nothing to say to that. He stared at the pile of charcoal.

The coals were ready now and Rich spread them evenly around the bed of the barbeque. He held his palm over them to make sure they were good and hot. He nodded to his brother and Nick put the gleaming chrome grill in place over the coals.

"Tell me about the rowboat heist. Rowing out to that damn barge. What was that all about?"

"I don't know . . ." Nick was starting to sound like a broken record. "Just the challenge, I guess."

"You guys are out there on the bay in the middle of the night, no life jackets. Do you realize all the things that could have gone wrong? You know how the current rips through the Strait when the tide changes."

"Yeah, but we planned it for high tide."

"And what if you planned wrong? What then? You could have ended up out in San Pablo Bay, or over at the mothball fleet."

Nick didn't say anything. He knew Rich was right.

Rich nodded his head again, indicating the grill was ready and Nick went through the garage and into the kitchen to retrieve the steaks. They had been marinating all day in the special sauce that he and Rich had concocted. They called it their "kitchen sink" marinade, a little bit of everything: catsup, mustard, some red wine vinegar, brown sugar, Worcestershire, Tabasco, minced garlic, chopped onions, maybe half a can of beer. They would let the steaks rest in this mixture all day, and save a little to brush on just before they came off the grill. It was all good.

Nick was back with the steaks now—three nice-looking sirloins. The meat sizzled as it hit the grill. The sauce that clung to the meat began to caramelize and the aroma made their mouths water.

"What did you guys do with the Budweiser sign?" It seemed that Rich had a checklist he was determined to cover.

"It's in the clubhouse—the shed—over at Brent's place."

"And Brent's old man is okay with that?"

"Uh . . . not really."

Rich just shook his head. He flipped the steaks, wanting to get a good sear on each side to seal in the juices. He glanced up at Nick. "You know none of this would be happening if Dad was alive."

Nick had nothing to say. Rich was right. Their father had been a stern man, not someone you wanted to cross, and he didn't tolerate bullshit from his kids. You behaved like a Good Sailor or you shipped out. Nick remembered that night in October of 1958, a little more than a year ago, when Rich came to pull him out of a dance at the high school. As they walked to the car, his brother turned to him, put his hands on his shoulders, and said, "Brace yourself, Nick. Dad had a heart attack. He's dead." Rich was only 25 at the time, just nine years older than Nick, yet so much responsibility had fallen on his shoulders since that night. Nick knew he was just making it worse.

Rich was watching the steaks carefully. He and Nick preferred medium-rare, while their mom liked hers well done. "Look," he said, taking his time, choosing the right words, "you guys are good students. You get good grades. You're not in trouble at school. You're good athletes. Hell, you're good kids! So why act like juvenile delinquents?"

Nick was quiet. Rich took two of the steaks off the grill. He would give the remaining steak a few more minutes. Mom would have the baked potatoes and salad ready when they came in and, of course, there would be chocolate cake for dessert.

"Why don't you just dial it back a little? You know?"

"Yeah . . ."

"I mean, I know you guys like to have your fun. Just dial it back some. Okay?"

"Okay."

Rich took the last steak off the grill and they headed into the house. Their mother was hurrying around the kitchen, putting the heaping salad bowl on the table, pulling the potatoes and garlic bread out of the oven. Nick thought about his brother's words as they sat down at the dining room table. Dial it back? Make it easier for Rich? Make it easier for the whole family, really. Yeah, he could do that.

And so he did.

There are some stories from your youth that you love to share with your family, tall tales and adventures, most of them having lots of good laugh lines. But Nick never shared the stories from 1959, that wild and chaotic year. He didn't want to be the dad who had to say, "Do as I say, not as I do." He didn't want to be disciplining his kids over some infraction and have them say, "Oh yeah, well what about what *you* did when *you* were a kid? What about *that*? Huh?" So he never told them about the Budweiser sign, or the rowboat trip to the fight barge, or that crazy Halloween night when he tore up the car. He never told those stories. It was best to keep them to himself.

ASPIRATION

I'm not going to tell you my name, or where I live, or even what part of the country. If I did, you'd probably say, "See, I told you those people are crazy." I don't think we're any crazier than anybody else. I think everybody has a story to tell, and sometimes it isn't pretty.

I guess my story starts with Momma. She got up one Sunday morning when my little sis and I were still in grade school and she said, "It's Sunday morning and these children belong in church." With that, she cleaned us up and marched us off to Sunday school and that's where we've been nearly every Sunday since.

Daddy never goes. Oh, he may go on Christmas, or maybe Easter, and he always plants his vegetable garden on Good Friday. Other than that, he doesn't hold much regard for organized religion. He likes to read the Sunday paper and have a cup of coffee, and maybe catch an early football game on the TV. Most of all, I think he just enjoys having the house to himself. That's his idea of a good Sunday morning.

Our little church is about the prettiest one in town. It sits back off the street with a nice green lawn on three sides and parking out back. The old plaster walls are painted white-on-white and the roof is Spanish tile. There is a steeple up front with a little cross on top, and down both sides of the building are pretty stained glass windows. The pews inside are sturdy oak and can hold about one hundred and twenty souls, and if you can sit there and not be inspired by the light coming through those windows, well then, you're probably at home watching football like my daddy. The social hall is downstairs and has a full kitchen, and along the south wall are the classrooms for the Sunday school. Reverend Parsons says our church is "the perfect marriage of form and function." I think he's right.

I used to fight with Momma every Sunday because I didn't want to get out of bed early and get dressed up and all. I wanted to stay with Daddy and maybe watch some football. But Momma wouldn't hear of it. She'd pull me out of bed by the ear if she had to.

When I was about to start my sophomore year at the high school, things started to change. That's when I began to notice Nola Belle Whitt. Nola Belle is a widow woman, about thirty-five or so. She lost her husband in the Korean Conflict. We're not supposed to call it a war. Anyway, she is a long-time member of the congregation and a real dedicated Sunday school teacher. Nola has a daughter, Lola Mae, who is a senior at our high school. Some folks say it was a mean trick for a woman named Nola to name her daughter Lola. But it isn't too confusing, so long as we use both names: Nola Belle and Lola Mae.

Nola Belle is about the prettiest woman I've ever seen. She has short brown hair, and soft brown eyes, and the nicest smile. And she is a kind person, too. You can tell just by talking to her. And, oh, does she have a shape on her! It is the best I've ever seen. I mean, I've seen movie stars in the magazines and all, but none of them has a shape to compare to Nola Belle Whitt. It's a shape that can keep you awake at night, take my word for it.

Lola Mae is another story. She is pretty enough I guess, kind of a young version of her mother, but that's where the resemblance ends. Lola Mae is a moody, stuck up, snotty brat of a girl as far as I'm concerned. I see her every day at school, and every Sunday at church, and do think she ever speaks to me? I'm just some lowly sophomore runt and she'll never let on that she even knows me. There's a word for girls like Lola Mae. Starts with a "B," but I won't repeat it here.

Anyway, start of sophomore year, I finagled things so that I could be Nola Belle's assistant with her Sunday school class. I just help keep the kids in line and help with class projects and such.

I can't wait to get to church on Sundays, just to be in the same room with Nola Belle. She has a good job over on the shipyard and she always dresses real nice. In the winter, it's really pretty sweater sets, and in the warm months, it's nice cotton dresses with those scoopy necklines. No matter what she puts on, it always shows off her shape. And that perfume she wears: just a touch, but boy does she smell nice.

I love being in the classroom with Nola Belle, being close to her, helping her with the kids, brushing against her from time to time. And she is so sweet, too. Once she reached up and touched my cheek and said, "You know, sweetie, there is medication that can help with your breakouts. Lola Mae uses it. I'll get some for you, if you like." And she did, and it helped. At first I was embarrassed that she noticed, but after I thought about it, I realized how sweet it was for her to even care. She is just that kind of person.

Well, one fine spring day Joe Don Jackson showed up at our church, driving his jet-black 1956 Chevy Bel Air hardtop. Joe Don is big, real big, like a football player or something, and nice looking too, if you like that type. He has dark hair and a big smile with these gleaming white teeth, and all the ladies immediately went into a twitter. He has this way of looking them in the eye and smiling the big smile and making whoever he's talking to feel like the only person in the world. But I saw something else: most of the time, those bright blue eyes were darting around the room, like he's expecting somebody to jump him or something. Real shifty-eyed, if you know what I mean.

Reverend Parsons welcomed Joe Don with open arms and introduced him to the entire congregation. It wasn't long before Joe Don was in tight with the Men's Club. He became a regular usher and passed the plate every Sunday. I heard that collections went way up, cause all the ladies liked him and all the men were a little scared, him being so big and all.

That was all fine with me, until I saw that he had his eye on Nola Belle Whitt. Right then and there I took a strong opinion of Joe Don Jackson, and it wasn't a high one either.

A few weeks later, it was all through the congregation that Nola Belle and Joe Don were "seeing each other." I think we all knew what that meant. Sure enough, you'd see them after services, downstairs in the social hall, holding hands and smooching and stuff. And him all the while with those shifty eyes.

One Sunday after services, we were heading for the parking lot in back of the church and I realized I'd left my bible in the Sunday school room. I didn't want to leave it there all week, so I told Momma I was going to get it and I'd be right back. I went down stairs into the social hall and started across to where the classrooms are located. All the lights were out, but there was some daylight from the ground-level windows along the side of the building. As I got close to the classroom, I could hear a voice and I realized it was Nola Belle. She was saying, "Oh . . . Oh God . . . Oh God," and I thought something must be wrong. The door to the classroom was open about half way and I started in to see what was the matter. Then I stopped dead in my tracks. At the far end of the room, there was a countertop and sink, and Nola Belle was perched up on the countertop, her legs wrapped around Joe Don's waist, and him with his slacks down around his ankles.

I stepped back out of the doorway and pressed myself against the wall, gasping for air. It was like somebody punched me in the gut and I couldn't breathe. Then I heard Joe Don calling, "God, oh God . . ." I couldn't stand to listen, so I ran out into the social hall and waited for them to finish. Finally, I heard Nola Belle's heels clicking on the wood floor and she and Joe Don came out of the room. I started toward them as if I just got there.

"Oh hi, honey. What are you doing down here?" She gave me that sweet smile of hers.

"I forgot my bible," I said, and nodded at Joe Don as I passed.

I went into the room and found my bible, right where I left it. I stood there for a while, looking at that countertop and thinking what an asshole Joe Don Jackson is, doing it right here in the church. But then I thought, well, if God gave us these feelings, then maybe church is as good a place as any. At least that shifty-eyed sonofabitch could have locked the door. Right there I started to cry, and I really wasn't sure why.

Not long after that, Nola Belle and Joe Don announced that they'd gone off to a Justice of the Peace and got married. All the church ladies were disappointed because they didn't get the chance to put on a big wedding, but they consoled themselves by throwing a real nice reception in the social hall. I didn't want to go, but Momma insisted. We all brought presents and the happy couple greeted us at the door. It was nice, with punch and cake and lots of little sandwiches with the crust cut off. I thought the cake was first rate.

After a while, Joe Don came over to me and struck up a conversation about fishing. I told him I'd been out to Lake Chabot a few times, but had no luck. He started giving me lots of pointers and told me how he usually caught his limit out there. He said he'd take me some day, maybe after church, and show me how he did it. I could see how people were drawn to Joe Don, what with all that charm going for him. Pretty soon, he wandered off and went to talk to Lola Mae.

Lola Mae was sitting by herself and looking real pouty, but I noticed something new about her. Her shape was really coming in. She was going to be just like her momma, maybe even prettier. But that didn't matter, cause she was still a stuck up snot. So Joe Don walks over and starts chatting her up, and all the while his shifty eyes are scanning the room. All I could think of was him with his pants down to his ankles.

A few Sundays later, I was up and showered and all ready for church, and I went into the kitchen to get a piece of toast and some orange juice. There was Momma, still in her housecoat, standing by the sink taking deep drags on her cigarette. Daddy was at the kitchen table with his coffee and his Sunday paper.

"Hey, Momma," I said, pouring myself a glass of juice. "Why aren't you ready for church?"

"We're not going today," she said, blowing the smoke out hard, the way she did whenever she was mad.

"Really? Why not?" I was looking forward to seeing what Nola Belle would be wearing that morning.

"Go ahead," Daddy said. "Tell him why."

"Hush up," she said, and blew another hard stream of smoke.

I stared at Momma and she finally stubbed out her cigarette and looked me in the eye.

"It seems that Joe Don Jackson got caught taking money from the collection plate. Seems he's been doing it for some time."

I turned away from her so that she couldn't see me smile.

"Tell him the rest," Daddy said.

She paused for a second and then went on. "It seems that Joe Don and Lola Mae have run off together. She left a note for her momma saying they was in love and they're going off to Nevada somewhere to get married."

"But how can they do that?" I said. "He's already married to Nola Belle."

"It seems the two of them wasn't married after all. They was just living over there to Nola's house like . . . like . . ."

"Like a bunch of bunny rabbits," Daddy said.

"I said hush, Harlan!" Momma was angry with him now. Daddy just chuckled and went back to his newspaper.

I took a long drink of juice and smiled again. *Well, she's quit of him now, and that's a good thing.*

When Nola Belle finally came back to church, all the ladies rallied around her. They hugged her neck and kissed her cheek and gave her tissues to dab her eyes. Let's face it: it was the most exciting thing to happen in that church since the foundation was poured.

Me, I took a different track. I bought Nola Belle a card at the supermarket where I work after school. It said something about "you got a friend," or some such. I signed it and slipped it in her purse one Sunday. I know she found it, though she never said anything.

One of my friends called her Nola Nitwit one time and I punched him real hard in the arm. "What was that for?" he yelped. I told him nobody was going to talk bad about Nola Belle when I was around.

So that's my story. I'm her friend and protector—for now. I'm getting my drivers license real soon, and I've got some money saved up. I'm going to get me a nice hardtop, or maybe even a convertible. She'll take notice then.

TAHOE BLUE

I.

Darin sat up straight in the back seat, craning his neck, anticipating the summit. Was it around this curve, or the next? Finally he saw the sign proclaiming they had reached Echo Summit. Soon Highway 50 would swing to the north and the scene he was waiting for would come into view. And now there it was, the great Tahoe basin and the south end of the lake laid out below like a picture postcard. He never tired of this panorama, no matter how many times they made the trip. To Darin, it was the most beautiful sight in the world, a world he'd seen very little of. Still, it was an opinion he shared with many world travelers. And there was the proof, just outside the window of the car, the incredible blue of Lake Tahoe, constantly changing with the sunlight and the puffy white clouds sailing above, as they headed down from the summit, the sheer cliff all along the right side, down toward the town of Meyers.

Darin and Nick both strained to look out the window as they crossed the Upper Truckee River. It had been a good snow year and even now, in mid August, the water level looked high and the stream flow strong. Fishing would be good this year.

They passed through Meyers and continued on past the turnoff for the Tahoe airport, and then they were into the home stretch, the view that Darin's parents, Dante and Bea Maneri, looked forward to: that last, long drive through the towering pines and into the

Tahoe "Y." There, Highway 50 branched east toward Stateline and Highway 89 headed north along the west shore of the lake toward Emerald Bay. To Dante and Bea, it meant the long hard drive from Vallejo was done. Soon they would be relaxing in the cabin with a tall cold drink and their summer vacation would be on.

Darin was eight years old when his parents bought the cabin near the Tahoe Y. Every year since then, his family had spent the last two weeks or so of August at the lake, and brought his friend Nick along to keep him company. His parents were not snow people, so come Labor Day weekend, they would put shutters on the windows, pour anti-freeze in all the drains, and head for home.

Darin never tired of it—doing the same thing year after year—because there was so much to do! There was the ping pong table in the garage, and the stickball game he and Nick had devised, and hiking in the woods in back of the cabin. At night, they could head for the miniature golf course down along Highway 50, or they could go into Stateline with his parents and be checked into the theater at Harrah's for a first-run movie. Of course, there was trout fishing on the Upper Truckee, and the activity that took on greater importance as they grew older: going to the beach at Camp Richardson every afternoon where there were lots of girls their age to ogle. If his parents had ever suggested that they go somewhere else and do something different, he would have protested vehemently.

This summer would be the same, only bigger and better. Darin now had his drivers license. The anticipation of the freedom to go places and do things and roam without parental supervision was almost too much to bear. He'd had his license for more than a year and had proved himself to be a responsible driver. He had gained his parents' trust. This year, the whole world of South Lake Tahoe would be his oyster.

The cabin was just off Highway 89, within walking distance of the Y. A single car garage was situated out on Rogers Street, and behind it stood the rustic little cabin with its green shingled roof. Originally it consisted of a large living room, a kitchen and a bathroom. The Maneris had added a room big enough to contain two full-sized beds, a set of bunk beds and a walk-in closet. When

Darin and Nick were younger, they would sleep in the bunk beds. Now they preferred to throw their sleeping bags on two couches that formed a right angle in the living room where they could talk late into the night and not disturb Dante and Bea.

Dante was taking one last box loaded with groceries into the cabin when he heard the garage door swing open, followed shortly by the sound of a ping pong ball bouncing back and forth across the table. He knew that Darin and Nick would launch a lively competition that would continue until Labor Day. It was a good sound, a happy sound, and Dante smiled a little as he opened the front door. Now it was time for that tall cold one.

II.

It was nearly 1:00 PM when Dante dropped them off. He synchronized watches with Darin and said he'd be back to pick them up at 5:00. He watched them head off toward the stream, fishing gear in hand and hanging from their bodies. It was a warm afternoon and they wore T-shirts, their gym shorts from school, and old beat-up Chuck Taylor high-tops with no socks so they could wade in the stream. They were pretty good at this and Bea was already planning the dinner menu for that evening with rainbow trout as the main course. Dante had no interest in fishing, so it was good to have Nick along to share the adventure. Ray Fulmer, an old family friend, had taken Darin under his wing when they first purchased the cabin and taught him everything he knew about stream fishing, how to read the water and—as he put it—think like a trout. "If you were a trout," he would say, "where would you hold up in the current, waiting for the stream to bring your dinner?" Each year, Darin and Nick had raised their game a little. Now they always came home with fish for dinner, plus a few to wrap and freeze for another day.

The Upper Truckee River was a fine trout stream, well stocked by the Department of Fish and Game, tumbling beautifully through the long valley. Maybe twenty yards across at its widest, it rushed over rocks and logs and tree roots between banks lined with willows and tall pines. Every so often there would be a long, deep pool, usually formed by a great tree that had fallen in a storm. East of the river along the flat floor of the valley was a development of summer cabins known as the Rainbow Tract. On the west bank, the land began the steep ascent up the mountainside toward Echo Summit.

Darin and Nick knew this stretch of the river by heart. They could close their eyes at night and work their way upstream, picking out the holes and rapids and eddies where they knew trout were holding. They each carried a long fly rod rigged with a clear six-foot leader and a #12 trout hook. Two or three split shot at the end of the leader, just above the hook, provided the weight to take the bait down to the sandy streambed. The bait of choice, proven over the years, was a single Atlas brand salmon egg carefully worked onto the curve of the small gold hook. They had tried many other offerings—worms, grasshoppers, helgramites harvested from the streambed, even dry or wet flies—but the large, pale pink Atlas egg was the consistent winner.

They crossed to the west bank of the stream and began their well-practiced routine. Darin would fish a promising riffle, tossing his line upstream at a forty-five degree angle and letting the bait drift down to the waiting fish. Meanwhile, Nick would take the next spot upstream along the bank. And so, they worked their way up river, fishing carefully, thinking like trout, making sure to fish every promising stretch of water.

The white water was the best. That tasty Atlas egg tumbling down through the rapids would be slurped up by a waiting trout with little hesitation. The long slow pools were less productive, even though there were some large fish holding there. Those fish were smarter and harder to catch. You didn't get to be a nice fat rainbow trout by being stupid. Occasionally they would hook a German brown, but that species was rare in this stretch of the river. "Good size" meant nine to twelve inches. Most of the fish they caught were in the six to eight inch range, just right for Bea's frying pan.

Of course, they had a standing bet, because every activity had to be a competition. It was two dollars for the first fish, two dollars for the biggest, and two dollars for the most. They kept a running tally that was never actually settled; at last count, Nick owed Darin about twenty dollars. The simple truth was that Darin was a better fisherman.

Darin hooked a nice rainbow at the second riffle he fished. He played it carefully toward the bank, drawing the line in with his left hand, his right hand holding the rod tip high, his right forefinger gripping the line as he drew it in. As the fish neared the bank, he could see that it was a nice rainbow, about twelve inches in length. Finally, he lifted hard with his right hand and the trout shot out of the water and onto the grassy bank behind him. He laid his rod down quickly and went to the fish, which was flopping wildly in the grass. He gripped it around the gills and removed the small hook. He had lined his creel with grass and now he dropped the fish inside on the sweet green bed. He relaxed for a minute, feeling the fish still moving strongly in the creel against his left leg. It was then he realized that his heart was beating rapidly. The thrill of it never got old for Darin. He smiled and reached for his rod. This would be a good day.

Nick landed one shortly thereafter, and so it went. They would fish upstream for about two and half hours, then turn around and start back down. Fishing downstream always went faster because they were retracing their steps, going over water they'd already fished carefully.

They took a break before turning back, sitting down on a sandy beach created by a bend in the stream. Darin had six nice fish in his creel and Nick was putting up a good fight with five of his own. They lay back in the sand and listened to the sound of the river and the wind whispering high up in the pines, talking quietly and making plans to see a movie that evening.

Pines really do whisper if you listen carefully. They say, *It's okay. You're okay. You have time to figure it out. You'll do the right thing, make the right decisions when the time comes.* They listened closely for a while. Then it was time to head downstream.

III.

"They're here again," Darin said. He and Nick had dropped their stuff, spread their beach towels on the coarse granite sand and were busy applying sun lotion. The beach at Camp Richardson was crowed as usual.

"Who?" Nick didn't bother to look up. He was pretty sure he knew the "who" Darin was talking about.

"Those girls we saw yesterday. You know, the pretty blonde and the other one."

"Yeah? Where?"

"Don't look, dummy!"

"Hey, bite me. How am I supposed to see 'em if I don't look?"

"They're to the left at 10:00 o'clock."

"Oh, yeah. Not bad. The 'other one,' as you call her, is pretty cute too."

"Does she remind you of anybody?"

"What? Which one? Remind me of who?"

"The blonde girl. Look again. Who does she look like?"

"I don't know. Give me a clue."

"Sandra Dee. Tell me she doesn't look like Sandra Dee."

"Oh for God sakes, Darin, give it up! This obsession with Sandra Dee is out of control, man." Darin had confided many times to his best friend that Sandra Dee was his idea of the perfect woman. "Besides, I thought you were pissed at her over *A Summer Place*, for doin' it with Troy Donahue." Nick laughed out loud.

"Yeah, well what does she see in that pretty boy? Makes me sick . . ."

"Look, Darin, it's a damn movie. You know—playacting on film? It's not real!"

Darin was quiet for a few seconds. "So don't you think she looks like her?"

"Okay, so they're both blonde. That's it. Give it up."

"I'm goin' over there . . . and you're coming with me."

"Yeah, right."

"I'm serious. We're going over there and talk to them."

"Let me ask you something, buddy. How many years have we been coming to this beach?"

"I don't know . . . maybe about seven or eight."

"And how many years have we been checkin' out the chicks, saying we were going to go talk to them?"

"Maybe . . . the last three."

"And how many times have we actually gone over to the cute girls and struck up a conversation?"

"Okay, so it's zero. I don't care. I'm going over there and you'd better be right behind me."

"I've got five bucks says you won't go." This was a direct challenge and Nick grinned at Darin, waiting to see him back down.

"You're on. You're gonna' owe me five more dollars, pal."

Darin was quiet for a minute, mentally trying out opening lines. How about . . . *Hi, my friend and I took a poll and you two were voted the prettiest girls on the beach.* Nah, too corny. Or . . . *Hi, your daddy must have been a thief, cause he stole the stars from the sky and put them in your eyes.* Nah, way too long. Let's see, how about . . . *Hi, I'm a reporter for the Tahoe Times and . . . and . . .* Shoot! And what? Then he thought he had a good one. "Hey, Nick, how about this: 'Hi, this must be heaven, cause you two are clearly angels.'"

"Oh, stop, you're killin' me, man!" But Nick was thinking too. "Try this: 'Hi, Miss Dee, sorry to bother you . . . I loved your work in Gidget and I was wondering if I could have your autograph?'"

Darin thought about that one for a few seconds. "You know, that isn't half bad. I might use that one."

Nick rolled over onto his stomach, continuing to work on the tan that would never be. "Yeah, sure. Wake me when it's over. Like when they throw sand in your face."

Darin stood up, gathered himself, and started across the beach for what seemed like the longest walk of his life. He heard Nick scramble to his feet and then his footsteps crunching in the sand behind him.

"Hi, how ya' doin'?" He could barely get the words out.

The girls looked up from their beach towels and smiled. They responded with something like, "Hi . . . okay . . . how's it going?" Darin couldn't hear over the pulse pounding in his temples.

"Are you guys staying at the campground here?" That sounded better. A rational question at least.

"No," the blonde girl replied. "My parents have a cabin over by Meyers."

Her friend with the short, dark brown hair grinned at them and said, "Yeah, we just come here to hang out. There are usually some cute guys around, but not today. Just a bunch of dogs!" She waited a beat and let loose a hearty laugh. "Oh, my God! You should see the looks on your faces. Come on, I'm just kidding." That did it. The ice was officially broken.

"My name's Darin. This is Nick."

"Hi, I'm Sandy and this is Becky."

Darin glanced at Nick and saw him roll his eyes a little. Of course! Her name had to be Sandy.

"You guys want to swim out the raft?" Becky stood up and nodded toward the large wooden raft supported by pontoons that was anchored about 100 feet off the beach. She tugged at the top of her black suit, shaking out the lean, taught muscles of her legs like a sprinter about to step into the blocks.

"Yeah, I'll go," Nick said.

Darin was surprised because Nick was never a fan of swimming in the ice-cold waters of Tahoe. He and Becky trotted off down the beach, sprinted the last few yards and dove head first into the lake, leaving Darin alone with Sandy. They laughed at what was obviously a race to the raft, which Becky won handily.

"Becky is a real jock," Sandy said, laughing easily. "So where are you guys from?" It was the first of a long series of leading questions, which Darin found himself answering at length. The questions came with a genuine curiosity that made him feel important, like someone worth knowing. He quickly learned to turn the questions around, to learn about the life of Cassandra "Sandy" Hansen who lived in Palo Alto, near Stanford University where her father was a professor. She made it seem so easy, so effortless, that he found himself relaxing and enjoying the conversation. It was a new experience.

He began to notice details. Her hair was the color of honey with lighter streaks from the sun, and she wore it pulled back and up off her neck, tied in a ponytail. Her bathing suit was a deep blue, much like the color of her eyes, and she was even prettier than he thought when he first saw her from across the beach. They talked for a while longer and then decided to walk up to the market that faced Highway 89 for a cold drink. She stood up to pull on a loose-fitting T-shirt and a pair of denim shorts and he saw that they were nearly the same height, about five feet six. They headed up the beach to the road, talking casually all the way.

"So, what are your plans for the fall?" he asked.

"I'll be a freshman at Stanford. My dad wants me to go there. How about you?"

"I'll go to Vallejo JC. Probably a couple of years, while I figure out what I want to do."

"So, do you have a girlfriend, Darin?"

"No, not really. Not now. Not anytime, actually." He felt compelled to tell this girl the complete truth. A simple "No" would have been enough. "How about you? Are you going with somebody?"

"I was. But we broke up. He's going back east for college in the fall and it didn't make sense to try to have a cross-country relationship. We're still friends, though."

Comfortable, relaxed, easy, the conversation went on. Why was she so easy to talk to? What was it about her that put him at ease? They came back to the beach with a bag full of snacks and soft drinks to share with Nick and Becky who were busy laughing and poking fun at each other. And so the afternoon passed, four new friends in the process of discovery.

As the sun began to fall behind the mountains to the west, Darin cranked up his courage one more time. "Hey, do you guys like miniature golf? Can you meet us tonight at the place down by Bijou?" In spite of a great afternoon, he was prepared for the big rejection, something along the lines of *umm, no, we have to wash our hair.*

The girls looked at each other, shrugged in unison, and said "Sure. What time?" Of course, they'd have to work it all out with their parents, but they made tentative plans to meet around 8:00 PM.

Riding home from the beach, Darin thought about the night ahead and suddenly felt like a dozen butterflies had taken flight in his stomach. In time, he would recognize it as the feeling that came with the anticipation of being with Sandy.

IV.

The light green 1959 Pontiac sedan sat in the parking lot of the movie theater, pulled forward into a space that faced out onto Highway 50. It had been a warm day that lingered into the mountain evening and the windows were rolled down, The Drifters "There Goes My Baby" playing softly on the radio. Darin and Nick were stationed in the front seat, carefully watching any cars that turned into the lot, waiting for Sandy and Becky to arrive. They'd made arrangements to meet for a movie that night after another afternoon at the beach. The week had gone by quickly, marked by time together at Camp Richardson, miniature golf, and a visit to a driving range at the golf course in Meyers where Becky wowed them with drives that sailed past the two hundred yard mark.

Darin's parents were staying in tonight and this was his first opportunity to "borrow" the car, as he put it to his father. A dark Chevy pulled into the drive leading to the theater and they saw the girls riding in the back seat. They waited until they were out of the car and the driver had pulled away.

"Okay, let's go," Darin said. He pushed the button to lock the driver's side door, checking to make sure the keys were in his pocket. The girls didn't know he'd be driving tonight, and neither did Sandy's parents. Darin was pretty sure what their reaction would have been had they known. Sandy was about to open the door to the theater when Darin and Nick came up behind them. They turned and smiled and said their hellos and suddenly Darin felt like the wind had been knocked out of him.

"Ohmygawd," he mumbled in Sandy's direction, "you look great!" Her hair hung down past her shoulders with a gentle curl that framed her face. It was the first time he'd seen her without a ponytail. But there was more: a bright red shade of lipstick that made him want to say the word *kiss*; eyes that were darker, fuller, her lashes longer and slightly curled; and a very becoming blush on her cheeks. *Makeup,* he said to himself. *She's wearing makeup.* And then those butterflies were back, launched into wild flight around his stomach.

"Yeah, go figure," Becky cracked. "A couple of beauties like us hanging out with Mutt 'n Jeff." She, of course, had opted for the natural look, not a trace of makeup to be seen.

The ice was broken again, thanks to Becky, and they stood talking and laughing on the steps of the movie house. The movie was *A Summer Place* and Darin didn't have much enthusiasm for it. He'd already seen it and really didn't want to sit through it again.

"Hey, do you guys really want to see this? I've got my dad's car. Why don't we just ride around for a while?"

Sandy and Becky did their famous shrug in unison. "Sure, let's go. But my dad will be back to pick us up around 10:00," Sandy added. That gave them about two hours. They hurried out to where the Pontiac was parked, each of them experiencing the thrill that comes with doing something forbidden.

Darin merged into the traffic on Highway 50 crawling toward the casinos at Stateline. Sandy found a Top Forty station on the radio and turned up volume as Wilbur Harrison sang about goin' to "Kansas City." Then it was the Coasters turn to sing about "Charlie Brown," followed by the Crests with "Sixteen Candles." They were solemn when The Big Bopper sang "Chantilly Lace," and they all agreed that the plane crash that February was a major tragedy. The parade of hits continued with the obligatory summer songs thrown into the mix, songs such as "Sum Sum Summertime," and "Summertime Blues," and even Nina Simone singing "Summertime" from *Porgy and Bess.*

Finally they hit Stateline and cruised slowly down the main drag, casinos lining both sides of the street, the neon signs turning night into day. The large white marquee at Harrah's advertised "Louis Armstrong and his All Stars" in bold black letters. Further down the street another marquee proclaimed "Louis Prima and Keely Smith," and the smaller subtext, "With Sam Butera and the Witnesses."

Sandy changed the station on the radio and, as if on cue, there were Louis and Keely doing their rendition of "That Old Black Magic." Nick immediately took Louis's vocal and Becky chimed in with Keely's part. They were pretty good, except for a few blown lines and Nick's lame attempt to copy Louis's New York Italian accent. Darin stopped at a crosswalk while this was going on, the summer gamblers streaming in both directions across the road. They glared into the car where all the commotion was coming from with that annoyed look that said *damn teenagers*. Darin and Sandy raised their palms and hunched their shoulders as if to say *what can we do, they're out of control.*

They cruised back and forth several times, making sure to be seen and heard, and then headed west, back toward the theater. Highway 50 swings close to a beach along the way and they pulled into the lot and parked facing the lake. A new moon hung in the sky, sending a river of white light across the surface of the water. Nick and Becky hopped out to take a walk on the beach, a walk that immediately turned into a romp and a wild game of tag. Darin and Sandy sat laughing, watching their friends darting around on the beach.

"Have you and Nick been friends forever?"

"Yeah, since he was six and I was seven."

"You're really close, aren't you?"

"Yeah . . . we've been best friends since we met." She had a way of opening him up and he went on without prompting. "I remember . . . we were walking down the hill from my house one day and I just blurted out, 'You're my best friend . . . I love you. And Nick said, 'Yeah, I love you too.' Do you think that's . . . you know, queer or something?"

"No. It's great that you have a friend like that. Becky and I love each other, and we tell each other all the time. Our parents became friends when we were babies. We've always been together. She's the greatest, isn't she?"

Maybe it was the moonlight on the lake, or the way it lit her face sitting there in the front seat of the car, but suddenly there was a direct connection from Darin's thoughts to his tongue with no filters in between.

"*You're* the greatest," he said, "you're so beautiful . . . the most beautiful girl I've ever known."

"No," she said, dropping her eyes, "I'm not . . . not really. I've got this bump on my nose . . . my ears are like Dumbo . . . my butt's too big and my boobs are too small."

He thought she was kidding at first, fishing for a compliment, but he saw that she was serious. How could it be that this gorgeous girl looked in the mirror and saw something different than what he was seeing now?

"Sandy, you're—"

"Hush," she said, turning toward him and putting her finger on his lips.

He moved toward her to kiss her, but their noses bumped.

"Here," she said, tilting her head slightly to kiss him. "Relax a little," she said and kissed him again. "Better," and then another kiss. "Try this," and he felt the tip of her tongue dancing against his. The lesson continued for several minutes. "Oh, that was nice."

"Really?"

"Yeah . . . you went from a one to a ten in about five minutes flat."

Just then Becky came tearing up to the car, having obviously defeated Nick in a foot race from the beach. They piled into the back seat and continued their game of slap and tickle. Darin checked his watch. It was time to get the girls back to the theater. He started the engine and let it idle for a minute, waiting for that intoxicated feeling to pass.

V.

They hiked deliberately, carefully on the path beside the river, avoiding the rocks and roots and willow branches that guarded the trail, heading steadily upstream in search of a picnic spot. This would be their last day together; the girls were heading back to the Bay Area in the morning. They'd decided to spend the day picnicking along the Upper Truckee near the Hansen's cabin.

Darin couldn't believe how fast the days had gone by. The four of them had found good reasons to be together every day and most of the nights, and since that night parked at the beach, he and Sandy had always found time to be alone together. He realized that he was addicted to the smell of her hair, the taste of her kisses, and the way it felt when he held her in his arms. He was not ready for summer vacation to end.

They came upon a promising stretch of sandy riverbank and Nick and Becky elected to stop there. Darin had a particular place in mind that he wanted to show Sandy, and so they continued on the path. Finally, they rounded a bend and there it was: a long, deep pool with a lovely stretch of white sand. At its head, there was a great pine tree that had fallen across the stream, its giant root base exposed on the west bank. They spread an old blanket on the sand, dropped the beach bag that held their lunch, and walked carefully out onto the fallen tree to a point about mid-stream. There they sat peering down into the dark water below the massive trunk.

"Just watch for minute, until your eyes adjust. You'll see. There! See them?" Darin pointed down into the pool where two large trout were swimming lazily by.

"Ohmygawd, yeah, I see them. They look kind of little, though."

"No, those guys are about twelve, maybe fourteen inches. That's good for this stream. But they're hard to catch in these pools. They're really picky . . . they won't hit just anything."

Further downstream, a fish broke the surface and glinted in the sunlight, disappearing back into the dark water, concentric waves moving out across the pool. They sat on the log watching, waiting for more of the brightly colored trout to pass by.

"This pool is too perfect," she said, standing up and heading for the beach. "I'm going in!" She reached the blanket, stripped off her khaki shorts and unbuttoned her sleeveless blue cotton blouse. "Don't worry," she called, "I'm not going to get naked." She waded into the stream up to her knees, wearing a white cotton bra and briefs, and then dove headfirst into the quiet pool. "Oh!" she yelped as she came to the surface, "this water is freezing!" She swam downstream with a smooth, well-practiced breaststroke, did a neat kick turn and started back.

Darin was waiting for her on the beach when she stood up and stepped out of the water. He handed her a beach towel from the bag and watched her dry off quickly, goose bumps breaking out all over her body, her teeth chattering slightly.

"This must come right from the snow pack. Here, feel my hand." They sat down on the blanket while she dried her hair, combed it out smoothly, then pulled it back and fastened it in a ponytail. "Oh, look," she said, glancing up at the sky.

They lay back on the blanket, side by side, gazing up into the cloudless blue sky. High above them, a tiny silver dot marked the progress of a jetliner, a long white contrail trailing behind. The tall pines surrounding the stream formed a rustic picture frame and the silver plane was the lone subject.

"If I was on that plane . . ." she started, pausing to consider, "I'd be on my way to Paris . . . and I'd wait tables in a café on the Left Bank at night . . . and write short stories and work on my novel all day . . . and I'd prowl through the bookstalls and sit in the sidewalk cafes and watch the tourists go by . . . and I'd meet Ernest Hemingway and he would become my dear friend and mentor . . . and I'd call him Papa and he'd call me The Kid . . . and we'd motor out into the countryside through the beautiful little villages . . . and we'd stop for a fabulous meal, with a different wine for every course . . . and when we got back to the city, there would be a cable waiting to tell me that my latest story had sold . . . and soon, I could afford to quit my job and write full-time." She finished emphatically, waited a few seconds and then turned toward Darin. "How about you?"

"Me? If I was on that plane . . . I'd be on my way to New York . . . to see the Yankees play at Yankee Stadium."

Sandy laughed out loud. "Oh, how romantic! You and I are like oil and water."

"No, listen . . . I'm not through. You'll be with me, and we'll go to the stadium, 'the house that Ruth built,' and I'll show you the monuments in centerfield to The Babe and Lou Gehrig and all . . . and we'll have seats behind the first base dugout, and we'll see all the great Yankees—Casey, and Mickey, and Yogi, and Whitey, and Moose, and Hank, and Don Larson . . . and then we'll fly up to Boston for a series with the Sox, and I'll take you to Fenway Park and show you the Green Monster . . . and you'll see the great Ted Williams play, and you can tell all your friends 'I saw the greatest hitter that ever lived' . . . and I'll teach you about the offense—when to steal, and when to bunt, and when to hit-and-run . . . and the defense—how it sets up for different hitters, and how the shortstop and second baseman turn a double play . . . and I'll teach you to keep score, and you'll sit with your pencil and your scorecard, wearing your Yankee cap . . . and you'll love the game as much as I do."

She looked at him for a long time, studying his face. "Okay . . . but do I have to wear the cap?"

They laughed as she stood up to get dressed, stepping into her shorts and picking up the blue blouse. He stood in front of her, folding the wet towel, preparing to stuff it into the beach bag. Then she took his right hand in hers and placed it on her left breast.

"See . . . my bra's nearly dry."

He could feel her nipple like a little stone in the palm of his hand. She took his hand away and put on her blouse.

"Come on, let's go find Becky and Nick." She looked at him and saw that he had something to say. "What? What is it?"

"You were wrong," he said.

"About what?"

"You said your butt was too big and your boobs were too small . . . wrong, on both counts . . . and I'm never going to wash this hand again."

Sandy laughed out loud and Darin laughed with her as they headed downstream to find their friends.

The sun had fallen behind Echo Summit leaving the valley in deep shadows, yet still reflecting brilliantly from the mountains to the east. They made their way up from the river and onto the road leading to the cabin. Nick and Becky lined up for one last sixty-yard dash down the road to where the Pontiac sat waiting. When Darin said "go," she broke away to a five-yard lead and held it for the length of the race, leaving Nick to shake his head in wonder and admiration.

Now they were at the driveway to the cabin and the time had come to say goodbye. Darin wrapped his arms around Sandy and held her close, swaying slightly in the gentle breeze, knowing that when he let go, summer and Sandy would be gone. She stepped back and looked at him and he could see that her eyes were welling with tears. One broke free and ran down her cheek.

"You told me I was beautiful," she said, "but it's you, Darin . . . you're the one who's beautiful . . . with your brown eyes and your perfect curly hair and those freckles across your nose. You'll always be beautiful to me." Then she turned and hurried away toward the porch and the front door, Becky following closely behind, waving goodbye to the two of them.

Darin turned the key in the ignition and rev'd the powerful V-8 engine, dropped the gearshift lever into drive and hurried away toward Highway 50 and the Y. They rode in silence for a while until Nick switched on the radio, to a station playing classic rockabilly.

"Are you and Sandy okay?" Nick asked, tentatively.

"Yeah, we're good. How 'bout you and Becky?"

"We're good too. Just good friends. Hell, every time I kissed her, she cracked up laughing. What can you do with a girl that runs faster, jumps higher, throws harder, and hits a golf ball two hundred and fifty yards?" He laughed and shook his head. "What are you and Sandy gonna do?"

"We're going to Paris. Then to Yankee Stadium. Maybe up to Fenway."

"What?"

"I really don't know," he said honestly. He reached for the radio and hit one of the pre-set buttons, and on came the tail end of Louis and Keely doing "That Old Black Magic." Nick immediately jumped in for the big finish . . .

Under that old bla-a-ack magic
Ca-all-ed love

VI.

Darin turned the letter over and over in his hands, admiring the familiar handwriting, so graceful and precise. He and Sandy had stayed in touch for a while, but this was her first letter in several months, and when he called, she was never in. He had a pretty good idea what was inside. He made his way to his bedroom at the back of the house, flopped down on his bed and ripped open the envelope. As he suspected, it was a classic "Dear John" letter.

Sandy said that she and her boyfriend were together again, that he had decided not to go east for school, that they were both at Stanford now and realized that theirs was a serious and committed relationship. She said she would always cherish their time together last summer, and she didn't want to hurt him, but she didn't want to string him along either. And so this would be her last letter. She hoped he'd understand.

Darin locked his hands behind his head and stared up at the ceiling, her letter resting lightly on his chest. He wasn't hurt, or even disappointed, just a little blue. He had already taken the summer of 1959 and stored it away carefully in a place for special memories. He knew that at any time, he could close his eyes and she'd be there, swimming smoothly across that deep still pool, sunlight reflecting from her body, white gold in a Tahoe blue setting, perfect forever.

THE LESSON

Senior year, fall semester: Nick walked up the ramp that led to the second story of the main building. He found the room designated for the class—U.S. History—and took a desk in the middle of the room. The instructor would be Mr. Sauer, and he had the reputation of being a tough taskmaster.

Earl entered the room and took the desk next to Nick. They'd had a few classes together and, though they weren't close friends, they'd always gotten along well. They chatted casually as the room filled, waiting for the instructor to arrive.

The bell rang and Mr. Sauer made his entrance. Nick had seen him around campus, with his tweed jackets, his horned-rim glasses, and an expression on his face that suggested chronic indigestion. He dropped a stack of books on the desk and then took his stance behind the old wooden lectern. He proceeded to call roll, constructing a seating chart in the process. When he finished, he wrote rapidly for a minute, ripped a piece of paper from his pad, and then walked down the aisle to Earl's desk.

"*You* are *not* in this class." He dropped the folded piece of paper. "Take this note to your counselor and get reassigned." He turned and walked away.

Nick was shocked. It seemed like Mr. Sauer was angry, as though Earl had done something to offend him.

Earl looked at Nick and grinned. "See ya around, Nick." He picked up his books and headed for the door.

Nick looked around at his classmates. Earl's departure left the class lily white; not a black face in the room.

Mr. Sauer began his opening lecture. *We are going to study U.S. History, from the founding of the nation until the present. You will be issued a textbook. There will be supplemental texts. Do your reading. Come prepared. Participate in class. Turn in your work on time.* From the expression on his face and the tone of his voice, Nick could tell this was serious business.

"What form of government do we have in the United States?" Mr. Sauer launched into a classic Socratic discussion, using his seating chart to call out names and shine the spotlight in their eyes. He let the discussion roll on for a few minutes. "Okay. Good. What we have . . . ," he paused for effect and everyone got ready to make a note, "is a republic. Or a representative democracy, if you will. Let's take that word 'democracy.' What does that mean?"

Again, he worked his way through the seating chart, letting students offer definitions. "Okay. Good. What democracy means to me is this . . . ," pencils poised again, "the recognition of the worth and dignity of every individual."

It was an electric moment for Nick, one of those ideas that clicks in your brain. He wrote it down and he would remember it for the rest of his life. In Nick's mind, every ideal that we believe and pursue in this country flows from that definition. Equal rights under the law. One man, one vote. Civil rights. Women's rights. Freedom of speech. The right to assemble peacefully. The list goes on, but it all comes from that idea.

Earl went on to have a fine career as an educator, rising to be an administrator at the community college level. Nick never asked him why old man Sauer had summarily booted him out of the class. But he never forgot either one of them, or the lesson he learned that day about the worth and dignity of every individual.

FANTASY CAMP

Claire's father dropped her off at the Greyhound bus depot with time to spare. She could purchase her ticket, buy a magazine, and have a few minutes to kill before the bus was scheduled to depart. Vince Ryan helped his daughter retrieve her suitcase from the trunk of the car.

"Have a good weekend," he said. "Tell Sue I said 'Hi.'"

"I will. See you Sunday night."

She was on her way from Vallejo to Sacramento to visit a friend. At least that was the cover story. She waited in the short line at the ticket window and bought a round-trip ticket to Fairfield, just fourteen miles up the freeway from Vallejo. There she would meet her boyfriend Hank and they would continue on to spend the weekend together in Sacramento. Claire had planned this down to the last detail, making sure they were covered for all contingencies. If her parents called to check on her, Sue was ready to provide cover. Sue's parents were out of town and she would be at home with her boyfriend, spending romantic nights in her parents' bed.

Hank, of course, had his own cover story, supposedly meeting a friend in Santa Rosa. All of this was necessary if you were barely old enough to drive and lived at home with your parents. It was 1961, and though the sexual revolution was on its way, it hadn't arrived just yet. Claire had hatched this plot out of frustration. She was tired of stealing moments alone with Hank, tired of making love in the front seat of a 1951 Ford with one eye open, expecting that any minute someone would come rapping at the window and shine a flashlight in her face. And so she planned this weekend with the utmost care, a chance to live with Hank from Friday night until Sunday afternoon with no one to interrupt or question the right or wrong of it.

Claire was patiently reading the latest issue of *Seventeen* when the loudspeaker in the depot came to life. "Now boarding at Gate 1 . . ."

Hank was waiting at the station in Fairfield when the bus from Vallejo pulled in. He did not believe for a minute that he and Claire could pull off this weekend together without being caught. Surely her parents would check up on her and find out she was not at Sue's. He knew there would be some measure of hell to pay, but he really didn't care. Claire's plan was too intriguing and exciting to dismiss. He had gone along with it as though riding an ocean wave: once committed, it was impossible to resist.

The bus pulled into the station on schedule. Hank grinned at Claire as she stepped down from the bus, wearing a straight gray skirt and a black sweater, carrying her coat over her arm. Her short brown hair had been set and combed and teased in the style of the times. She looked so together, so pretty, so proper.

"So far so good," he said, still smiling.

They waited holding hands while the bus driver retrieved her bag. As they headed toward the parking lot, Hank saw several men in the small crowd glancing at Claire, admiring her figure. He didn't mind the looks. He was used to it. He knew they would look at Claire and think *Wow!*, and then look at him and think *lucky guy*. He didn't mind at all. Minutes later, they were on the freeway headed for Sacramento.

Hank drove across the Tower Bridge and into downtown Sacramento. The sun had fallen from the December sky and it was growing darker by the minute. A week after Thanksgiving the city was bright with Christmas decorations. They admired the lights as they found their way to the downtown Travelodge. There a reservation awaited them under the name of Mr. & Mrs. Hank McKay.

Claire had a plan for this juncture as well. She reached into her purse and pulled out the simple gold bands they had purchased at the five-and-dime in downtown Vallejo. They slipped them onto their ring fingers and admired them in the dim light. Who could tell that they weren't real gold?

A young woman greeted them in the motel office. Hank told her they had a reservation, his voice breaking just a little, and in a moment it was confirmed. He asked if they could see a room before they checked in. This too was Claire's idea, supposedly to look more authentic, less like a couple just looking for a love nest. The girl led them to a room near the office on the first floor, smiling slightly as she opened the door for them. Hank was sure she wasn't fooled in the least.

"The room I have for you is on the second floor, but it's just like this one," she said.

Yes, it was fine they said, and a few minutes later Hank unlocked the door to their room. It was standard Travelodge: a full-size bed with headboard, a bedside table on either side, a credenza with four drawers and a tall mirror offset to one side and a television offset to the other. There was a small round table and two chairs near the window as they entered. At the end of the narrow room were two doors, one to a small closet and the other to the bathroom. A large framed print adorned the wall above the bed. The best thing to be said about the room was simply that it was clean.

They busied themselves with unpacking, hanging clothes in the closet and stowing things in the drawers, settling in for the weekend. Claire called Sue to give her the phone and room numbers, just in case. Finally, everything was done and they stood face to face near the end of bed. Claire moved close to Hank and looked up at him.

"Well," she said, "here we are."

He leaned down and kissed her, gently at first, then with growing insistence. She felt his hands slip under her sweater and caress the small of her back. Their weekend had begun.

Hank was the first to open his eyes the next morning, glancing around the room, trying to judge the time without looking at the clock on the bedside table. He looked at Claire, sound asleep on the pillow next to him, and smiled. He reached up to brush back a lock of hair from her face and her eyes opened slowly, becoming aware of the place and the time, causing her to smile too.

"How did you sleep?" he asked.

"Okay. You?"

"Pretty good. I kept waking up. I'm not used to bumping into someone in my bed."

"Me either. I think I can get used to it."

They talked quietly for a while, planning the day ahead, a little embarrassed to be sharing morning breath for the first time. Finally, they did "odds or evens" to see who would use the bathroom first. Claire won and scampered across the room wearing the top to Hank's pajamas, the sleeves rolled up several turns on her arms. He watched her go with wonder in his eyes. What had he done to be so lucky in this life?

When it was Hank's turn, he washed his face and made a half-hearted attempt to comb his hair. Then he brushed his teeth, and brushed them again, making sure morning mouth was gone for the day. He opened the bathroom door and started into the room, then stopped short and leaned hard against the doorframe.

"Dear Lord," he heard himself say. It sounded like someone else's voice.

Claire was sitting in the middle of the bed, her legs tucked under her, the pajama top dropped casually behind her. She sat with her back very straight, her arms at her sides, shoulders drawn back slightly. It was as though she had been posed for a painting, waiting for a Rubens or a Picasso to put brush to canvas and make her immortal.

"Stay there for a minute," she said. "I want you to stay there . . . and look at me. Really look at me." She looked away from his eyes so that he could stare at her and she could be stared at without embarrassment. "Do you like my body? Am I beautiful to you?"

Hank was sure she knew the answer, knew that she was firm and full and soft in ways that only a girl her age could be. Yet it seemed she needed to ask the question and needed even more to hear his answer. She had other questions, a long and surprising list, and Hank answered all of them in a soft, thick voice.

It occurred to him that in their time together as a couple, he had never had this luxury, the time and the place to just look at her and absorb her beauty. He was truly seeing her for the first time. Hank was no painter, but he knew that the image of her, sitting there so naked and vulnerable and proud, would be etched on his brain from that moment on.

"Come and sit here on the bed," she said, "with your back against the headboard." Hank did as she asked, wondering if this was another item on a long checklist she had prepared for this fantasy weekend. She moved over him and sat across his lap, face to face. Standing apart and looking made touching now even more exciting.

"Can we make love this way?" she asked.

"We can try."

This was new for them and they took it slowly, as though learning a new dance step, awkward at first, then beginning to get the hang of it, finally letting the rhythm take them away.

BAM, BAM, BAM came a sudden pounding on the door. "Housekeeping! Housekeeping! We make up room now." It was a woman's heavily accented voice, just outside the door on the landing. Hank and Claire froze. Their immediate reaction was to stay perfectly still and hope she would go away. BAM, BAM, BAM! "Housekeeping," the voice came again. A second later they heard the sound of a key rattling in the lock.

"No!" they shouted in unison.

"Come back later!" Hank added.

The rattling stopped and they heard the key slide out of the lock. They heard the woman's voice again, now fading, moving away from the door. Then they looked at each other and dissolved in laughter, a full-blown case of the giggles that took several minutes to control. But by then the spell was broken. It was time to shower and dress and head out to explore the city.

Sacramento is a city with a colorful history, from the gold rush to the Pony Express to the transcontinental railroad, not to mention the famous and infamous politicians who made their reputations there in state government. In the sixties, it was very much a government town, home to the state capitol, two Air Force bases, an Army depot, and a handful of major defense contractors. Out in the tree-lined suburbs, it was known as a good place to raise a family, and close to everything—the mountains, the coast, Lake Tahoe, San Francisco. In all the ways to describe Sacramento, the words "pretty" or "beautiful" never came into play. Yet that December in 1961, it was a beautiful place to a young couple in love.

Hank and Claire found a coffee shop for a late breakfast, then wandered through the downtown streets, admiring the department store windows glowing with holiday scenes in bright red and green. Neither of them had much money to spend but they managed to buy a few small gifts for family members, and drop some coins in the kettles of the Salvation Army bell ringers who seemed to be posted at every door. Even the gray, threatening weather couldn't bring them down as they went from store to store, lugging holiday shopping bags.

Claire made a point of checking in with her friend Sue. No, there had been no calls from Vallejo to check on her. Everything was going according to plan. Late that afternoon, they drove across town and found their way to Sam's Ranch Wagon on Broadway, a place that a friend had recommended. There they filled their bellies with delicious prime rib, then headed back to the Travelodge to cuddle in bed and watch TV. They ended this perfect, stolen Saturday making love and falling asleep in each other's arms.

Sunday morning was a good time to linger in bed, exploring and experimenting, ignoring the clock moving toward the end of their weekend. This time they made certain the "Do Not Disturb" card was hanging outside on the doorknob. Finally, they could put it off no longer: it was time to pack and check out.

Claire headed for the shower first. "Give me a few minutes, then come wash my back," she said. When Hank joined her in the little shower stall, the stream of hot water felt good against his skin. They washed their bodies until the small bar of Travelodge soap was nearly gone.

They timed their departure from Sacramento carefully to be in Fairfield in time for the bus to Vallejo. They talked and laughed about the events of the weekend, both of them a little amazed that it had gone according to plan. The closer they came to Fairfield, the more serious the conversation became.

"Hank, I know I'm going to end up pregnant from this."

"You don't know that. How could you know?"

"I just know. I have that feeling."

"Women's intuition?"

"Don't laugh at me! Don't you think it's possible?"

"Of course it's possible, but how can you say that you know?"

"For one thing, it's the right time of month for me. For another, we didn't use any protection most of the time." She was right about that. Hank had brought along a supply of condoms, and even used a few. But for the most part their lovemaking was spontaneous and unprotected. "What would we do if I was pregnant?"

"Geez, I don't know, Claire. You know I've got to decide on scholarship offers, and then four years of college and football— somewhere. I'm not sure where yet."

He went on, but it was not what Claire wanted to hear. She knew what was at stake for Hank's future and knew what that meant for her as well, but four years—or more—was beyond what she could deal with right now. She grew very quiet as they approached the bus station in Fairfield.

A young medical student from San Francisco sat on the hard maple bench in the bus station, quietly observing the scene. Chun Li was on his way back to Chinatown, to his family and his studies, after a weekend visit with friends. He watched the young couple say their good-byes, and then watched the girl board the bus with measured, careful steps. He boarded the bus after her and took a seat across the aisle next to the window. He noticed that the girl had removed her coat, folded it neatly and placed it on the empty seat next to her.

Chun Li opened his book bag and removed a notebook and a fountain pen. The pen was a gift from his parents in honor of his graduation from college and he thought of it as a fine writing instrument. His parents chose medicine as his career, but his secret ambition was to be an author, a writer of moving short stories and epic novels. He uncapped his pen, wrote the date at the top of a blank page, and made the following entry in long, elegant strokes:

Fairfield, Calif., Greyhound station
Handsome young couple say goodbye
Loving embrace, lingering kisses
Across aisle now
Pretty girl, distant and mysterious
Right hand placed low across abdomen
Protective, caring, loving
Perhaps with child

He capped his pen, waited for the ink to dry on the page, and then returned both pen and notebook to his book bag. The bus was merging onto the highway now, gathering speed. He looked through the window at the rolling hills, just now turning a light green after the November rains. He thought about the entry in his notebook and a brief smile crossed his face. *So many possibilities! What a wonderful story this will be.*

THE BALLAD OF
HANK MCKAY

At first he could only sense it, then he could hear it, then he could feel it, coming from behind him and to his left. The linebacker had broken clear and was closing on him at full speed, closing the last yard between them. The ball was leaving his hand now, leaving his fingertips, on its way to his receiver streaking down the right sideline. He would not see the end of the play. He never did. In an instant, he would feel helmet and shoulder pads dig deep into his back, just below his own pads, his head snapping back in a violent whiplash. Then he would be driven forward and down, face first into the dirt at mid-field, his attacker's weight crashing down on top of him with the terrible sound of crushing flesh and bone.

"Hank . . . Hank, wake up. You're dreaming again." His mother shook him firmly by the shoulder. His eyes snapped open, then closed again, relieved to realize it was only a dream, the one he had nearly every night. "Wake up, Hank. I need you to do something for me. Wake up!"

"Yeah, Mom. What is it?" This had to be important. The clock on his bedside table read 7:00 AM and it was a Sunday morning.

"Are you awake?" Mary McKay waited for her son's eyes to stay open. "I need you go track down your father. He didn't come home last night. You know the places he likes. I need you to go find him."

He could see the stress in his mother's eyes. His father had gone off on many a bender, but to Hank's knowledge, he'd always managed to find his way home.

A few minutes later, he was dressed and nearly ready to go, a baseball cap pulled down over his sleep-matted hair. He went to the kitchen where his mother had toast and orange juice waiting for him, and while he wolfed it down, he glanced at the front page of the morning paper. The headlines in the *Vallejo Times-Herald* trumpeted the news of a hit and run accident that had left a five year-old girl fighting for her life in Vallejo General Hospital.

"You get going now, and call me if you find your father." His mother cleared the dishes and wiped the table in front of him.

"I'm sure he's just sleeping it off somewhere. I'll call you." Hank gave his mother a peck on the cheek and headed for the door.

Outside, he started the engine of his 1951 Ford Victoria hardtop and let it idle for a few minutes. The car had been a present from his parents on his sixteenth birthday, and he'd put a lot of time into cleaning it up. He listened with pride to the throaty rumble of the flathead V-8, then turned the windshield wipers on and off a few times to clear away the morning dew. It was nearing the end of October and the mornings were decidedly cooler. Finally, he pulled away from the curb and headed down the block to the intersection with Georgia Street.

Hank knew just where to look for his father, having made the rounds with him so many times when he was younger. Starting when he was about five years old, his father would take him on a regular Saturday morning journey. They called it ". . . going downtown to cash the check." It was one of Hank's favorite things to do and he looked forward to it every payday. It involved cashing his father's paycheck from the shipyard, but it was more than that.

They would ride the local bus down to the ferry building at the foot of Georgia Street where his father would cash his check at the Skippers Club. While his dad had a beer with his friends, Hank would hang around outside on the dock and watch the water taxis race back and forth across the Mare Island Strait, taking the weekend workers to the shops on the shipyard.

After a while, they would walk up Virginia Street to a bar called The Relay where Hank could play shuffleboard if there were no adults using the table. His dad would have a couple more with his friends, and then they'd be on their way over to Georgia Street to a bar called the Towne House, Hank's favorite stop.

The bartender at the Towne House was a guy named Pete Bennett, and Hank thought he was the best. He would climb up on a stool at the bar and wait for Pete to come over. Pete would look him in the eye and say, "Have you been a good boy, Hank?"

"Yes, sir!" Hank was sure to be emphatic with his reply. Then Pete would hand over a pack of Juicy Fruit gum. "Thank you, Pete!" He would jump down from the stool to enjoy his gum and watch the men playing pool in the back room.

Finally, his father would come and get him and they'd catch the bus headed back home to Steffan Manor. His mother would have lunch waiting for them when they got home.

Hank loved going to cash the check and he loved being with his dad. He wondered exactly when a few beers on a Saturday morning turned into drunken binges for his father. Why did it turn out this way? Or, could it have turned out any other way? At least it was better when his father rode the bus, before he started driving again. Now there was that to worry about.

He was heading west on Georgia when he saw two familiar figures waiting at a bus stop. Hank pulled over to the curb and reached across to roll down the passenger-side window.

"Hi, can I give you a ride?" It was his ex-girlfriend Claire Ryan, looking prettier than ever, and their mutual friend Carol Crane. "Come on, I won't bite." He smiled, and at that, Claire smiled back and the two girls approached the car.

"I suppose a ride won't hurt," Claire replied.

Carol, painfully shy as always, climbed into the back seat with barely a "Hi" to Hank. Claire settled into the front seat and closed the door. Hank pulled back into the light Sunday morning traffic.

"You look great," he said to Claire, and it was true. "I'm going downtown. How about you?"

"We have to work at Crowley's today. We're doing an inventory, getting ready for the holidays." She ignored his compliment, but offered one of her own. "Hey, great game Friday night. You were terrific."

"Thanks, Claire. You were there? I didn't see you around after the game."

"Yeah, I was there. I've seen all your games. No need to miss any now." Claire had broken up with him a little more than two months ago, but Hank wasn't ready to let go. "Have you decided who you are going to sign with?"

"No, not yet. It's between Southern U and Cal Poly. Coach Harris from Southern is coming to visit with my folks next week." Hank McKay was the hottest high school quarterback in Northern California and there had been a spirited battle among the colleges competing to give him a scholarship.

"Do they even play football at Cal Poly?" Claire sounded slightly puzzled.

"Yeah, they have a good team. It's not Division I, but I really like their engineering program. You know I've always been interested in engineering."

She turned to look at him for a moment, as if seeing him for the first time: six feet four, two hundred and twenty pounds of muscle, and an arm that could throw a football sixty yards in the air. *As if they are going to let you become an engineer*, she said to herself.

They rode in silence for a while, up over the Georgia Street hill and down toward the main shopping district. Crowley's department store was at the corner of Georgia and Sonoma Boulevard. He pulled up in front of the entrance to the store.

"Thanks for the ride, Hank." Claire opened the door and stepped out onto the sidewalk, holding the seat forward as Carol scrambled out of the back. Carol called a quick thank you over her shoulder and headed for the store entrance.

"Claire, wait a minute." He knew he should probably keep quiet, but . . . what the hell. "Why does it have to be this way? Why can't we be together? You know how I feel about you."

She stared back at him from the curb and her eyes were suddenly very wet. "You've got things to do, Hank, places to go and I can't go with you." She paused for a minute, started to leave, then leaned closer to the door of the car. "You've got too many people with their hooks in you, Hank. Just . . . just be careful." With that she slammed the door and headed toward the entrance to the store.

Hooks? What hooks? God, go figure what girls are thinking. When they were together, he used to fantasize about earning his engineering degree and settling down with Claire. Maybe they could even get married when he was in his senior year. There was no question that he'd have job offers with an engineering degree. At least they could be together.

For some reason he never told her, or anyone else, how much he hated football. Maybe he had just figured it out himself. Oh, the games were fun, making big plays, being around all the guys. But the rest of it, the practices and the beating your body takes, and the endless hours in the weight room—he despised all of it. If he could just stick it out long enough to trade four years of football for an engineering degree, that's all he really wanted.

Hank continued to the end of Georgia Street and pulled into the lot at the Skippers Club. He walked into the dark bar and stood near the door, letting his eyes adjust to the light.

"Hank! Hey, guys! It's Hank McKay." He recognized the bartender, Mickey, an old friend of his father's. "Hank, great game Friday night. It's always great to beat those sonsabitches. Come on over. Can I get you a Coke?"

He hadn't been in Skippers for a long time, but he could see it hadn't changed much. He wondered if the old sign still hung over the toilet in the men's room: "We aim to please. You aim too please."

Several of the Sunday morning drinkers came over to pat him on the back. It was something he'd grown used to, and he remembered what his father taught him: always say thank you to a compliment. Everybody loves a modest hero.

Mickey brought a tall glass of cola and set it on a coaster in front of Hank. "So, Hank, what brings you here?"

"Has my dad been in, sir? I'm trying to find him."

"Will? Yeah, he was here yesterday morning, like usual. Cashed his check, had a couple of beers. Hey, have you decided who you're going to sign with? I bet it's Southern, am I right? You could win a national title there, kid."

"Uh . . . no I haven't decided, sir. Did my dad say anything? Like where he might be going?" He could see that it was going to be hard to keep Mickey on task.

"No . . . he didn't say anything. Just had a couple and left." Mickey looked up suddenly, his attention drawn by the television above the bar. There was a news report about the hit and run accident. No further word on the girl's condition, but the police reported having an eyewitness. "Can you believe that shit? I hope they nail whoever did that, eh kid?"

"Yes, sir. Well, I gotta go. Thanks for the Coke." Hank headed to the door while several patrons shouted congratulations his way. He pulled out of the lot and headed for Virginia Street and The Relay. Somebody had to know where his father ended up.

He parked at the curb just down the street from bar and went inside. The welcome scene from Skipper's was played out once again. It was great to come around these places after a big win. He thanked everyone politely and made his way to the bar. The bartender's name was Marion Bronson, but everyone called him Ace. Ace Bronson had been an outstanding football player himself at one time.

"Hi, Hank. Great game the other night! Were you calling the plays on that last drive? That was classic." Ace knew the game better than most fans.

"Yeah, I called most of 'em. Coach sent in a few, but I had to audible a lot." Hank changed the subject as quickly as he could. "Sir, have you seen my dad? I have to find him."

"Yeah, he was here yesterday. Listen, I've got to tell you, if he doesn't calm down a little, I'm going to have to tell him not to come back. He punched a guy in here yesterday. Busted his nose. I can't have that shit, Hank. Know what I mean?" Ace moved to the back bar and leaned close to a small radio. "Get this, kid, they have a partial license plate on that hit and run driver. They're gonna get whoever did it, am I right?"

"Mr. Bronson, about my dad . . ." Hank tried to get his attention.

"Hank, I like your old man, but if anybody looks sideways at him, he's ready to fight. I know he'd listen to you. Can you talk to him?" Ace let the question hang in the air.

"Okay, sure, I'll talk to him. Any idea where he went when he left here?"

"Not really . . . but you know he always goes by the Towne House."

"Thanks, Mr. Bronson."

Hank made his way through the well-wishers and out the door. He thought for a minute about walking the few blocks to the Towne House, but decided to drive instead. He parked about a half block up Georgia Street from the bar and made his way along the quiet Sunday morning sidewalk. He glanced at Crowley's just across the street and thought of Claire for a moment. Then he saw the gold Cadillac Coupe de Ville parked at the curb. "Oh, crap," he said out loud. Ralph Moretti's car. Just the guy he did not want to see. He paused for a second to weigh his options, then pushed open the door to the Towne House. Pete Bennett was behind the bar and saw Hank come in. He motioned him over and reached across the bar to offer his hand.

"Hi, Hank. How's my favorite quarterback?" Pete had a great smile and a way of making you feel at home.

"Hi, Mr. Bennett. How are you?" Hank shook his hand firmly, the way his father had taught him.

"Can't complain, kid." Pete turned to the men sitting along the bar. "Hey, guys! It's Hank McKay." Again several men came over to clap him on the back and talk about Friday's game. All but one: Ralph Moretti sat at the end of the bar, papers spread in front of him, hard at work on his bookmaking operation. Pete nodded in Ralph's direction. "He's been asking about you, Hank. I think he wants to talk to you. I wish he'd take his business and his fat ass somewhere else. I don't like that shit in here." Pete moved away to help another customer.

Ralph Moretti was a second-generation Italian-American, born and raised in Vallejo, and groomed to take over the family business. Nominally, that business was a string of small neighborhood markets, but the real business had always been elsewhere. In the Prohibition years, the family prospered selling whiskey and wine. And when Prohibition ended, they shifted to bookmaking, which quickly expanded into loan sharking. If you wanted to place a bet on a sporting event anywhere in the country, and borrow the money to do it, the Morettis had you covered. As a young man, Ralph had been an accomplished football player himself, good enough to earn a scholarship to Southern University. At six one, two hundred and sixty pounds, he became a starting lineman with pro ambitions, until he blew out both knees in his junior year. And so, he returned to the family business, which flourished under his leadership. Ralph loved two things: Southern University football and good Italian food. And while his weight grew to well over three hundred pounds, so did his influence in the Southern U Boosters Club. Ralph saw to it that talented players all over the North Bay were in touch with Southern's recruiters. Hank McKay had been a special project of his.

Hank just wanted to ask Pete if he had seen his father, but before he could get his attention again, he saw big Ralph heading his way. He took a deep breath and braced himself.

"Hank! How's it goin'?" Ralph slapped a heavy hand on his shoulder.

"Fine, Mr. Moretti." Hank saw no way to escape what was coming.

"Take a walk with me, kid. Let's go outside for a minute." He kept his hand on Hank's shoulder as they headed toward the door. Outside, he stepped to his car, the gaudy gold pimpmobile, and opened the door for Hank. "Sit inside, let's talk a while." Hank got in and closed the door while Ralph rumbled around to the driver's side. The car rocked and dipped dramatically as Ralph climbed in.

"Great game Friday night, kid. You were terrific."

"Thank you, sir."

"Listen, Hank, I've got to ask you, have you made up your mind who you're gonna sign with?"

"Not yet, sir. I'm interested in Southern, of course, but I'm still thinking about Cal Poly."

"Cal Poly? Hell, they're not even Division I, Hank. At Southern you can wind up playing for a national title. Think about that, kid. Not gonna happen at Cal Poly." Ralph had been after Hank for a long time and he was losing his patience.

"Well, I like their engineering program, sir." Hank tried to avoid looking at Ralph.

"Listen, Hank, I know Coach Harris is coming to see you next weekend. He wants to sit and talk to you and your folks. He's gonna tell you all about the program and where you fit in. Hell, you could be starting QB in your sophomore year! But there are some things he can't tell you that I can. If you need spending money while you're at Southern, it's taken care of. If you'd like a newer set of wheels, that's taken care of too. Harris can't be into that stuff; that's where the Boosters come in. So, you've got tuition, books, room and board, spending money, and a car. Hank, you tell me: what more is it gonna take for you to sign that letter of intent?"

Hank felt his face flush. He wanted to tell fat Ralph Moretti where he could shove his money and his car. But he knew what his parents thought and how much the offer from Southern would help them financially. The offer from Cal Poly was only for tuition and books. He bit his tongue. He could sense that Ralph was losing patience, near the end of his rope.

"Listen, Hank, remember a couple summers ago, you came to me asking about a summer job? Did I set you up, kid?"

"Yes, sir."

"And what did you have to do for the last two summers?"

"Groundskeeping, sir."

"Actually, what you did was turn on the sprinklers at the ball park and make sure the grass stayed green, right? What was that, about six hours a week? And how many hours did you get paid for?"

"Forty hours, sir."

"Forty hours. So you had some money in your pocket for clothes, or to spend on that pretty girlfriend of yours, right?"

"I gave the money to my mother, sir. My parents give me an allowance." Hank enjoyed throwing it back in Ralph's face.

"Okay," Ralph said, the anger evident in his voice. "And what was your real summer job?"

"Hit the weight room."

"Right, you lifted weights. And you went from a beanpole one hundred and sixty-five pounds to—what are you today? Six four, two fifteen, two twenty? Where do you think your paycheck came from, Hank?"

"I don't know." Hank had dropped the "sir." God, how he despised this man!

"From the Boosters, kid, that's where."

Hank didn't doubt Ralph's assertion for a minute. He and his friends in the weight room joked about their summer jobs, and not all of them were with Ralph Moretti. Everybody was doing it.

"And that car your parents gave you when you turned sixteen," Ralph continued, "did you wonder how they paid for it?"

Hank was stunned. He couldn't answer. So his parents were in on this too?

"See, Southern has an investment in you, Hank. Now they want that investment to pay some returns. You understand, kid?" Ralph paused for a moment, but he wasn't through yet. "I didn't want to bring this up, Hank, but you leave me no choice. Remember the little problem you and your girl had last summer?"

Hank jerked his head to look at Ralph. "What do you know about me and Claire?"

"Just that you had this little problem and neither one of you was ready to be a parent, that's all."

"How did you know about that?"

"You confided in Coach Slade, told him you wished she'd make it go away, and he called me for help. That's the way it works, kid. Coach needs help, I'm there."

John Robert "Jackie" Slade was the offensive coordinator for the high school football team, but his ambitions ran far beyond high school ball. When he first laid eyes on Hank as a raw-boned sophomore, he saw a potential star, one that would surely shed light on his coaching skills. He took Hank under his wing, worked with him constantly, befriended the young man, and saw that potential develop beyond his wildest dreams. Hank McKay was Jackie Slade's ticket to the next level. In turn, Hank trusted Slade like a second father. When he learned that Claire was pregnant, he confided in his coach and asked for help. Not long after that, Claire called to tell him it was over, that she wasn't pregnant anymore. And not long after that, she told Hank they were through.

Hank had to get out of this car and away from Ralph Moretti. The thought of Ralph having anything to do with his Claire made him sick to his stomach. "I've got make a phone call," he blurted, putting his hand on the door handle, waiting for Ralph's okay.

Ralph nodded. "See me before you leave, kid. I know you're looking for your old man. I can help you." Ralph barely suppressed a smile.

Hank slammed the door of the car behind him and walked quickly into the bar. He headed for the payphone on wall near the restrooms and called his mother to tell her he was still searching. Then he dropped in another dime and dialed the number he'd called many times.

"Hello." It was Coach Slade's familiar voice.

"Coach, this is Hank McKay."

"Hi, Hank. Say did you read Don Gleason's column on Saturday? Nice tribute to you, kid. That's one you should save for the scrapbook."

"Coach, I have to talk to you . . . I have to ask you something." Hank didn't know how to start.

"Sure, Hank, anything. What is it?"

Just get to the point, he told himself. "Coach, did you talk to Ralph Moretti about Claire and me?" The line was quiet for several seconds.

"Hank, you came to me and confided in me, and you told me this is what you wanted. I knew Moretti knew people, real doctors, Hank. Not some back alley thing. I knew she'd be well taken care of . . . Hank? Are you there?"

"Yes, sir . . . I . . . I've got to go now, Coach." And with that, he hung up the phone, not waiting for a reply.

Hank headed back out to the street, crossing at the end of the block to the entrance of Crowley's Department Store. The front door was locked and he tapped loudly on the glass with his keys to catch someone's attention inside. Finally, Carol heard the commotion and approached the door.

"Hank, what is it? We're not open." She looked at Hank through the glass, slightly annoyed.

"Carol, I need to speak to Claire. Can you let me in?"

"Wait a second and I'll get her." She walked away and after a minute, Claire came to the door.

"What is it? What do you want, Hank?"

"I need to talk to you. Please let me in. Please!"

Claire paused for a second, looked around to see who was watching, then unlocked the door. "Let's go in the back. We can talk there."

They went through the store and the stock room and found the employee entrance that opened onto an alley in back of the store. Claire propped the door open with a small box and they stepped out into the alley.

"What is it, Hank?" She glanced around, as though someone might be listening.

"I just had a talk with Ralph Moretti. And with Coach Slade." Hank stopped, not knowing what to say next. "Is it true, Claire? Tell me the truth. Is it true?"

She dropped her eyes and looked away. "Yes," she said quietly.

"Why didn't you tell me? I could have at least been with you. I didn't know what you were going to do."

"Didn't know?" Her voice was rising now. "You didn't *want* to know, you big jerk! All you wanted was to protect your precious football career . . ." She had more to say, but her voice trailed away. No one spoke for what seemed a very long time.

"Are you okay? Is everything okay?" Hank finally got the words out.

"Yes," she said quietly. "I'll give them that. It was all very clean and very professional. And I'm fine . . . so get the hell out of here before I get fired." She looked up at him, and then went back into the store, closing the door behind her. Hank stood in the alley, staring at the metal door, locked out of the store and out of her life.

She was right, of course. He had been so relieved when she called to say the pregnancy was over that he didn't ask when or where or how. He remembered saying, "Thank God," and feeling the weight of the world fall off his shoulders. When, he wondered, had he become one of those people he despised? He knew the answer, of course. It started when he was barely a teenager and he accepted the idea that he was special and deserved all the privileges that were coming his way. It continued with things like the summer jobs, where he took their money and barely had to work. And it continued to this day, when he seldom had to attend class or turn in an assignment and still received A's and B's. Why? Because he could win football games, and they could all fatten their resumes.

Hank remembered seeing a college athletic director being interviewed on TV. The reporter asked why top athletes received the scholarships, the special attention, and the financial resources of the great universities. Why not, for example, top scholars? The AD flashed a *you dumb shit* look at the reporter and said, "Because you can't get seventy thousand people to pay good money on a Saturday afternoon to watch some kid fill up a test tube." Honest answer. Case closed.

He turned and walked out of the alley to Sonoma Boulevard, then back toward Georgia Street. He had to see fat Ralph Moretti one more time. Ralph was waiting in front of the Towne House as Hank approached.

"You said you could help me find my dad?"

"Yeah, kid. Do you have your car? Okay, follow me. We're going up on Napa Street. It's just a couple of blocks."

Hank got in his car and fell in behind Ralph's Cadillac. They turned left on Sonoma, then right on Virginia and started the steep climb up the hill. At Napa Street, they turned left and continued the climb. Finally, Ralph pulled over to the curb and Hank parked behind him.

Hank stood a little behind Ralph as he rang the bell for Apartment A. A woman opened the door and nodded at Ralph in recognition. She was wearing a short, white terrycloth robe and her blonde hair was pulled up and piled loosely on her head. Hank looked at her in the late morning light and found it impossible to tell her age. She could be twenty-five or forty-five. All he could tell for sure was that she had nice legs.

She looked at Hank for a moment and said, "Well, well . . . if it isn't the quarterback himself."

Ralph spoke up to make the introductions. "Hank, this is Honey Wells. Honey, this is Hank McKay." Honey pulled open the door and motioned them in.

"Is he still here?" Ralph asked.

"Yeah, he's in the shower." She turned and saw Hank staring at her. "Don't look at me that way, kid. He was too drunk last night to do what you're thinking."

Hank looked away, slightly embarrassed. He could hear water running behind a door just down the hall.

"Are you gonna show him the car?" Honey looked at Ralph for the answer.

"Yeah. Hank, come with me." Ralph led the way through the living room and into the kitchen, to a door that opened onto a small yard. There a short walkway led to a garage that faced the alley in back of the building. Ralph opened the door to the garage and found the light switch. The light was poor, but Hank recognized his father's dark green sedan. Well, Hank thought, at least he had the decency not to park on the street. He looked at Ralph, for some explanation.

"Walk around to the other side."

Hank went around the front of the car to the passenger side. There he stopped short, staring at the broken headlight, dented fender, and scratched paint. Then he began to feel a little queasy.

"Is my Dad the driver they're looking for?" He locked eyes with Ralph, dreading the answer.

"Yeah, he is."

"How do you know?"

"Honey was with him. Your dad was driving."

Hank pitched forward slightly, catching himself against the damaged fender, as if he might pass out. He stood there for a long time, his mind racing, then stalling, then racing again. *An eyewitness, a partial plate, probably paint chips. Who knows what else the police have?* He steadied himself and looked up at Ralph. "Do you know a lawyer? Someone who could represent my Dad?"

Ralph was surprised by the question. "Yeah, kid, I know a lawyer."

"Is he any good?" Hank didn't have much to bargain with, but he didn't want just any hack.

"He's a good attorney, just a bad handicapper." Ralph chuckled a little at the truth of his statement.

"Okay, you asked what it would take for me to sign with Southern? Well, that's my price. Forget the money, forget the car. Your attorney represents my Dad all the way through, beginning to end. I want guarantees."

"It's not the kind of thing you can put in writing."

"He stays with my dad all the way. Hear me? If not, I don't care what the situation is, what Southern's record is. I don't care if it's half time at the friggin' Cotton Bowl, so help me God, I'll walk. Understood?"

Ralph seemed impressed; the kid could really get his Irish up. "Okay. I'll have to make a phone call."

They closed the garage and headed back towards the apartment. Ralph stopped in the kitchen to make his call, many thoughts running through his mind. *A lawyer? How naïve is this kid? Hell, the car could be fixed quietly. Or wiped down and abandoned, reported stolen. Witnesses could change their minds. Honey could provide a good alibi. The kid has no idea how much he's leaving on the table. Damn, maybe he is a Boy Scout after all. So, he wants a lawyer for his dad. Well, I know just the guy: a good attorney with a bad gambling habit. Owes me big time! But hell, the Boosters will make me whole, if I can deliver Hank McKay. I wonder if Coach Harris will think he's damaged goods? Nah, the kid didn't do anything. In fact, he wants to do the stand-up thing. We've got friends in the press who can spin this the right way. Hell, it could end up being good PR. Some country boy down there in Texas could turn it into a damn song!*

When Honey saw Hank approaching the front room, she promptly left for the bedroom. Will McKay sat on the couch, fumbling to put on his shoes, his hair still wet from the shower. He looked older than his fifty-five years.

"Hank, what are you—?" He cut off his question in mid-sentence. "Son, I'm sorry . . . I am so sorry . . . I swear to God, Hank, I didn't know I hit that little girl. Right hand to God, son, I never would have driven away."

Hank sat down on the couch and put his arm around his father's shoulders. He leaned forward and their heads bumped lightly, then stayed together. "I know, Pop. I know." Hank could not remember when he and his father had cried together, until now. "Pop, you know they have a witness, and a partial plate. I'm sure they have paint from your car. You know there is only one thing we can do. We've got to start doing the right things."

"Son, I swear I didn't know."

"I believe you. Look, we'll get a lawyer for you. You'll be represented. But you know you have to turn yourself in."

They sat like that for a minute more, father and son, sharing the same nightmare. Then Ralph entered the room.

"Okay, you got your attorney. I just have to tell him where and when to meet you."

"Tell him we're going to the police station. We're going there now." Hank turned to his father. "Give me the keys, Pop. I'll drive us there in your car. I don't want them finding it here."

It was nearly 1:00 PM as Hank drove down Virginia Street, heading toward the downtown police station. He had called his mother and explained as much as he could without mentioning where he had found his father. Now they were within a block of the station.

"Hank, I'm sorry to put you through all this. I never wanted to hurt anyone." His father's voice was heavy with emotion.

"I know, Pop," he said. "Neither did I."

BOOK 2

Sliding headfirst into adulthood . . .

INNOCENCE

S arah listened to his acceptance speech at the convention and thought it was the best she'd heard. She followed the campaign closely and was struck by his ready wit and his grace under pressure. And of course, she thought he won the debates hands down.

None of this prepared her for his inaugural address. When he said ". . . the torch has been passed to a new generation of Americans . . ." she knew he was speaking to her. When he said ". . . ask not what your country can do for you, ask what you can do for your country . . ." she felt the goose bumps break out all over.

In November of 1963, Sarah was a Peace Corps volunteer working in a remote village in Kenya when she heard the news from Dallas. Until that day, she believed with all her heart that her generation would change the world and make it better, and she fought hard to hold onto that belief. Then came the war in Vietnam, and the burning ghettos at home, and the violent anti-war protests, and more assassinations. First, Martin was shot dead, and then Bobby. The decade that began with such promise now had a single, enduring icon: a body bag.

Sarah came home and married well and settled into her life as a wife, mother, and school teacher. She was thrilled by the bright and eager faces and the boundless energy that filled her classroom every day. Her station wagon was always loaded with kids, carpooling from one event to another. It was a full and busy life.

But in the quiet times, alone with her thoughts, she felt despair settle in like a fifty-pound weight on her chest. Her despair was for the children and their future. Her belief in a better world died, finally, with Bobby Kennedy on the kitchen floor of the Ambassador Hotel in 1968.

BUTTERFLY, PART 1

Dinner and a movie . . .

Carol was shocked. She wanted to pinch herself and make sure she was really awake. Randy Haman had walked right up to her desk in History of Western Civ and asked her for a date. Randy Haman, the coolest, hippest guy on the campus of Vallejo Junior College! The instructor had dismissed the class and Carol was making one last note from the lecture when it happened.

"Hi, Carol. Hey, what are you doing Friday night? I'm thinking dinner, maybe a movie. Are you free?"

"Uhnnn, umm, yes . . . sure," she said, nearly choking in the process. What else could she say? Randy Haman, starting forward on the basketball team, BMOC, Mr. Cool. It didn't matter that he'd never spoken to her before, never acknowledged her presence.

"Great. I'll pick you up around 8:00. That is if you'll write down your address and phone number for me." With that, he gave her his best Randy Haman smile and then chuckled as she fumbled to tear off a piece of paper from her notebook. "See ya Friday night." He stuffed the scrap of paper in the pocket of his jeans and strolled away as casually as he had arrived.

Carol noticed her hands were trembling a little as she gathered her things and prepared to leave the classroom. Friday night he said, 8:00 o'clock. She had two days to pull herself together. She headed down the hall toward her next class, thinking that surely this confirmed what she had just recently allowed herself to believe. Her life was changing at last, and she was never going back.

Carol Crane had barely survived high school. In her mind, it had been three years of unrelenting hell. It seemed she had never found a place to fit in or a friend that she could relate to. There were other girls she connected with briefly, but for some reason it never seemed to last. They always drifted away and found other people to hang out with, other things to do. They simply stopped calling and didn't return her calls. And as for boys, she could not recall ever having a conversation with a boy in her class. Her classmates gave her a nickname: Olive Oyl, after Popeye's girlfriend, and she heard them call her Olive as she walked through the halls between classes.

There was only one exception: Hank McKay had been her next-door neighbor growing up, and he'd always treated her like a kid sister, even though she was a year ahead of him in school. Hank was a gifted athlete and popular with his classmates. He would walk with her between classes when their schedules were in sync, and nobody called her Olive when Hank was around.

Carol was sure that it was her appearance, that people just didn't want to be seen with her. She had always been tall for her age and painfully thin, unable to gain an ounce, her bones protruding at odd places. And then there was her skin, which was in a constant state of eruption, and no amount of makeup could conceal the damage. She saw a dermatologist regularly and did everything he ordered with little or no effect. At times she could barely stand to look in the mirror.

Carol and her mother lived alone in a house on Tuolumne Street, just a few blocks from Vallejo High. Her parents had divorced when Carol was in grade school, and though her father provided for them and made sure they wanted for nothing, he was not a factor in her life. Her mother did the best she could, working part time to keep busy and generally relying on Carol to fend for herself.

More than once, Carol thought about the most efficient way to kill herself. She could loop a rope over the crossbeam on the patio, stand on a chair and fashion a noose around her neck, then simply kick the chair away. When her mind wandered into these thoughts, she had a habit of scribbling notes in her spiral notebook, notes she would read later and not remember writing.

"Will it hurt when I kick away the chair?" She had written that question in her English notebook during junior year. She'd had enough of pain. Even if it lasted only a minute, she was determined not to die that way. There was a better idea: she could wait until her mother refilled a prescription for sleeping pills, then just take the entire bottle. The fear of *not* dying prevented her from doing it. With her luck, she'd just end up with brain damage.

During her freshman year in high school, Carol took up running, loping along the streets of her neighborhood like a wobbly stork. It was not for athletic or health reasons, but simply because it allowed her to be totally alone, without the slightest possibility of being questioned or confronted or teased. It started with a mile or so on alternate days and grew to a near-daily regimen and more than twenty miles a week. She could not wait to get home from school, change into her running clothes and hit the street, releasing all the frustration and anger of being Olive Oyl in a world of Barbies.

Late in her senior year, just before graduation, Carol began to notice changes. She was showering one day, shaving her legs, and she noticed the shape of her calves. It caused her to stand on her tiptoes later and look at her reflection in the mirror above the sink. The hipbones that once protruded, and the rib cage once so prominent, were less evident now. Even more surprising, her complexion was changing. The awful pimples and welts began to subside and she could look at her face without flinching. And wonder of wonders, she could not help but notice her breasts, once nearly non-existent, now beginning to look and feel like a young woman's breasts.

Carol's mother had a full length mirror fastened to the back of her bedroom door, and Carol began to visit her mother's room after showering, locking the door carefully so as not to be interrupted. She would drop her robe and stare at herself, unable to believe the changes she was witnessing, the firm, toned flesh and the curves where before there had only been sharp angles. She would step close to the glass, close enough for her breath to cause brief patches of fog, and touch her face, wondering at the large expressive eyes, the high cheekbones she'd never noticed before, and the full, sensuous mouth.

She was well into her freshman year at Vallejo JC when, after a shower and visit to her mother's room, she sat at her desk and slowly, deliberately wrote in her notebook:

> *I am a pretty girl.*
> *I will be a beautiful woman.*

Carol shook her head sharply and began to cross out what she had written, then stopped and read it again. She would not cross it out. Instead she drew a bold box around the two sentences. Because they were true.

Randy Haman was having more fun than the law allowed. When he left Vallejo after high school, he was sure he would never live there again, yet here he was at Vallejo JC, having the time of his life. Randy had enlisted in the Army right after graduating from Vallejo High. He had finished his tour of active duty and now was completing his service commitment in the National Guard. Randy had been sent to Korea during his active stint, and it was there, freezing his ass on guard duty somewhere above the 38th parallel, that he decided he would get serious about school when he got home.

He enrolled at Vallejo Junior College and found himself among some old friends, guys he had grown up with in Carquinez Heights during the post-World War II years. They were older and more experienced than the average community college student fresh out of high school, and it didn't take long for Randy and his friends to make their presence felt on the campus.

Randy loved all sports, but his game of choice was basketball. At six feet four, he was big enough and talented enough to be the starting forward on the Vallejo JC team. A knee injury in his first year caused him to redshirt, saving eligibility. He came back to be a starter during the season just ended and looked forward to starting again the following year.

That would make three full years on the Vallejo campus, a little too long except for the fact that it was so much fun. He and his friends had it made, as long as they kept their GPAs above 2.0, high enough to stay eligible for sports. Old enough to hang out in their favorite bars and drink themselves shit-faced, they raised serious hell around town. And, best of all, there was a steady stream of sweet young women flowing their way, lovely high school graduates, easy picking for men of their experience.

Randy was still committed to the idea of getting serious about school and preparing for a career of some sort. The idea was simply on hold. He was tall and well built and considered himself ruggedly handsome in a Robert Ryan sort of way. But without question, it was his attitude that sealed the deal. He learned quickly that if you acted like the biggest, baddest man on campus, it soon came to pass that you were.

Carol was ready for her date with Randy Haman with at least fifteen minutes to spare, but only because she started two hours earlier. She tried on nearly every spring outfit she owned, finally deciding on a simple blue cotton dress. It was sleeveless, fitted on top and full in the skirt, and it was perfect for dinner and a movie. It was warm, unseasonably warm for mid-May in Vallejo, but Carol felt cool and relaxed as she waited. She thought long and hard about what makeup to wear, but she had no experience with eye shadow or mascara or any of that. Lipstick, a light red shade, was all she wore. She checked her hair, short and wavy and nearly black, thought of combing it differently, then changed her mind. She stood in front of her mother's mirror, took a long, measured look, and was pleased with what she saw.

Randy pulled up at the curb in front of Carol's house in his metallic red pickup with the chrome wheels and dual exhaust. She'd seen him driving it around campus, up and down Mini Drive, the windows rolled down and the sound system blasting away, and she knew it was considered a "cool set of wheels," even though she wasn't a fan of pickup trucks.

"Mom, I'm leaving now. Don't wait up." She headed out the door, not waiting for Randy to knock.

"Carol? You're going now? Have a good time," her mother called from the back of the house.

Randy met her on the walk leading to the front door. "Hey," he said, giving her an up-and-down appraisal. "You look nice."

Carol felt her face flush as she mumbled a thank-you. Randy was wearing khakis and a short-sleeved button-down shirt, and she caught a whiff of Old Spice aftershave. It registered instantly that her father wore Old Spice, then she put it out of her mind. He opened the door for her and she stepped up into the cab and slid onto the leather seat. Randy pulled away from the curb, made a U-turn at the first intersection, and headed south toward Nebraska Street. The sun was down and the sky was beginning to darken as he turned right onto Nebraska and headed west toward the Vallejo High campus.

"Warm today, isn't it?" He adjusted the volume on the radio, turning the Everly Brothers down to a quiet roar.

"Uhnn . . . yes it is. Really warm for May." Carol's mouth was dry and she was finding it hard to talk. "You mentioned dinner or a movie, Randy. Have you ummm . . . decided?" She felt her face flush again, certain she was making a fool of herself. What she really wanted to say was *Why? Why did you ask me out? Me, of all people?*

"Yeah," he said, "but first we've got to make a stop." He looked at her and gave her his killer grin. She saw that his eyes were very blue, an unusual blue in this light.

They approached Vallejo High School on the north side of Nebraska Street, looking like a small college campus, with its stately two-story main building surrounded by the Science Building, the Women's Gym, the Library and the Men's Gym. On the west side of the campus was the football stadium, Corbus Field, with its hulking concrete grandstand.

Randy suddenly turned left, into the parking lot across from the campus. Filled to capacity on school days, it was empty this Friday night with no special events taking place. He drove to the middle of lot, away from Nebraska Street, pulled into a parking space and stopped. With the engine quiet and the headlights off, Carol was acutely aware of the silence.

"Randy, why are we . . . ?" she started, then stopped and looked at his face for answers.

"Carol, I've been watching you, all this semester in Western Civ . . . and I just wanted to . . . you know . . . be alone with you." He had moved very close to her on the seat, facing her. She felt her heart begin to race and the blood pound in her temples. Then he kissed her very gently on the lips, just a tiny, innocent kiss.

"Randy, I . . ." She started to say that she never knew he was aware that she existed, but he kissed her again, the same little innocent kiss. Then again, and again. Her mind began to race now, just like her heart, and the thought that filled her head was *Randy Haman is kissing me . . . Randy Haman is kissing Me!* She raised her right hand and cupped his neck, pulling him to her very gently, and now the thought that crowding out everything else was *I'm kissing Randy Haman!*

It took just a minute or so for Randy to teach her the mechanics of the French kiss. She'd heard of it, read about it, and thought the concept was kind of gross. Now she couldn't believe how wrong she'd been. She was aware of his hand, caressing her shoulder and her side, and she was aware of his tongue deep inside her mouth. Then his hand was covering her breast, his fingers searching for her nipple and finding it, and she felt a surge go through her body that she'd never known before. Somewhere, way in the background, nearly inaudible, a voice was coming to her saying *What is happening . . . what is he doing . . . why are you letting him do this?* He eased her down onto the seat, his left leg clamped firmly between her legs. Then his hand was under her dress, moving along her thigh, then pressing hard, probing deep between her legs. Now the background voice came screaming to the fore.

"Randy, wait . . . wait . . . Randy, wait . . . please."

"It's okay . . . it's okay . . . shhhh . . . it's all right." His voice was soft and reassuring, and ever so slightly, she relaxed, which was the wrong thing to do. Randy had no intention of waiting. He was about to roll over her like a runaway train.

When he finished, he pulled away from her and sat up behind the steering wheel, fumbling with his pants. Carol covered her face with her hands and felt the tears spilling from the corners of her eyes, running down across her temples.

"Here," he said. "Use this."

She moved her hands and saw that he was holding a neatly folded white handkerchief, offering it to her. She took it and wiped herself quickly, then struggled to sit up in the seat. She groped on the floor of the truck for her panties, too embarrassed to admit she couldn't find them. She had to settle for straightening her skirt and fighting for composure.

Randy started the engine, backed the pickup out of the parking space and headed back to Nebraska Street. He turned right on Nebraska, and it soon became clear that he was retracing the path they had taken. He was taking her home. Carol realized this quickly and was grateful. All she wanted then was to be away from him, to be alone, to be back in her cocoon. She looked at him, sitting behind the wheel with a wry smirk on his face, and the anger began to rise in her from the very bottom of her soul.

"Dinner and a movie?" she said, her voice shaking noticeably.

"We didn't need all that now did we, babe." He looked at her and grinned.

Carol turned away and fought back the tears. She opened the door almost before the truck stopped in front of her house. Her key was in front door when she heard the wheels screech as he pulled away from the curb. No one was in the front room as she entered the house and she hurried down the hall to her room.

"Carol, is that you? I thought you were going out?" It was her mother's voice from the kitchen.

"Change in plans, Mom. I'll be in my room," she called. She closed the door to her room and locked it, then leaned back hard against the door. *Why did he do this to me? Why did this happen, God? Why me?* She felt something in her hand, looked down to find Randy's handkerchief, and she saw the dark red stain.

"Hot damn!" Randy yelled in the cab of his truck, the sound reverberating around him as he pounded his right fist on the steering wheel. He cranked up the volume on the radio where Jerry Lee Lewis was destroying his piano, singing about a whole lotta shakin'.

He was on his way to find his buddies, knowing they'd probably be out at Kentwig Lanes, shooting pool and having a few beers. He hurried east on Tennessee Street, heading toward the freeway. They will never believe this story! He looked at his watch and laughed out loud. Forty-five minutes, door to door! They'll never believe it. But they'll have to . . . didn't he have her panties carefully tucked away in his pocket? He rehearsed telling the story, listening to them say "Get the hell out . . . No way . . . You're full of shit, Haman." Then he'd pull out her panties to wave in their faces. They'd believe him then, and they'd have to pay up too. After all, he'd won the bet fair and square.

"Hot damn!" he yelled again, as Jerry Lee rocked on, singing all about chicken in the barn.

Carol wrapped the thick terrycloth robe around her damp body and sat at the small desk in her room. Her books and notebooks were stacked neatly to her left, but she wasn't there to study. She had taken a long, hot bath, refreshing the hot water several times. Then she had drained the tub and started the shower and scrubbed herself from head to toe. Only then did the smell of Old Spice begin to fade from her body and her senses. She fixed her eyes on the calendar tacked to the cork board above her desk and tried to focus, not on what had happened, or why, but on what would come next. She knew that Randy would tell his friends, and they'd tell their friends, and by Monday the story would be all over campus. She could picture them sniggering, laughing at her, talking behind her back.

I won't go back! I won't give them the satisfaction. I'll tell my instructors that I'm sick, and I'll find a way to finish the semester without going near that campus. Sooner or later, Randy and his posse will move on. She felt her grip tightening on the arms of the chair.

No! I'll go to class on Monday, just like any other day, with my head up, and I'll look them straight in the eye, and they can all go to hell.

Slowly it began to dawn on her: either way, she would win. They could defeat her, but she could not be destroyed, not now. She reached for a particular notebook, the one for Western Civ, and thumbed through the pages until she came to the one she was looking for. There it was, the dark box drawn around the two simple sentences:

> *I am a pretty girl.*
> *I will be a beautiful woman.*

Carol leaned back in her chair and closed her eyes. She felt herself reaching, reaching deep down inside, to that place that the Randy Hamans of the world could never touch.

BUTTERFLY, PART 2

What goes around . . .

Hank finished his warm-up pitches in the bullpen just as the inning ended. He trotted out to the mound for the start of the fourth inning while his team, the Benicia Mudhens, went through warm up drills in the infield and outfield. This was the first game of the summer season and their opponent was the Vallejo Builders.

The league, if you could call it a league, was referred to as semi-pro, though Hank knew of no one who was getting paid to play. It was just a handful of teams representing cities around the North Bay for older guys who still loved to play the game. For Hank McKay, it was a chance to have a little fun before he headed off to Southern University for his freshman year. Hank's game was football and that would be his focus at Southern. This was likely to be his last opportunity to play baseball and he was looking forward to it. No pressure, just fun.

After today's game, that is. Today he was on a mission.

He got the first batter on a routine pop-up. Then the hitter he was looking for strutted into the batter's box: tall, left-hand hitting Randy Haman. Hank knew that Randy was a fair basketball player who played a little baseball just for fun and to hang out with his friends. He didn't think Randy was going to have much fun today.

Hank took the sign from his catcher, a fastball low and inside. He wound up and let it go, right on target. Randy turned quickly to his left at the last instant and took the pitch flush on the right cheek of his ass. Hank normally threw in the high eighties or low nineties and he knew that one would leave a mark.

Randy glared at Hank for an instant, then trotted down to first base. *That's one,* Hank said to himself. The next two batters went down in order. It would be a couple of innings before Randy came to bat again and Hank had more fun planned for him.

When Randy came up again, Hank looked in and grinned at him. *What will it take to get you to charge the mound? Let's find out.* He went into his wind-up and fired a waist-high fastball about a foot behind the hitter. The ball slammed off the backstop and Randy glared at Hank with a dumbfounded look. The umpire ripped off his mask and issued a warning. Any more pitches like that and Hank would be ejected. Everyone knew that throwing behind the hitter was intended to send a lethal message.

Hank grinned again. He could read Randy's lips: "What the fuck are you doing?" He was getting to him now. Hank wondered if Randy remembered to wear his cup, or if he would bring his bat when he charged the mound. Nah, Randy was a tough guy, one who grew up in the federal projects. He'd drop the bat and come running, ready to do battle.

With the next pitch, Hank took dead aim at that right butt cheek again, but the ball sailed a little high and caught Randy under the ribs on his right side. That did it. Just as Hank expected, Randy threw down his bat and charged the mound, screaming obscenities on the way.

The rest of it played out in slow motion for Hank. He dropped his glove, squared up and took a boxer's stance as Randy raced toward him. Randy's first punch was a wild roundhouse left that Hank easily sidestepped. Then Hank caught him with a left hook to the groin. As Randy bent over, both hands clutching his crotch, Hank shifted his feet quickly and landed a short right uppercut flush on the nose. Randy went down in a heap, one hand on his crotch, the other on his nose, which was now gushing blood.

Hank felt himself being grabbed and wrapped up by his teammates who had no idea what was going on. They pulled him away before he could do any more damage. Players and coaches from both teams milled around the mound, and someone had the good sense to run to the snack bar for a bag of ice to stop the bleeding. Things calmed down somewhat and the umpire found Hank to tell him he was kicked out of the game. No surprise there.

"Good call, Mr. Umpire. I deserve it. Hey, let me talk to Randy. I just want to shake his hand, say I'm sorry."

Randy was on his feet now, clutching a bloody towel to his nose as Hank approached with one of the coaches. "You guys shake hands, okay, and then let's play some ball."

"Geez, Randy, sorry about that," Hank said, extending his hand.

Randy hesitated for a few seconds, and finally extended his hand as well. Hank took it firmly and pulled Randy to him. They were about the same height and they came nearly nose-to-nose, close enough for Hank to smell the onions on Randy's breath; that and the rancid mix of sweat and Old Spice aftershave. No one else was close enough to hear when Hank whispered to Randy: "Carol Crane is a friend of mine, you cocksucker. That was for Carol." Randy's eyes widened for an instant, and then closed as the pain overwhelmed him. Hank let go of his hand and walked away.

He gathered his gear and headed for the parking lot where he tossed his things in the trunk of the car. He stood there for a minute taking stock. Carol would be mad at him—for a while at least. He'd have to deal with that. As for Randy, he ran a quick tally: a bruised butt cheek, sore ribs, aching testicles, and a broken nose. Was it enough? No. Not nearly enough. Then again, he knew it wasn't over.

Hank lined up the shot carefully, drew the cue back and forth a few times, then sent the cue ball gently on its way to kiss the 4-ball. The 4 pitched to the left and fell quietly into the leather side pocket. It was a good shot, the kind Hank usually found a way to miss. Nick thumped his cue on the floor a few times to show his appreciation. They were engaged in a friendly game of 8-Ball in the billiards room at Kentwig Lanes and Hank was holding his own, though pool wasn't really his game. He scratched on his next shot and Nick stepped to the rail with a good chance to run the table and win—again.

Hank glanced at his watch and saw that it was nearly 11:30 PM. He thought sure they would be here by now. Maybe he'd been too subtle. Maybe Randy didn't get the message. The first thing Hank heard when he arrived home for winter break was that Randy Haman was looking for him. So he let it be known where he'd be this Friday night and when he'd be there. All that was needed was to tell the right people and he knew it would be reported back to Randy.

Nick was lining up the 8-ball, about to finish the game, when Hank looked up to see a group of six guys enter the room with Randy leading the way. Hank was impressed: his pal felt the need to come as a gang of six, a real show of respect. Randy approached and stopped about six feet away, a silly little grin on his face.

"You have to answer for this, McKay," Randy said, pointing to his nose, which exhibited a noticeable bump somewhere near the midpoint.

"Looks like an improvement to me, Randy." Hank smiled as he assessed the damage.

"Do you want it in here, or outside?" Randy wasn't smiling now.

It grew quiet now except for the sound of shuffling feet as the other pool players left their games and gathered around. The room began to fill as more guys crowded in, leaving the bowling lanes or the coffee shop at the far end of the building. Hank recognized most of the new arrivals, good friends and former teammates of his. He had given them a short list of suggestions: wear your oldest, grubbiest clothes; wear your stomping boots; wear a cup; and bring a mouthpiece to protect your teeth. He pulled his own mouthpiece out of his pocket and stuffed it in his mouth. All around the room, his buddies did the same. Hank gave them a thumbs-up and grinned. It was an awesome sight to look around the room and see a dozen or more Apache-red mouthpieces grinning back at him.

Randy saw it too. "What the hell is this, McKay?"

"You brought your friends. I brought mine."

Randy's friends, having done the math, chimed in now: "This is crap, Randy . . . Let's get outta here . . . You didn't say it was the whole football team, Haman."

"Okay, we don't want any trouble," Randy said. "We're leaving."

"Not yet, Randy. I have something I want you to sign." Hank reached into his back pocket and removed a neatly typed, carefully folded letter. He opened it and handed it to Randy who read it slowly with several of his friends looking over his shoulder.

Dear Carol:

I apologize for my behavior toward you on our date. I acted like a scum sucking pig, which—let's face it—is exactly what I am. If there was justice in this world, then my genitals would be removed, pickled, and delivered to your doorstep in a jar.

Please accept my humble apology. You deserved better.

Sincerely,
Randy Haman

"Are you crazy? I'm not signing this!" Randy held the letter out toward Hank.

Randy's friends disagreed. "Just sign the damn letter, Randy . . . Yeah, sign it and let's go."

Hank reached in his pocket again and took out a ballpoint pen. Then he removed his mouthpiece in order to speak clearly. "You only have to sign it," he began, slowly, pronouncing each word carefully, "if you want to walk out of here on your own two feet."

For several seconds, the only sound to be heard came from the bowling lanes—the thump of the balls hitting the lanes, crashing into the pins, the clatter of the automatic pin setters.

"Gimme the damn pen." Randy took the pen from Hank, placed the letter on the green felt surface of the pool table and scrawled his signature.

"Now . . . you can go," Hank said, as he retrieved the letter and refolded it carefully.

Behind Randy and his entourage, a pathway opened leading out of the room. As they made their way through the gauntlet, someone in the crowd began to hum the "Death March," which was quickly taken up by the rest of the group: *Dum dum da-dum dum/Da-dum da-dum da-dum . . .*

Hank went around the room and shook hands with his friends, thanking them for turning out. The near-unanimous response was to let them know if they were needed again. He reflected that it was good to have friends, especially friends who spent half their lives in the weight room.

Hank and Nick went back to their game where Nick was about to sink the 8-ball. Was it over now? Maybe. Maybe not. Would he ever show the letter to Carol? Not likely. She had too much class to get involved in such things. It was just another way to rub Randy's nose in it. Was the score even now? Not really. But it was sure as hell better than nothing.

JOJO

R ich could feel a buzz coming on already. He sipped his beer from the longneck bottle and resolved to slow down a little. There was no way he was going to get wasted tonight. The place was quiet on a mid-week night, only a few regulars sitting at the bar, drinking beer and smoking cigars. Rich and Mike sat at the corner of the bar where they had a view of the front door through the blue haze.

There wasn't much to recommend the 714 Club, a simple working class neighborhood tavern, except that the beer was cold and the restrooms were clean. The only embellishments were the neon beer signs in the windows and the vintage Wurlitzer jukebox loaded with classics from the big band era. If you wanted to hear The Beatles or the latest Bob Dylan, well, you were in the wrong bar.

"Well, whataya say?" Mike asked, grinning at his friend. "Should I make the call?"

"Yeah, why not?" Rich replied. "We'll see if you're full of shit or what."

Mike had been pushing Rich to make a date with a particular girl who worked at Glen Cove, going on and on about her looks and her prowess. He was not going to let up until Rich availed himself of her services. Now the time had come, they were here at the 714 Club, and all it would take is a simple phone call to seal the deal.

The Glen Cove brothel was an institution in the Vallejo area. It had been in business for as long as Rich could remember. If anyone said they were going to Glen Cove, it was for one of two reasons.

Either they were going fishing for striped bass at the cove along the Carquinez Strait, or they were going to the best cathouse around. The stately old Victorian was located on Glen Cove Road in the rolling hills a couple of miles south of Benicia Road and about halfway to the cove itself. It had the reputation of being a clean, well-run establishment. If you drove by on any given day, you would see sparkling white bed sheets drying on the clothesline in back of the house, and you'd be struck by the well-maintained look of the place. The old mansion was set well back off the road and a long, paved driveway led the way in. It was rumored that if you passed by at the right time, you would see trucks from the Vallejo Street Department and city work crews busily working on the driveway, keeping it in good repair. This was not a comforting sight if you were a Vallejo taxpayer.

Potential customers could not simply drive up to the house and knock on the door. The business had worked out an interesting arrangement that required a phone call from one of several bars around town, including the 714 Club. When you called the unlisted number and gave the current password, a car would be dispatched to pick you up. The whole process took on a cloak and dagger aura that seemed to work well for the business and its patrons. Rich wondered about the VIP customers. He'd heard there were quite a few and he was sure they had a separate procedure, one that didn't involve waiting around in neighborhood bars.

Mike returned from the payphone at the back of the club and sat down on the barstool next to Rich. "Okay, Richie baby, you're all set. The car is on its way and you're booked with JoJo."

"What about you?"

"I'll take whoever is available. No big deal. But you, my friend, are getting the number one girl." Mike could not suppress his grin.

Rich and Mike had been buddies since grammar school and they had shared many an adventure, especially during their high school years. After a short time at Vallejo Junior College, they enlisted in the military, Mike heading off to the Army and Rich to the Air Force. Four years later, Mike was back knocking around in his father's business while he decided what to do with his life. Rich had landed a job in the State Controller's office in Sacramento, but still dreamed of returning to college to complete his degree.

They ordered another beer and were nearly finished when a small, gray-haired man entered the bar and approached the bartender. After a brief conversation the bartender called out in their direction. "One of you guys named Mike? Your ride is here." Rich thought this was a little too obvious, but they settled their tab and headed for the door with the driver. Outside, they climbed into the back seat of an old Chevy sedan for the short drive to Glen Cove. Rich was a little nervous. He wished now that he'd had a shot with that last beer. After all, he'd never been to a brothel, even though there were several that were well established here in his hometown.

The route the driver took, out past the Auto Movies and through the open hills and grazing land, reminded him just how remote and isolated this place was. When they finally reached the drive leading to the old house, Rich was thinking about all the names society had for places like this: brothel, bordello, cathouse, whorehouse, bawdyhouse, house of ill repute. Had he missed any? Probably. It was a testament to the fascination we have with the world's oldest profession

The old man led them up the steps and opened the front door. The small entry hall led to a staircase and to the right there was a large sitting room. The décor was about what Rich expected, with lots of crushed red velvet upholstery and lamps with fringed shades laced with colored beads. The walls were hung with large oil paintings in heavy gold frames, depicting voluptuous nudes in various poses. Rich supposed they were intended to set the mood. They sat down and he tried to look as though he had been there before.

In less than a minute, a tall, elegant woman in a floor-length red dress entered the room and greeted them. Her gray hair was piled high on her head in an up-swept do, and Rich could easily picture her as a great beauty in her day, perhaps the subject of one of the paintings.

"Hello, boys. Welcome to Glen Cove. Now you I recognize," she said, pointing toward Mike. "Which one of you asked for JoJo?"

"That's me," Rich said. He didn't recognize his own voice.

"Good choice! She'll be right here. And I suppose you'll be wanting a line up?" The question was directed to Mike. "Should we take care of business first, boys?"

They discussed sex and money with the affable madam, paid in advance, and took their seats in the sitting room, waiting for the girls to arrive. Rich heard the click of high heels on the wooden floor of the entry hall and looked up to see a striking young woman enter the room. He knew immediately from Mike's description that this was JoJo. Mike had not exaggerated a bit. She was tall and very pretty, and her easy smile revealed gleaming white teeth. She wore a cream-colored satin robe, tied at the waist, which extended to a point just above her knee. Her skin was the color of coffee with a generous shot of cream, just a shade or two darker than her robe. Her black hair was cut in a short shag with bangs that touched her dark, full eyebrows. Rich swallowed hard and tried to return her smile.

"Hi, I'm JoJo," she said, extending a delicate hand.

"Hi," he said, feeling more awkward with each passing second.

"Okay, come with me." She turned and still holding his hand led him toward the entry hall and the staircase. As they made their way up the stairs, following a couple of steps behind, he found that he was short of breath and it wasn't entirely from the stairs. She opened the door to a room at the top and led him in. He sat down on the large brass bed while she busied herself at a sink to one side of the room, all the while carrying on a steady stream of chatter. There was something familiar about the voice, soft and warm, with a tinge of Southern Comfort. Then she turned to face him straight on.

"You don't recognize me, do you Richie Shane?"

"What?" he replied, the surprise evident in his voice.

"You don't recognize me . . . Josephine Jackson . . . Josie . . . I sat next to you in Mrs. Dunn's English class."

The name registered, then the picture slowly began to come into focus, the shy little girl with the mouth full of bright metal braces: Josie Jackson. "Oh my God," he stammered. "Josie . . . I never would have recognized you . . . I mean you're . . . you're gorgeous, drop-dead gorgeous!"

"Oh, Richie, that's sweet," she said, mocking him playfully.

"Josie . . . can we talk for a minute? Mike—that jerk—didn't say anything. I mean, I don't know if I can do this." Rich felt his libido melting like an ice cube in a skillet. He had not counted on running into a former classmate.

"Okay . . ." she said, tentatively. She crossed the room and sat next to him on the bed. The conversation was a bit awkward at first. They got through the usual *so how have you been* phase and he told her about his stint in the Air Force, his so-far unsuccessful attempts to finish college, and his current job with the state. They talked about the usual suspects in their high school class, the athletes, the cheerleaders, the student body officers. Rich knew that she was holding back, revealing very little of herself. Finally, he blurted the question he'd been holding in.

"Josie, why did you . . . I mean how did you . . . you know . . ."

"Why did I become a whore?" She said it without a trace of resentment, but it seemed to touch a nerve. She was quiet for a moment, and then let her defenses fall ever so slightly. She spoke about growing up in a family with a black father and a white mother, about feeling estranged from both sides, about never feeling that she belonged, about a lifetime of family gatherings where she was odd girl out. She summed it up for him: "My daddy's folks thought I wanted to pass for white. And my momma's folks . . . well, they thought I was just another . . . just another colored girl."

She brightened quickly and continued. "It won't be long now, though. I'll be outta here. I'm saving my money and real soon now I'll be off to New Orleans. I read they got a whole culture there, a whole Creole community, and lots of people that look just like me. I'll fit right in!"

They talked a while longer and as he listened to her, he wondered about her plans. He hoped she was right, that there was a community that would embrace her and make her feel wanted and at home. There was a break in the conversation—another awkward moment—and then she flashed her perfect smile as if to say *it's time to go to work.*

"So, what do you think, Richie? You know, there are no refunds. You should get your money's worth." She stood up and returned to the sink across the room. "You know I have to check you out, make sure everything is okay. Just let me run some warm water here." She carried a basin over to the bedside table. Next to it, she placed a white towel and washcloth. "Now, Richie, you're gonna be okay with this aren't you? I promise I won't bite or anything." She flashed that brilliant smile again as she knelt in front of him. "Now stand up for me . . . there, that's it." And then she reached for his belt.

JoJo went about tidying up the room while Rich got dressed. He found that he could not pull his eyes or his mind away from her. He wanted to ask her about New Orleans, if she would be a working girl there too, but he kept the question to himself. In the end, about all he could do was to give her a hug and wish her well. He stuffed some bills in the pocket of her robe as they left the room.

Mike was in the sitting room, grinning from ear to ear, when Rich came down the stairs. Rich shot him a look that could kill. The driver appeared and motioned them toward the door. As they walked across the driveway to the car, Rich whacked Mike hard on the shoulder. "You asshole! You could have told me. Josie Jackson, for God's sake. You could have given me a clue."

Mike laughed out loud, enjoying his prank to fullest.

As the car headed down the drive and onto the main road, Rich was quiet, peering out the window at the darkened countryside. This night was more than he had bargained for. He would forgive Mike; he always did. But there were thoughts and images he couldn't push out of his mind, about the girl who sat next to him and shared a classroom but lived in another world, a world he could never know or understand.

He thought again about New Orleans. He'd spent several weekends there while he was stationed in Biloxi, and it was a city that he loved for many reasons: jazz and blues; red beans and rice; café au lait and beignets at Café Du Monde in the wee hours of the morning; the beautiful, funky, dirty French Quarter, a brass band swinging its way up the street, coming from a funeral, a second line forming in its wake; breakfast at Brennan's, or dinner at Arnaud's—for his money, the best damn restaurants in the country.

And now, another reason to love The Big Easy: JoJo!

BONEHEAD ENGLISH

B rent sat at his desk reading the professor's prompt: "Write a story, 750 words minimum, about something interesting that happened to you during summer vacation." Bonehead English—what a pain in the butt. He met with the professor after class and told her he didn't know what to write about.

"Didn't anything interesting happen last summer?"

"Well, yeah."

"Well, then, just write about it. Tell me a true story about what happened."

Okay sweetie, he said to himself. *You asked for it.* He would write the damn thing longhand and then type it later. He flipped open a pad of lined paper, picked up his pen and began:

MY SUMMER JOB

by
Brent Barlow

"Burlingame? I don't want to go to Burlingame. Why can't I go to Sequim again, up to Uncle Stan's place?" I was really pissed at my old man.

"Because, Brent, you're going to Burlingame and that's it," he said. "It's a summer job and you need to help out around here, not just piss away the summer sittin' on your ass."

I knew what was going on. He and Jan, my stepmother, wanted me out of the house for the month of August so that they could have some time alone, time without me in the next room listening to them fool around. Cal, my old man, was in his mid-forties and Jan was only about thirty. She tolerated me but that was about it. Any time they could ship me out it was a good thing in her book, and if I made some money to buy my own school clothes, well that was even better. It was no use arguing, but I still wanted to give my old man some grief, so I kept it up for a while. Got him really steamed, too.

I'd just turned eighteen and would be a freshman in junior college in the fall. For the past several summers, I'd spent the last couple of weeks in August at my Uncle's place up in Washington. I loved it up there, with horses to ride, lots of shoreline to fish, and woods full of critters to hunt. It was a great way to end the summer.

My job in Burlingame would be to do some house painting for this couple that Cal and Jan were good friends with. Their names were Craig and Tina. Craig was going to be in Chicago for four weeks, attending some kind of training. I would live at the house, paint the eaves all around, and help take care of their two bratty kids; kind of a live-in handyman and babysitter. What fun! So, I kept up my crappy attitude and let my old man know it was a crappy thing for him to make me do. That is, right up until the barbeque.

Jan invited Craig and Tina to our place in Vallejo for a Sunday barbeque. This was about a week before I was supposed to start the job. Jan thought it would be good for them to get to know me a little. I was ready to be my usual crappy self, and then I saw Tina.

What a doll! I mean it. She was barely five feet tall, shoulder-length blonde hair, pretty blue eyes, and oh my, did she ever look good in a pair of white shorts! Right away I started to change my mind about my summer job.

Jan introduced us and then hurried off to the kitchen to do something. I found out right away that Tina liked to flirt, and to be told how cute her little bottom looked in those white shorts, though I didn't say it just like that. She had a couple of drinks and started to have way too much fun with me, laughing and cutting up. Craig came over and pulled her away, but that was all right because I knew I'd made a beachhead, so to speak.

So, a week later, my dad drove me down to Burlingame and I started my summer job. I'd get up in the morning, have breakfast with Tina and the kids, and then get out there and start my painting chores—hosing down, scraping, sanding, and painting. The weather was nice down there on the Peninsula—cool overcast mornings, warm sunny afternoons, temperatures in the sixties and seventies. It was a good gig, really. And, I kept up the constant chatter with Tina, letting her know how pretty and sexy she was. She was eating it up.

Tina had the kids booked in some sort of summer day camp, so she'd take off about 8:30 to drop them off, then pick them up around noon. Candace was five and Jeffery was seven and they were pretty good kids. They had terrible table manners, but otherwise, not too bad to be around. In the evenings, I taught them how to play card games—fish, casino, hearts—and they thought I was pretty cool.

One day, after the kids were at camp, Tina called to me to come and help her in the kitchen. She had to get a cake plate from on top of a cabinet and she wanted me to steady her while she climbed up on a step stool. I mean, come on! Why not just have me get it down? So, she got up on the stool and reached way up, and I held on to her waist and let my hands slide down a little. She got the plate and started climbing down, and I was still holding on to her hips. She put the plate on the counter, spun around in front of me and looked up with those big blue eyes. Then she threw her arms around my neck and the next thing I knew, her tongue was half way down my throat. A minute later, we were in her bed, wrestling around under the covers. That's how it started.

After that, we had a new morning routine. We'd have breakfast, she'd take the kids to camp, and when she got home, I'd be waiting for her in bed. We'd stay there all morning, until it was time for her to pick up the kids. I started to fall way behind on my painting.

She had the finest little body I'd ever seen—absolutely perfect proportions. The only flaws I could find were some tiny stretch marks from when she was pregnant, but other than that, she was perfect. I told her she was like Tinker Bell with boobs and she thought that was funny.

Another funny thing: she wouldn't let me sleep in her bed at night—she was afraid the kids would come in—but she'd come sneaking into my room and take me really fast, like a wild animal. I think she did her own foreplay. Less than ten minutes and she'd be gone, back to her own bed.

If something seems too good to be true, well, it probably is. After two weeks in Chicago, Craig's company gave him a little bonus and let him come home for the weekend. He flew in Saturday morning and had to fly right back Sunday night. That Saturday night was one of the worst nights of my life. I had to lay there in my bed and listen to Tina and Craig make love until about 2:00 in the morning. I felt like jumping up and banging on the walls, telling them to knock it off. I'd never been so hurt and angry in my life. Then I finally put it into words and said it over and over again: "Tina is cheating on me with her husband." That helped me calm down a little.

I was still in a bad mood on Monday morning at the breakfast table, and Tina wouldn't look me in the eye. The kids were up to their usual stuff, slurping their cereal, and chewing their toast with their mouths open. So I barked at them and told them their manners were awful. They stopped dead still and looked at me, then at their mom. When I looked at Tina, she was glaring at me with fire in her eyes. She told the kids to go brush their teeth and they left the table in a hurry.

"Don't *ever* lecture my kids!" She said it through clenched teeth. "You are not their father."

"Their father?" I said. "You mean the guy you were screwing Saturday night?"

As soon as I said it, I knew it was over. But there was no way to put the bullet back in the gun. Tina stormed out of the room, loaded the kids into the car and headed off for day camp. I went outside and tried to pick up where I left off with the painting.

She was gone for a long time. When she finally came home, she called me down from the ladder and told me I should clean up and put things away, that she had called my dad and told him it wasn't working out. He was on his way to pick me up and would be there in about two hours.

I was packed and ready to go when my old man arrived. He was standing at the door with a puzzled look on his face, hoping for an explanation from somebody. I shook hands with Tina, said thanks for everything, brushed past my dad and headed for the car. He stood at the door and had a long, intense conversation with Tina. When he finally came to the car, he was madder than hell. We pulled out of the driveway and started down the street, and then he really let me have it.

"Goddamn it, Brent, how did you screw this up? A good summer job and you blow it halfway through! An easy thing like painting the damn eaves—how'd you manage to screw that up? You stupid, lazy . . ."

He went on, yelling at me in the car, cursing me six ways from Sunday. I finally decided enough was enough. "Yeah, well it's hard to get any painting done when you're in bed all morning with the boss!"

He jerked the wheel to the right and pulled over to the curb, stopping so fast he nearly bounced me off the dashboard. "What? What did you say? You've been sleeping with her? Goddamn it, don't you know she is Jan's best friend? You stupid, goddamn . . ."

Off he went again, calling me every name he could think of. I saw his right hand come off the steering wheel and I figured he was going to backhand me. I was ready to raise my fists, to block the backhand if I had to. I wasn't going to just sit there and get hit. Then he turned away, still cursing a blue streak, staring out the windshield. I knew what he was thinking, that somehow this would get back to Jan and she'd make his life miserable. I think he was actually afraid of her. He turned to me again and I was ready for the backhand.

"How the hell could you do this? You stupid little jerk!"

"Well, tell me something, Daddy," I said, with a special emphasis on *Daddy*. "I'm eighteen . . . she's thirty-something . . . who was fucking who?"

He stared at me for a long time, and then he said, "Whom."

"What?"

"It's 'Who was fucking whom.'"

"Are you sure?" I mean, suddenly he's Mr. English Major.

He thought about it a few seconds. "No," he said. Then he turned, checked his mirrors, and pulled back out into traffic. We cruised along in silence for a while, finally merging onto the freeway for the long ride home. I could read him like a book and I knew exactly what was coming. I waited . . . and waited . . . and finally he spit it out.

"So, tell me," he said, "how was she?"

I tried not to laugh out loud, but I couldn't help it. And that's the story of my summer job.

The End

Brent read his composition again and made a few corrections. He reached for a couple of sheets of typing paper and rolled them onto the carriage of the old Underwood typewriter, making sure the little bottle of White-out was close at hand. The professor said she wanted the truth. *Let's see how she likes the truth,* he said to himself. Back in high school, this one would have landed him in the vice principal's office. Maybe the VP would have called in Cal and Jan. Maybe he would have read the story to them. What a hoot that would've been!

TERRY

W e had a fine bowling team back in the fifties. We'd travel around to tournaments all over the place, including some of the big ones: Frisco, LA, Reno, and Vegas. Terry O'Hara was our captain—a great guy and a solid bowler. He had a sanctioned 300 game and you get a nice big ring for that. He made it a point to wear that ring whenever we traveled to tournaments out of town. We never won much of anything, but we had our share of good times, and then some.

The trip that none of us will ever forget was to San Francisco in '55. We checked in at the tournament site, got settled in our hotel, and then went out to dinner at Lefty O'Doul's down on Market Street. There we ran into a bunch of guys we knew from past events. We had a few cocktails and that got the ball rolling, so we invited everyone back to our hotel. Before long we were all packed into Terry's room and the party was in full swing.

Around midnight, the hotel sent up their security guy. He said we had to quiet down or they'd throw us out. We took a liking to this kid right away and it only took a few minutes to convince him to join the party. About 2:00 AM, the S.F.P.D. showed up at the door and they weren't nearly as friendly. To calm things down, Terry went into his repertoire of Irish ballads. He had a tenor voice like an angel! We sang along some, but mostly we just listened. He finished up with "Mother McCrea."

> *God bless her and keep her,*
> *Mother McCrea!*

Hell, there wasn't a dry eye in the room.

Then Terry stomps over to the window at the back of the room, throws it open and says, "Ah, to hell with it!" He climbs out on the ledge and jumps off. Mind you, we're on the fourth floor! You never saw a room full of drunks sober up so fast in all your life. We ran to the window expecting to see Terry splattered all over the pavement four stories down. But there he was, a little below the ledge, arms spread wide and a big grin on his Irish mug.

"Ta Da!" he says.

See, he'd checked it out earlier and found that the hotel was built up against the side of a hill. The drop was only about five feet. Well, we hauled him back into the room and had a great laugh. Except for a couple of guys who were really mad and one who took a swing at Terry, said he nearly gave him a heart attack. It all ended with handshakes and hugs.

We lost Terry to a car accident a few years later. At his wake, I was asked to tell the story of the Frisco trip. I gave it my best, with a few flourishes thrown in. It got a huge laugh and everybody said it was pure Terry. I think he would have been proud.

If I could sing a lick, I would have closed with "Mother McCrea."

QUICK EDDIE

T he sun was breaking through a thick gray overcast and it
looked like it could turn into a decent afternoon. Eddie
Clark drove across the Carquinez Bridge, then took the
Sonoma Boulevard exit and headed toward downtown Vallejo.
He had time to kill before heading on to Napa. In fact, he had all
Sunday afternoon and evening. His meeting wasn't scheduled until
the next day. He had recently moved back to San Francisco and
been assigned a territory that extended into the North Bay.

Eddie had not been in Vallejo in nearly twenty-five years, since
November of 1941, and he wanted to check out some places he
remembered. He approached the downtown area not knowing how
much might have changed. Then he saw the old Vallejo Bowl, still
standing at the corner of York and Sonoma. A little up the block
and across the street was the Greyhound Bus station. Things had
been cleaned up and painted, but at least these two landmarks were
standing. *The scene of the crime*, Eddie said to himself.

He continued across Georgia Street, the main drag of town, and
up the hill to the Casa De Vallejo hotel at the corner of Sonoma and
Capitol. By God, it was still there too, and looked to be in pretty
good shape. As he passed the front of the hotel, he saw the coffee
shop inside the lobby on the street level. That's where he had met
Jodie.

Eddie turned left onto Capitol and found a place to park at the
curb. Just down the hill from the hotel was a bar, now called the
Ritz. He pushed open the door and went inside. It was dark, but

he could tell there had been changes—probably remodeled many times over the years. There were a handful of patrons sitting at the bar or in booths along the wall. He sat at the bar and waited for the bartender to approach.

"Hi, what can I get for you?" The bartender was a young man and Eddie wondered for a moment if he was old enough to serve drinks.

"Gimme a draft," Eddie replied, letting his eyes take in the interior of the bar as they adjusted to the light. The bartender returned and set his beer down on a coaster. Eddie extended his hand across the bar. "Name's Eddie. Eddie Clark."

The young man shook his hand. "Hi, I'm Don." He sized-up the middle-aged man sitting across the bar: slick hair, slick clothes, too much jewelry. Had to be some kind of salesman. Or a pimp.

"Donnie, tell me something, when is a woman like a good draft beer?" Eddie smirked a little, waiting for the answer.

"Don't know," Don replied. He could tell a punch line was coming.

"When she's got a good head and goes down easy." Eddie let the line sink in, then he laughed a little too loudly. Don laughed too, then glanced away, a little embarrassed. He moved away to help another customer at the bar.

Eddie sat at the bar and nursed his beer. He was in no hurry today. He picked up a copy of the *Vallejo Times-Herald* and thumbed through to the movie section. He noted that *The Hustler* was back in the theaters again. *Great flick*, he thought. *Fast Eddie Felson, Minnesota Fats. They don't make 'em like that anymore.* Eddie laughed out loud. That's what he needed when he was hustling in bowling alleys, a good nickname. *How about Quick Eddie? Quick Eddie Clark.* He wondered how many people knew there were hustlers in bowling, just like pool, and lots of other games. Any game where you could get somebody to put down a bet, there you'd find hustlers making a living.

He remembered the sweet little hustle he and Pete had going back in '41. Pete Pannel! What a guy, may he rest in peace. Pete was thirty years older than Eddie, big and barrel-chested with his stomach hanging over his belt. Bigger than life, that was Pete. Eddie could still hear Pete's voice booming through a bowling establishment, challenging anybody to bowl him for money. Then he'd bust out with that huge laugh of his.

Eddie recalled how Pete could hold a sixteen-pound bowling ball on his palm, let it roll down his forearm, pop it up in the air with his biceps and catch it in his hand. He saw a lot of guys wreck their arms trying to match that stunt. Pete was powerful man, and a great bowler. He taught Eddie everything he knew about the game—angles, lane conditions, how to find the groove, how to adjust—but especially how to get into the other man's head. Pete was a master at that. He knew just where to stick the needle.

Bowling was a different game then. Lane conditions were rough, the pins were heavy, lots of variables to consider. You had to "hit 'em to get 'em" in those days. Not like today, with these plastic coated pins flying around like ping pong balls. Hell, in the thirties and forties, if a bowler could average 180, he was damn good. Now guys are carrying 210, 220 averages like it was nothing. It's a damn circus.

Eddie looked around and he thought about Jodie. They used to come in here for a drink. God, she was a doll! Auburn hair, beautiful little figure, and light, light green eyes. Those eyes: that's what did it to you. What a doll.

He and Pete were working their hustle down at the Vallejo Bowl when he met Jodie. He remembered how their little game used to work. They'd pick a bowling establishment in one of the smaller towns, well outside of Frisco. In any good house, when the league bowlers wrapped up around midnight, the pot games would start. A bunch of guys would get a couple of lanes, hire a pin setter and a scorekeeper, throw a few dollars in the pot, then bowl winner take all.

There was nothing like it, after midnight in a good house, all the lights turned off except for the lanes where the action was taking place. The bowlers, all kind of nervous and jumpy, messing around with their gear. And there'd be a few people watching, enjoying the action, maybe waiting to jump in when the stakes got high enough. Eddie focused the picture in his mind, right down to the sign on the wall saying, "No Gambling On These Premises." It was a beautiful thing to see.

Well, the games would go on and the stakes would go up. Pretty soon, guys would be tapped out and it would come down to a couple of bowlers. Finally, all the money would go in the pot, and somebody would walk away a little richer. By that time, the sun might be coming up.

Eddie had seen men lose their paychecks. They'd put up anything—rings, watches, golf clubs, pink slips—to stay in the action, sure that in the very next game, they'd come out on top. It was sad to watch sometimes. Unless you had an edge and knew you'd be the winner. He never found a bowler in any one of the small towns they worked—Orinda, Walnut Creek, Pacheco, Fairfield—who could beat him when all the money was in. Hell, this was Eddie's job! These other Joes had to put in fifty or sixty hours a week on a damn shipyard or some other gig.

So, Eddie would go into a town first, start hanging around the lanes and getting into the pot games. After a couple of days, he'd have a reputation built up. He was good and none of these small town guys could touch him. Then Pete would blow in on the weekend and start shooting off his mouth about how nobody could beat him for money. The hometown boys would go find Eddie and the match would be on. Of course, nobody knew they were connected. So Eddie would win a few, and Pete would win a few, and there would be other bowlers that would be in for while, until they tapped out. Finally, Pete would start talking up the stakes until the pot got nice and big. He'd be drinking beer and going to his bag for a silver flask he carried, and he'd be nipping at that flask and getting louder all the time. There wasn't anything in the flask but water. He'd scare off everybody but Eddie, and finally, all the money was in. Pete would make a few mistakes and Eddie would win. Then it was time for Pete's big speech.

"I've got five hundred dollars says you can't beat me again," Pete would bellow, and he'd flash a roll of bills.

"Hell, I don't have that kind of money," Eddie would say.

"What's the matter, kid? Tell him, guys. No guts no glory!" Pete was something when he got going.

Eddie would flash some anger then: "You old fart, I've been beating your ass all morning, and I can keep on beating your ass. I just don't have that kind of money."

Five hundred dollars was a fortune in those days. But sure enough, somebody in the crowd would offer to put up the stakes for Eddie. It could be a bunch of guys going in together, or it could be the manager of the house. They wanted to see Eddie beat this loudmouth drunk, and make a little money in the process.

Then the game would start and Eddie would miss a shot or two and suddenly, Pete was the winner. And that was it. They were careful not to be too greedy. After the big finale, it was time to make an exit. Eddie would tell the men who put up their money that he'd be back that night with a new stake, and that they'd all get their money back. He'd challenge Pete to show up and try to take him again. Of course, Pete would accept, at the top of his lungs. What a guy, Pete.

They'd leave separately and Eddie would beat it back to wherever he was staying and grab his suitcase. Pete would be waiting for him in the car when he came out, and they were gone. It was a sweet hustle, and they worked it through a bunch of small towns during the summer and fall of 1941.

That's what brought them to Vallejo that November. And that's when he met Jodie. Eddie checked into the Casa De Vallejo—everybody called it the "Casa Dee"—then walked downstairs to the coffee shop. Jodie was working behind the counter. They were about the same age, mid-twenties, and they hit it off right away. Her shift was over around 2:00 PM, and he asked her if she'd like to catch a movie. He had lots of time to kill before he went to work around midnight.

They saw a movie that first afternoon, then had dinner together with a nice bottle of wine, and ended up back in his room at the Casa De. They made love until it was time for him to head for the Vallejo Bowl, just down the street. Just like that, he thought. She was a beauty.

He saw Jodie the next day, then the next, and the day after that. He was really getting to know her. She wanted to go to college to study art and was working hard, saving her money. Her father didn't think girls should go to college, so she got no help there. She was about as nice a girl as Eddie had ever met, and smart too.

Eddie remembered his room at the hotel, looking out on Sonoma Boulevard, with the neon light from the hotel sign turning everything kind of a rose color inside, and he and Jodie snuggling and laughing after making love. There was an old steam radiator near the widow for heat and they'd turn it up to take the chill out of the room. Jodie would put her underwear on the radiator to warm up a little before getting dressed. God, what a girl!

Well, Pete rolled into Vallejo on Saturday and they were all set to do their thing that night. Eddie checked out of his room on Saturday morning and left his bag with the desk clerk. His cover story with Jodie was that he sold bowling equipment, and that he had to move on to his next customer. He made plans to come back and see her in about a week. He wasn't sure how he would work that out with Pete, but he knew he wanted to see Jodie again.

Things were going like clockwork that Saturday night. There had been some guys who wanted to try their luck and ended up donating lots of money. Pete was sipping beer and going to his flask, and getting louder and louder. And finally everybody was out but Eddie and the money was all in. Pete tanked a few shots and Eddie won the big pot. The beauty part was watching Pete just barely miss a critical shot or two. Pete was a master.

"I've got five hundred dollars . . ." Pete went into his big speech. And sure enough, a bunch of guys came to Eddie and said they'd back him, and for him to kick Pete's ass. The final game was moving along with Eddie about to miss a critical shot by a fraction, when he heard Pete curse under his breath.

"Jeezus, Mary and Joseph!" Pete looked like somebody had punched him in the gut.

"What is it?" Eddie stood next to Pete at the ball return.

"The house manager is up there talking to a guy that looks familiar. I think I saw him in Walnut Creek when we were there last month. Oh, shit! It *is* him. We've been made."

Eddie looked up and saw the manager in earnest conversation with a tall, thin man wearing a plaid jacket. The manager stepped out from the counter and began to talk to one of the men who had put money on Eddie.

"Okay, kid, we've got to run for it," Pete said. "Head across the lanes to the pit area and out the back door. My car is out there. You run for the bus station and I'll take the car. They'll follow me and I can lose 'em. We'll hook up later in Frisco. Go!"

With that, Eddie took off across the darkened, empty lanes, heading for the back of the house, skipping over the ball returns and trying not to trip in the gutters. Pete was right behind him, change and keys jangling in his pants, huffin' and puffin', his big belly bouncing along. They blasted through the back door and Pete headed for his car. Eddie sprinted around the building and across Sonoma Boulevard to the bus station. He peered through the plate-glass window of the station and saw Pete tear out of the parking lot and onto Sonoma, heading for Highway 40 and the bridge. Sure enough, a group came charging out the back door and jumped into two cars. They sped off after Pete.

Eddie waited a few minutes to let his heart rate return to normal, then he went to a ticket window and bought a one-way ticket on the next bus scheduled to leave. It was heading to Oakland and he knew he could get home to San Francisco from there. He boarded the bus and sank down in his seat. He didn't begin to breathe easy until the bus had crossed the Carquinez Bridge. He glanced down at his feet and realized he was still wearing his bowling shoes. His ball, his bag, his street shoes, and his jacket were all back at the Vallejo Bowl. And his suitcase was sitting with the desk clerk at the Casa De.

Eddie made it back to San Francisco the next day. Later he heard that Pete was back in town and they arranged to meet. Pete had ditched the posse by heading off of Highway 40, through Crockett and down past Port Costa. It was all pretty funny and they had a good laugh over their adventure. Except for one thing: Eddie couldn't go back to Vallejo and he didn't know what to do about Jodie. It wasn't long before his dilemma was resolved. On December 7, the Japanese bombed Pearl Harbor. A week later, Eddie enlisted and shipped out for basic training at Fort Ord, near Monterey. He never saw Jodie again.

Eddie called Don over to settle his bill. When the young man returned with his change, he had a question waiting for him: "Donnie, why doesn't a rooster have hands?"

"Don't know, Eddie." Don could see it coming again.

"Because chickens don't have tits." Eddie let it sink in, then let loose his best Pete Pannel laugh and got up to leave. "I'll be coming through from time to time. See you later, kid."

"Not if I see you first," Don mumbled under his breath.

Eddie started for the door, then stopped and stared at an empty booth in the corner. He hoped Jodie got everything she wanted: art school, a career, a great guy, a bunch of little green-eyed kids, and happily ever after. She was a great kid and nobody deserved it more than her. She deserved better than Quick Eddie Clark.

The door swung open and a well-dressed woman with flowing brown hair walked briskly into the Ritz. She waved to several of the regulars at the bar and they called out her name in greeting.

"Whoa, who is that?" one of the barflies asked his friend. "What a knockout!"

"Forget it, man. The lady is all class and she's way out of your league."

Don exchanged smiles with the woman as she sat down at the bar. He scooped ice cubes into a tall glass, dropped in a wedge of lime and filled the glass with club soda. He placed the drink on a coaster in front of his new customer.

"How's it goin', Mom?"

"Good, honey. How's your day?"

"Not bad. Hey, you wouldn't believe the guy I just had in here. What a piece of work! Oh, yeah . . . answer this: why doesn't a rooster have hands?"

THE ROAD TO MOONLIGHT

I had no idea what was in store for me when I walked into The Vintage that afternoon. I just wanted to see what Jesse was up to and if he wanted to go get something to eat, then maybe watch a game on TV. It turned into one of the all time great road trips, one we still talk about. Funny how the best times are the ones you don't plan.

Jesse was behind the bar, getting ready to hand-off to one of the bartenders who worked for him. He bought The Vintage in 1964 and turned it into the best bar in town, at least as far as I was concerned. It was like Grand Central: if you stayed there long enough, everyone you knew would come through the front door. After three years, The Vintage was doing very well and all of Jesse's friends were happy for him.

Let me tell you about Jesse. You see, he was born with some serious issues. The state declared him blind at birth—*legally blind* was the term that got tossed around. He could see, but not much. You'd think that would be a major problem, but not for Jesse. He refused to let it slow him down. He kept up with all the rest of us, in school and on the playground. I remember going over to the basketball courts at the park and playing for hours and hours. It was always me and Will against Lannie and Jesse. Lannie was a couple of years older and he and Jess made a great team. Jesse was tough under the basket: he could box out with that round body of his, and he could score off the rebound. They beat us most of the time. We'd play for hours.

As we got older and went out for school sports, Jesse became our team manager, taking care of the equipment, keeping score and keeping the official stats. He even got to travel with us on all the road trips. The important thing was that he was part of everything we did.

Some kids who didn't know Jesse would make smart-ass remarks and tease him. They would see him holding something an inch from his nose, struggling to read, and they'd think that was funny. They'd only do that once because we'd kick their asses. Anybody who messed with Jesse was in for a whipping. That's just the way it was. He was our friend and we took care of him. And here's the thing: it wasn't because we felt sorry for him. He was just a great guy and we all loved him.

So, I walked into The Vintage that summer afternoon and took my regular stool at the bar. Jesse popped open a cold Hamm's and slid it in front of me.

"Hey, Jess, how's it going?"

"Good, Jon. A little slow. Ronnie's taking over. It'll just be a couple of minutes."

"So what do you wanna do? Wanna grab some lunch?"

"Okay, but, you know, after that . . ."

"Yeah?"

"I'm bored, man. Ya know? I mean, we need to get out of town or something."

"Where to, Jess?"

"Let's go to up to Nevada. To the Moonlight Ranch."

"Carson City? Geez, Jess, that's a five hour trip."

"Yeah, so? Come on, let's do it."

Just then the front door swung open and our friend Danny strolled in. He came over and took the stool next to me. Jesse went to get a beer for him.

"Hey, Jon. What's up?"

"Hi, Danny. Jesse wants to go to Carson City. To the Moonlight Ranch."

"The cathouse? Okay, I'm in. Wait a minute . . ." Danny took out his wallet and cracked it open a little. "Damn, I'm a little short, Jon. How about you?"

"Yeah, me too. Let's talk to Jesse, see what we can do."

Jesse came down the bar with a beer for Danny. "What's up, Dan?"

"Not much, Jess. I hear we're going to the Moonlight Ranch?"

"Yeah, if we can talk Jon into it. Whataya say, Jon?"

It wasn't fair, because I knew it would be too easy, but I went into negotiation mode with Jesse, looking for the best deal we could get. "Damn, Jess, Danny and I want to go, but we're a little light, man. You can't have fun up there without some cash in your pocket."

Jesse's brow furrowed over that one. "Look, I'll spot you guys a c-note, okay?"

"Is that a c-note each?" I was having fun now.

"Okay, a c-note each."

I could see that Jesse really wanted to go. "It's a long drive, Jess. It's gonna take some gas, too."

"All right, damn it, I'll pay for the gas."

Now it was Danny's turn to weigh in. "I say we stop at Stateline too, spend a little time at Harrah's."

"Oh, man, I don't wanna stop. If we're going to The Ranch, let's just go."

"I don't know, Jess. A little stop at Harrah's can't hurt. The ladies will be waiting when you get to The Ranch."

Jesse knew he was being hustled, but he caved in anyway. "Okay, we'll stop for one hour at Harrah's. One hour and that's it! Done deal?"

Ten minutes later we were on the road.

We made a quick stop for lunch and I went to a pay phone to give Gina a call. Gina was Jesse's sister and they were really close. I knew she'd worry if she didn't know where Jesse had gone. The two of them fought like cats and dogs, but one thing was certain: Gina always had Jesse's back. She looked out for him like a mama lion.

"Hey, Gina, it's Jon. Just wanted to let you to know that Jesse is with Danny and me. We're going up to Nevada."

"Nevada? Where in Nevada?"

"You know, Stateline. We're goin' to Harrah's."

"Yeah, I'll bet you're goin' to Harrah's. Look, just be careful. Don't leave him alone in the casinos. It's too damn crowded. Okay?"

"Sure, Gina, don't worry. He's with Danny and me."

"This is on you, Jon." With that she hung up.

It was nearly 5:00 PM when we pulled off Highway 50 and into downtown Placerville. We were thirsty and Danny said he knew of a good bar near the center of town. It was a place called The Hanging Tree. They had a dummy hanging from a noose from the second story of the building, a not-so-subtle reminder that the original name of this burg was Hangtown. We went in, took a seat at the bar and ordered some beers. Jesse struck up a conversation with some local guys sitting at the bar and it wasn't long before he had them all laughing. Danny went to scope out the action at the pool tables in the back room, and he came back with a grin on his face.

"I think we can make some money here, Jon. Are you up for it?"

"Sure. You gonna talk us into their game?" Danny could shoot a mean game of pool and I was no slouch.

We left Jesse with his new best friends and went into the back room. Before long, we were in the game—Danny and me against two locals who smelled fresh meat. They were pretty good, but Danny was better and I was having a pretty good day. We played 8-ball, starting at $5 a game. Before long, it was up to $10. We were winning two games for every one of theirs and our pile of winnings was growing steadily. The locals weren't taking it very well. They didn't like the idea of some out-of-town guys coming in and messing up their Saturday evening and they started making some wise-ass remarks.

Danny walked over to me while one of their guys was lining up a shot. "Okay, they win the next two games. Got it?"

He smiled a little and I could see that he'd taken out his front tooth. He had a false tooth to plug a gap left by a fight a long time ago, and when he took it out, it meant that he expected trouble.

"Oh crap, Danny, I don't wanna fight these guys."

"Don't worry. Just follow my lead, okay? And go get Jesse back here—now."

I went and told Jesse that we needed him in the back room, even though I wasn't sure why. We tanked the next two games and the locals were really feeling it. They were laughing and slapping high-fives all over the place.

"Hey, guys," Danny started, "we've got to leave for a date with some Nevada ladies. What say we shoot one more game for . . . let's see . . . two hundred . . . no, make that two hundred and fifty dollars. Here's our stake." He counted out the money and dropped it on the table.

The locals looked kind of stunned. "What? Nah, you're full of shit."

"What's the matter, that kind of money scare you? You guys aren't afraid, are you?" Danny had them going now.

Sure enough, the two players and a couple of their buddies huddled up and came up with the two fifty. After all, they'd just won the last two games. They dropped their money on the table and Danny scooped it up and handed it to Jesse.

"Okay, Jesse here will hold the stakes. We'll lag for the break."

I was already racking up the balls. The local guys weren't happy about Jesse holding the money, but things were moving too fast for them now. Danny won the lag easily and got ready to break. He sent the cue ball into the rack like a sledgehammer and the 15-ball fell neatly into the corner pocket. He ran the rest of the striped balls and left himself an easy tap-in of the 8-ball for the win. And just like that, it was over.

"Thanks, guys," Danny chirped. "We gotta go."

We laid our cues on the table, Danny grabbed Jesse under his right arm and I grabbed his left, and we booked it for the front door. The locals didn't have time to react. Jesse called goodbye to his new friends as we passed through the bar. We were out the door, up the street and into the car by the time they regrouped and came after us. They just stood on the sidewalk, under that legendary hangman's noose, and watched us drive away.

"All right! That was sweet!" Danny was looking out the back window, laughing and waving at the Placerville boys. "Now we can afford some good, clean Nevada fun."

We pulled into Harrah's parking lot around 9:00 PM. Jesse wanted to see a lounge show while Danny and I gambled, so we helped him find the lounge. He wasn't comfortable trying to find his way around places he didn't know, especially with the crowds. I was itching to find the poker room and Danny was looking for a craps table.

"Okay, you guys, look: if you go and blow your stake, don't come to me for help." Jesse was laying down the law. "You're on your own. Got it?"

"Yeah, yeah, no worries, Jess. We'll be back in about an hour."

No worries, my ass! I sat down at a seven card stud table and I've never seen the cards so cold. It was a three dollar/six dollar limit table and I won a couple of small pots, but I was looking at rags most of the time. The hour was nearly up and my stack of chips was going south. On the next hand, I looked at my hole cards: a pair of 10's. Finally something to work with! The dealer turns up another 10 and suddenly I have a set. I make the small bet and watch most of the players around the table muck their cards. Except for a sweet-faced lady sitting across from me who reminded me of my grandmother; she calls my bet with a 7 showing. The dealer throws me an 8 and grandma a Jack. Now she makes the small bet and I call. My next card is another 8 giving me a full house. Grandma draws another Jack and checks. Damn, what does she have? Jacks showing, but what's in the hole? Didn't I see another guy fold a Jack? She's probably got a set. Okay, so I throw in the max bet, and she calls. The next cards don't help either of us. She checks again, I go for the max bet and she calls. The dealer throws the seventh card face down and I can't believe my eyes: it's a 10. I've got four 10's. Now she tosses in the max bet and I raise. Grandma re-raises, which puts me all in, but that's okay because I'm sure I've got her. I stand up to get ready to rake in the pot, and I'll admit my heart is thumpin' big time. She turns over her hole cards: a pair of Jacks. She's got four Jacks! I look up at her and she gives me the sweetest smile. "Sorry, honey," she says. I tuck my tail between my legs and limp away—flat broke.

I found Danny just as he was walking away from a craps table. "How'd you do?"

"I lost."

"How much?"

"All of it." Danny gave me a weak grin. "How 'bout you?"

"Same story. I had four 10's and got gutted . . . by somebody's grandmother. Can you believe that shit?"

What a roller coaster! We came out of Placerville riding high and now we were back to zero. There was nothing to do but go find Jesse. The lounge show was ending as we walked up and Jesse was saying goodbye to several new friends. What a guy! He made friends everywhere he went. We told him our sad stories and he cracked up. It was the funniest thing he'd heard all night.

"Okay losers, let's hit the road. It's about half an hour to The Ranch from here." Jesse was laughing all the way to the car.

When we pulled up to the Moonlight Ranch, it was close to 11:00 PM. The parking lot was nearly full, probably typical for a Saturday night. We went in and sat down at the bar. Danny and I had enough money for a couple of beers, but that was about it. So we nursed our beers while Jesse struck up a conversation with some of the girls. Before long, he went off to talk turkey with the madam and a cute little brunette. Then we saw him heading off down a long hall with the girl he chose. He looked back over his shoulder and waved to us, a big grin on his face.

We took our beers over to a couch across from the bar and visited with some of the ladies. They said it was a shame that we didn't have any money because we were nice looking guys. That didn't make us feel any better. Danny popped out his front tooth and grinned, and that made them laugh. One of the girls brought a deck of cards over and we gathered around a low coffee table and played gin rummy—dollar a point, though it was just for fun.

After a while, Jesse came back out to the bar and ordered a tall orange juice. We kept the card game going and about half an hour later, there was Jesse, heading back down that hall with another girl. We got tired of playing cards, so we just sat around and talked to the girls. One of them asked if we could at least put a quarter in the jukebox and play some music. Danny and I looked at each other and shrugged: between us, we didn't even have a quarter. The girl went over to the bar and brought back a couple of beers. She said our friend was doing so much business that the house could buy us a round.

Jesse came back out for more orange juice, and the next time he went down the hall, it was with two ladies. I settled back on the couch and closed my eyes. All the chatter and laughter at the bar was like a lullaby and in a minute, I was sound asleep. The next thing I knew, Jesse was shaking my shoulder, waking me up. He'd spent all his money and he was ready to go. All the girls came over to give him hugs and say goodbye. Like I said, he made friends everywhere he went. We stumbled out the door and headed for the car. The cold, crisp night air was like a slap in the face. I looked at my watch and saw that it was a little after 3:00 AM.

Finally, we were back on Highway 50, heading for home. I took the first shift behind the wheel while Danny stretched out in the back seat to get some sleep. Jesse was riding shotgun up front with me. I checked my watch and made a mental note to give Gina a call when we got to Placerville. When we hit Spooner Summit, I glanced over at Jesse and saw that he was out cold—with a smile on his face.

It made me think of the times when I was a kid and we'd go over to the Suisun Valley to pick apricots. It was a way to make a little extra money for school clothes and such. All day long, you'd be climbing up the ladder, picking apricots as fast as you could, climbing down to dump your bucket in a wooden crate, then scrambling back up the ladder again. The faster you picked, the more money you could make. At the end of the day, you'd go home dead tired—and dream all night long about picking apricots.

I looked at Jesse with that big smile on his face and knew that he was dreaming a sweet dream. And it had nothing to do with apricots.

THE LAWNMOWER

M
y brother Rich and I were on a mission, him behind the wheel of our mom's old gray Chevy Nova and me riding shotgun. We were heading north on the highway that cuts through the rich farmland of the Sacramento Valley, determined to find our friends Hugh and Jean Quinn, collect the lawnmower, and make it home to Vallejo before dark. It was late morning on a hot August day and the sun beat down on the bone-dry fields that lined the road. Now and then, we'd pass irrigated land where the row crops were nearing end of season. Looking up the highway, we strained our eyes to filter out the false vision of water covering the road, anticipating a grain elevator or a church steeple that would announce the town of Valley Vista. On Main Street, we were to look for a watering hole called Sunny's, then turn left and head west out of town up into the low foothills. Hugh and Jean had marked the entrance to their property with red and white balloons tied to a fence post. "You can't miss it," were their last words.

The town materialized out of the valley heat, we found Sunny's corner and headed west. We were out into rolling country now, populated by small herds of cattle grazing on the hillsides.

"Hey, Nick . . ." Rich was smiling, keeping his eyes glued to the road. "Remember when Brent's old man told you that these cattle are a special breed called Sidehill Gougers? With longer legs on one side so they can graze the hillsides?"

I couldn't help but laugh at the memory. "Yeah, I guess you'll believe anything when you're a kid."

The road began to twist and turn now as we wound through a stand of scrub oak that followed a dry creek bed. Suddenly, there were the promised balloons, bobbing about in the warm breeze. Rich turned right and began to climb a gravel road that curved gently up the hill. We topped a rise onto a flat, graded area and there were the Quinns, standing in front of their doublewide trailer, waving and smiling broadly.

I looked around as we got out of the car and was impressed by the setting. The trailer was situated facing east, looking out across the valley toward the Sierras. The valley itself looked like a brown and green quilt stretching into the distance. To the west, behind the trailer, the knob of the hill and a large valley oak promised afternoon shade, a welcome respite from the brutal August sun. Just outside the door to the trailer, there was a broad concrete patio, covered by a ribbed metal roof on a redwood frame. It was obvious that Hugh had been busy with these improvements to the site, and it was clear that he intended to stay. A little wooden sign that read "Dun Movin'" was nailed to one of the patio posts.

There were hugs and handshakes all around. After a quick tour of the doublewide, we settled into padded chairs on the patio and Jean handed each of us an ice-cold Coors. She made it clear that from that point on, we'd have to help ourselves.

We'd known the Quinns for about a dozen years, dating back to the time when Jean ran the neighborhood hamburger shack in our hometown. Hugh was a long-distance truck driver and was on the road much of the time. The little restaurant—called Alice's Place, in honor of the former owner—was initially intended to keep Jean busy while Hugh was away. It turned out to be a successful little business. The burgers and sandwiches were first rate, the Cokes, Nehis and Squirts were always ice-cold, and the juke box was loaded with the best music Tin Pan Alley had to offer, from Glen Miller's "In The Mood" to Frankie Lane's "The Kid's Last Fight."

Rich was the local news carrier in those days, delivering the morning and evening papers to the surrounding neighborhood. He would make Alice's Place his last stop every morning and every evening, and Jean Quinn came to love him like a son. As the "little brother," nine years younger than Rich, I would tag along every chance I got. As far as I was concerned, happiness was a pocketful of nickels to feed the jukebox and enjoy a Nehi Orange. As the old marketing pitch proclaimed, "A nickel for Nehi. How much for a dime?"

We relaxed on the patio now, catching up on what was going on in everyone's life. Hugh had finally retired from the trucking business, at least for the time being. He and Jean both knew that sooner or later, he'd run out of projects around their property. When that happened, she'd have to find something for him to do; either that or let him drive her nuts. Rich filled them in on recent happenings in his career with the State of California. I played the part of the good listener: the Quinns had always been Rich's "family," and I was fine with that. The beer was very cold, coming directly from a large ice chest next to Hugh's chair, and that was a good thing, because the temperature continued to rise, sure to hit triple digits by early afternoon.

There was one Quinn family member that had been left out of the conversation and I couldn't help but wonder why. The Quinns' daughter Roslyn, who must be in her mid-twenties now, was conspicuous by her absence, and I was waiting for the right time to raise the question. Roslyn was, and quite likely always will be, the substance of my fantasies. I would describe her as Elizabeth Taylor with brown eyes, and few people would argue with me. I first became aware of her when I was about thirteen and she was seventeen and a senior in high school. I was totally smitten, a fact which manifested itself by my inability to speak a coherent sentence whenever she was around. All she had to do was make eye contact and smile and I would be reduced to pile of warm Jell-O. While I carried that heavy torch, it turned out that Roslyn had eyes for Rich, a fact that I couldn't help but hold against my brother.

Rich, who was twenty-two at that time and well past his news carrier days, did his best to resist. But in the end, it became obvious to anyone with eyes that there was something going on between them. Jean, being a protective mother, found herself torn. She loved

Rich, thought of him as the kind of man she'd want her daughter to bring home, as long as it happened later. Much later.

And then life intervened as it is inclined to do. Rich went off to serve in the Air Force and Roslyn moved on with her life, never lacking for attention from male suitors. All of this left me with a fantasy woman who crept into my dreams from time to time, with her beautiful brown eyes, her gleaming white smile, and a figure that could keep you awake at night.

Hugh took Rich around to the back of the trailer to a shed where the lawnmower was stored, leaving me to chat with Jean. I filled her in on my attempts to work and go to school, determined to earn my degree. Jean brought me up to date on their most recent move, from a home in Quincy to this notch in the hillside overlooking the valley. The Quincy house had an expansive lawn, hence the lawnmower; it was clear that Hugh had no plans to do any lawn mowing here. It just so happened that we were in the market for a reliable mower to tend the lawns at our mother's place.

I finally found an opening in the conversation to ask how Roslyn was doing. As Jean was about to answer, we heard the mower start up in back of the trailer, coughing a little at first, then running strong and smooth as advertised.

"Roslyn is doing fine, Nick. She lives near here, so I get to see her a lot. But . . ." She looked away across the valley and it was several seconds before she continued. "Hugh and Roslyn had a falling out. She hasn't spoken to him for nearly two years now." She went on to explain that it was a dispute that centered on Roslyn's husband, a guy that Hugh could not stand. She started to say more, but then caught herself. Finally she added: "He's just not a very nice person, Nick. He doesn't treat her well."

This caused my imagination to run amok and I felt my cheeks flush with hatred for the rotten bastard of a husband. Who could possibly mistreat Roslyn? Just then Rich called me to help load the mower into the car. We folded the handle in half and lifted the nearly new machine into the trunk. We blocked the wheels with wood scraps and lashed the trunk lid down with some rope that

Hugh had handy. This effort out in the mid-day sun renewed our thirst and called for another ice-cold beer.

"Okay guys, finish your beers and then were heading down to Sunny's. It's too damn hot to sit up here, even in the shade." Jean got no argument on this point. A little air conditioning would be much appreciated.

Sunny's fancied itself to be a cowboy bar. The décor was classic western bunkhouse, with lariats and spurs, horseshoes and branding irons, and even an old saddle hung on the wall; this in addition to two large oil paintings behind the bar that depicted life on the range. Sunny herself dressed the part, looking like a sixty-something Dale Evans after a hard day's work. The jukebox was loaded with great tunes, as long as you adopted the house view that there are only two kinds of music: Country and Western. There was a nice crowd for a Sunday afternoon and Sunny was busy keeping everyone's glass full.

Hugh and Jean had donned their cowboy hats and fit right in with rest of the crowd. Rich and me—in our polo shirts, khaki shorts and tennis shoes—were the odd men out. None of that mattered as the Quinns introduced us to friends who stopped by to say hello and buy a round. Before long, I noticed that I had two beers waiting on the bar for my attention, in addition to the one in my hand. Rich, to his credit, had switched to club soda, anticipating the drive home.

The circle around Jean and Hugh expanded and contracted as friends came and went. They sat with their backs resting against the padded rail, as though holding court. Jean gave me a handful of quarters for the jukebox with instructions to play some Patsy Cline, or Tammy Wynette, or Johnny Cash. I selected "I Fall to Pieces," and "Crazy," and watched as several couples slow-danced on the small dance floor. I punched the numbers for "A Boy Named Sue" and smiled, wondering what kind of reaction it would bring. When I rejoined the group at the bar, a guy who'd been introduced as Dudley entered the circle behind me.

"Hey, Hugh." He said it loud enough to cut through the general chatter. "Roslyn is here, down at the end of the bar." And just like that, all conversation stopped as everyone turned to Hugh.

Hugh was quiet for a moment. "Is *he* with her?"

"No. She's here with some friends."

He took a long pull from his beer, looking very uncomfortable in this sudden spotlight. "Well . . . tell her we're right here . . . if she wants to say hello."

Dudley blinked a couple of times, then turned and headed back down the bar, honored to play the designated shuttle diplomat. It was quiet for a second and then the suspended conversations resumed and Tammy Wynette sang "Stand By Your Man." I looked around and tried to spot Roslyn, but the place was too crowed now. Jean got up and walked away, heading toward her daughter's end of the bar.

Five minutes later, Dudley was back, and again, all conversation halted. "Roslyn says she's right there if you'd like to say 'Hi.'" Dudley glanced around the circle, clearly growing less comfortable with his role.

I watched Hugh's face and saw a range of emotions come and go, probably somewhere between *Damn stubborn kid, just like her mother,* and *Aw shit, life is too short for this!* He cleared his throat and said, "Tell her I hope she's well . . . and that everything's okay at home."

Dudley smiled now and headed quickly away with this message. It wasn't long before he was back. "She says 'thanks, same to you.'" He paused a moment and then added, "They're gettin' ready to leave."

Hugh fixed Dudley with a steady gaze. "Tell her to take care. And tell her I said 'I love you.'"

The background noise continued and Johnny Cash sang "I Walk The Line," but you could hear a quarter drop in the circle around Hugh Quinn as Dudley hurried away. I shuffled my feet and stared at my sneakers. A few seconds later, out of the corner of my eye, I saw a white streak fly by. It was a girl in a cowboy hat and she ran into Hugh's arms so hard that her hat was knocked to the floor. I knew it was Roslyn. She wrapped her arms around Hugh's neck and he held her close for a long, long time. We were all quiet, except for Dudley who kept saying, "Ah, now that's the ticket . . . that's the ticket."

Roslyn let go of Hugh for a second and turned to me. "Nick! It's great to see you!" She gave me a quick hug and a peck on the check, and I instantly became Mr. Jell-O. I managed to say, "Hi, Roslyn. Great to see you too." I had picked up her hat and I handed it to her now. She was wearing a white western-style shirt and jeans, with a wide leather belt and a big silver buckle. If anything, she was prettier than I remembered.

Then she turned to my brother and gave him a full-body hug, one that went on a little too long for my taste. I couldn't hear what they were saying but my brother was grinning an embarrassed little grin. She turned back to Hugh, grabbed his hand and led him to a booth off across the dance floor for a private conversation. As she walked away in those wonderful fitted jeans, I could see that time had certainly been good to her. Dudley kept saying, "Now that's the ticket," and his eyes were shining with pride over his role in all of this.

Merle Haggard sang "Okie from Muskogee" and the whole bar joined in the chorus; that is except for Roslyn and Hugh. And then it was time for us say goodbye to the Quinns and all of our new friends at Sunny's.

We'd stayed longer than planned and the sun was about to duck behind the hills to the west as we headed down the highway, talking and laughing about the events of the day. But I had some questions for my brother, and after a while, I just couldn't hold back.

"So . . . Roslyn really looks great, don't you think?"

"Yeah."

"Is she still with that guy?"

"As far as I know."

"Ya know, I had a huge crush on her . . . when I was a kid."

"Everybody knows that, Nick."

I was a little surprised at first, but I knew it made sense. "That was some hug she gave you!"

Rich didn't reply.

"So . . . you guys kinda had a thing, you know, way back in the day?"

He was quiet for a few seconds, and then he spoke to me in his best big-brother voice. "Nick, give it up. I'm not gonna talk about it."

And that was my brother. A gentleman. Never kiss and tell. Not ever. I looked at him with a bag full of mixed feelings—curiosity, admiration, frustration, love, jealousy—but mostly love.

I leaned back in the seat and looked out the window to the west. We were cruising through the hills between Fairfield and Vallejo, and I watched a herd of those famous Sidehill Gougers moving along the steep hillside, heading home, wherever home might be. I let my mind wander a little and conjured up a daydream in which Roslyn came over to our mom's house and mowed the lawns, wearing those painted-on jeans.

My brother looked at me suspiciously. "What the hell are smiling about?"

It was an easy shot, too easy really, but I took it anyway. "Rich, give it up. I'm not gonna talk about it."

Rich cracked up laughing and I joined him. I could always make him laugh. We must have looked pretty silly, two guys rolling down the road, laughing our asses off, in a little gray Chevy with a lawnmower stuffed in the trunk. Just like those Sidehill Gougers—finding our way home.

ACCORDING TO PLAN

H e admired people who lived their lives according to plan. They knew what college they'd go to, what career they'd pursue, where they'd be at certain points in that career. They knew how many kids they'd have and when they'd have them. He could never make it work that way. He seemed to ricochet from one questionable choice to the next, always by chance, never by plan. Planning was for those other guys.

That is, except for baseball.

He coached his sons' baseball teams for ten seasons and it was the best hobby he ever had. It was all about preparation and planning and he threw himself into it completely. He read books and went to clinics in the off-season. He planned carefully for the draft each February. And his practices were mapped out to the minute: no wasted time, no standing around.

He had a program and it never changed: have fun; teach fundamentals; teach sportsmanship and teamwork; teach the value of hustle. If you did those things well, winning or losing didn't matter much.

He would gather his players around him before a game and go over the signs. Then he'd tell them a corny joke. They'd look at each other and laugh, even if they didn't get it. And they'd relax a little, which was the whole idea.

If it was an important game, maybe with a championship on the line, he'd give them the John Eaton speech. He remembered it from when he was ten years old, playing in his first All Star tournament.

He was scared spit-less, butterflies raging around his stomach. Coach Eaton said: "You guys have been a joy to work with. You're good kids. Whatever happens today, win or lose, it won't change the way we feel about you. Give it the best you've got today, and just have fun." It was exactly what he needed to hear—*It won't change the way we feel about you*—and he felt the butterflies settle down a little.

Whenever he saw that look in his players' eyes, he knew that Coach Eaton's speech was in order.

He would run into former players from time to time, grown men now, and they'd say, "Hey, I'm coaching a team and I wanted to tell the kids the joke about the largemouth frog. How did that one go?"

He loved to hear it. At least one small part of his life went according to plan.

HIGH AND TIGHT

S arge Martin looked around his hotel room, running down a mental checklist, nearly ready to head for the lobby. He grabbed the small duffle bag he had packed and was on his way to the door when the phone rang.

"Hello."

"Hi, Sarge, it's Shelley Goldstein."

"Hi, Mrs. Goldstein. I was just heading out to meet Barry. We're gonna share a cab to the ballpark. Looks like a great day for a ballgame."

"That's what I wanted to talk to you about, Sarge. Do you think . . . are you sure Barry is ready?"

"Absolutely, ma'am. You know I've been with him all the way, from Arizona on, through A and Double A ball, and believe me, he's ready." He hoped his voice didn't betray any of the doubts.

"It's just . . . well, you know, Sarge, if he ever got hit again . . ."

"We've spent hours on that, Mrs. Goldstein. You've just got to trust it now. And we've got the helmet I had made for him with the extension that covers his cheekbone. He's gonna be fine."

"I know, I know. You've been a godsend, Sarge. I don't think Barry would even have tried if you weren't there with him. You're a real *mensch*."

"Now, you know I'm just a coach, Mrs. Goldstein, just a batting coach. I say, 'do this, try that.' Barry had to do all the work."

"Sarge, after all this time, can't you please call me Shelley?"

"Uh . . . yes, ma'am." That made her laugh and he laughed along with her. But he had something more to say, something he needed to tell her, if he could find the words. "You know . . . Shelley . . . I don't have any kids. I was never blessed with any of my own. But if I had a son, I'd want him to be the kind of man that Barry is. And if I had a daughter, Barry is the guy I'd want her to bring home. Barry is the *mensch*."

"Oh, Sarge . . ." she said, and he heard her blow her nose softly.

They said their goodbyes and he hung up the phone and headed for the lobby. He had coached Barry Goldstein on his way through the minor leagues the first time around, and there was just something special about the young man. He was glad he was able to tell Shelley how he felt about her son. And he meant every word.

Barry stood in front of the mirror, the bath towel fastened snugly around his waist, waiting for the steam to clear. As his face came into focus, he leaned forward and looked closely at his left eye. *Kudos to the doctors,* he said to himself, admiring their work. His cheekbone looked fairly normal now, the left side nearly a twin to the right, and the scars from the surgeries were fading nicely. You had to be close and know what to look for to understand what he'd been through.

He wasn't worried about the scars. He'd wear them like a warrior. It was his vision that had been the real battle. For many months, his left eye had provided nothing more than a blur, and that's why it had taken so long to reach this day. You can't hit a baseball, especially not at the pro level, with only one good eye. At least Barry Goldstein couldn't do it.

Next week would mark the two-year anniversary, though there'd be no celebration. You don't celebrate being stupid. All he had to do was turn with the ball, turn his left side and his left shoulder in, roll with the pitch, take it off his shoulder, or at worst off the back of his helmet. It's one of the first things his father taught him, when he was barely big enough to swing a bat. Turn in with the pitch; turn hard and quick if you have to, get down and hit the dirt. The last thing you want to do is open up, open your face and your chest and your *cajones* to a fastball. But that's exactly what he'd done. The ball caught him flush on the left cheekbone, and then the world went black. When he tried to open his eyes, only the right one seemed to work, and all that red sticky stuff that was all over his face and uniform he soon realized was his own blood.

His season ended right there, a season that began with such promise, with talk about an All Star Game selection and possible Rookie Of The Year honors. Then came the surgeries and the battle to save his left eye, and with it the realization that he might lose more than his rookie season. He could lose an eye. More than likely, he would lose his career.

Barry looked in the mirror again, clear-eyed and confident. It had been a long, hard road, and he wasn't all the way back, but he was damn close. Today would be his first game since the promotion to Triple A. He was one step away.

Bonnie came into the bathroom, rubbing the sleep from her eyes, wearing one of his long T-shirts with a faded team logo across the chest. "Hey, you," she said, "everything okay?" She moved in close behind him and wrapped her arms around his chest. He could feel her head nestled between his shoulder blades and her long, lean body pressed against his backside.

"I'm good," he said. "You sleep okay?"

"Hmmm," she said, rocking gently against him.

Some people said he was unlucky, that he'd caught a bad break. How could they say that when this amazing woman was in his life, loving him unconditionally and oh so well? It didn't matter if he played ball or sold magazine subscriptions door-to-door, Bonnie was there for him; she always would be. He turned to face her and gathered her in his arms.

"Oh, my," she said, "I take it you're glad to see me."

"Uh huh. Do we have enough time?"

"Nooo . . . you've got to meet Sarge in the lobby in a few minutes. But keep that thought . . . for after the game."

"Is that a promise?"

"You got it. And you'd better bring your 'A' game, Buster. Now can I please have the room? I gotta pee."

Sarge stood behind the batting cage, watching the familiar progression of batting practice. Barry was slated to bat sixth in the lineup today, so his group of three would be hitting next. Sarge loved BP: the batting cage and the heavy tarp to protect the infield near home plate; the L-screen to protect the pitcher; coaches on either side of the cage, hitting fungos to the infielders and outfielders; players roaming the outfield, shagging balls and tossing them into a large screen behind second base; pitchers running along the warning track in the outfield, getting in their off-day work. It was a busy scene and Sarge was in his element.

"Well, if it isn't Ernest J. Martin, otherwise known as Sarge!"

Sarge turned to greet Billy Condon, a baseball writer who'd covered the game for three decades. "My God, Billy! Still at it after all these years?" They clasped hands firmly and Sarge tightened his grip until Billy cried uncle. Billy shook the pain from his hand and they shared a good laugh.

"So, I hear Barry G is back, and you're the man that got him here. All true?"

"Well, it's a big step for him, Billy. We'll know in a few days, maybe a few weeks, if he's back or not." He saw Billy scribbling notes on his pad. "Oh, for chrissake, are you gonna quote me on this?"

"Yep. I'm counting on you to fill up my book, Sarge. You know Buzz Adams is starting today. Should be a good test for the kid."

"Buzz and I go way back. I hear he's got a new pitch; gonna make another run at The Show."

"Yeah, he says it's part slider and part cutter. So it's a slutter. He just calls it 'The Slut.' I've seen him throw. He's been hot lately. And what about you, Sarge? Gonna make another run at The Show?"

"What, me? Nah, Billy, you know it's a young man's game today. I'm a dinosaur. Look at me in this damn uniform. I look like ten pounds of shit in a five-pound bag." He saw Billy writing furiously. "Geez, Billy, don't write that down."

Billy laughed and completed his notes. "It would help though, wouldn't it, Sarge? A couple of years and you'd have your full pension."

"Got me there, Billy, but it ain't gonna happen."

Barry's group was moving into the cage now, gathering balls and loading them into the ball bag for their BP pitcher. Billy saw Sarge's face grow serious, his eyes concentrated on the activity in front of him. He knew his interview with Sarge Martin was over until after his pupil was through hitting.

The pitcher was ready and Barry hustled into the cage. He bunted the first pitch down the third base line, bunted the second pitch down the first base line, and then hit the next two pitches hard on the ground toward right field, as though advancing a runner, just as he'd been taught. Now he was ready to swing away.

Sarge watched and listened, paying little attention to where the ball went. He looked for the coil of the hips, weight loaded on the back foot, the short smooth stride and the quick hands as Barry uncoiled into the pitches. He could tell from the sound of the bat exactly how well the swing had been executed, and the sound was sweet music to his ears. He believed that hitting a round ball with a round bat, and hitting it squarely, was the most difficult skill in all of sports. He felt a tingle run through his body. Even now, at sixty-six, he never tired of watching a great swing, and Barry Goldstein had one of the best he'd seen, certainly the best he'd ever coached.

Sarge Martin had a theory about hitting. Great swings are like snowflakes: no two are exactly alike. The trick was to know what a hitter was doing when he was hot, and then put him back onto it when things went bad. With a good film library, you could show a hitter the contrast between then and now, hot and cold. As Campy used to say, "A slump starts in your swing, goes to your head, and winds up in your gut." Sarge could fix the swing, talk it out of a guy's head and undo the knot in his gut. But it seemed that this was old school thinking, a theory that had gone out of style. They all looked at him now as though he'd passed away and didn't know it. It's definitely a young man's game.

Billy strolled back over to where Sarge was standing. "The kid looks good. Now let's see if he can hit The Slut."

Barry sat in the dugout, bat in hand, batting helmet firmly planted on his head. He would bat third this inning. As Buzz Adams took his warm up pitches, Barry let his mind drift back to that spring day when he had placed the phone call to the general manager of the big club, telling him that he was ready to play, or at least ready to give it a try. Terry Hines, a veteran GM and former ballplayer, listened carefully and responded with enthusiasm. It was great to hear that his former prized rookie was fully mended and ready to get back on the horse.

Barry had one request: could Terry bring in Sarge Martin to work with him on the road back? He knew that Sarge was retired and living somewhere in the Phoenix area. Nobody knew his swing the way Sarge did.

Within a few days, it had been arranged. Barry would meet Sarge at the club's training site in Arizona and they'd go to work. That was mid-April and the season was already underway. Terry knew it was a long shot, knew that the odds against Barry making it back to the majors were very long. But he remembered Barry's rookie year, and he'd been in the press box when the ball made contact with his left eye. The thought of it still made him sick to his stomach. He had to give the kid a chance.

And so it began, in the hot desert air: hours of banging balls into a net, first from a tee and then from soft toss. Then it was into the cage with a pitching machine, sweat pouring from his body, hitting until his hands were blistered and raw. In between these sessions, Sarge rigged a pitching machine to fire tennis balls at his body so that he could practice spinning out of the way, protecting his head, relearning the lesson he'd learned so long ago from his father. Then came the endless hours of batting practice with a corps of hired BP pitchers. And finally, the day when Sarge told him he was ready to play and they headed off for an assignment in short-season A-ball. Barry wore out the A-level pitching and within a month, it was on to Double A where the results were much the same. And now, in late June, nearly two years since his eye socket had been shattered, he was about to take his first Triple A at bat.

Buzz Adams appeared to have plans for spoiling the party. He'd put the Solons down 1-2-3 in the first inning, including two impressive strikeouts, and he got their number-four hitter on a weak popup to begin the next inning. That brought Barry out to the on-deck circle. He glanced up into the stands where he knew Bonnie and his parents were sitting and nodded quickly to them. Then he went to work, wiping the handle of his bat with the pine tar rag and sliding the weighted donut down onto the barrel. He took a few easy practice swings and studied Buzz's pitches. It was clear that his new pitch, whatever he called it, was his best weapon today. The batter was called out on a sharp breaking ball and Barry made his way toward the batter's box.

Barry looked to the third base coach for a sign, though he knew there'd be no play on with two outs and nobody on base. It was time to hit away. He planted his right foot, stepped into the box, and immediately began to recite the mantra his father had taught him in Little League: *A balanced stance tension free/Feet shoulder width with bended knee.* He'd done this through his entire playing career and it always served to relax him. *A little movement keeps you loose/ Now you're ready for the juice.* Buzz started his windup and Barry continued his ritual. *Bat back, weight back/Ready to stride.* Now Buzz was uncoiling, striding toward the plate, and Barry saw the ball clearly as it left his hand. *Now drive your weight to the pitcher's side . . .*

The next thing Barry knew, he was spinning away from the pitch, diving back and away from the plate, the bat launched from his hands as the ball flew within inches of his head. He landed on his chest, his hands bracing his fall, and without a second of hesitation, he was up, grabbing the bat, planting his right foot back in the batter's box, not even pausing to brush the dirt from his uniform.

The crowd gasped at the sight of the near bean ball and the Solon's bench erupted in shouts directed at Buzz Adams and at the umpire, demanding a warning, or even an ejection. Joe Betini, the veteran umpire, stepped out from behind the plate and ripped off his mask, glaring at Buzz Adams. He let lose a stream of expletives that began and ended with "sonofabitch." Buzz shrugged his shoulders and motioned that the pitch had slipped out of his hand. Joe stepped across the plate, his back to the mound, and brushed the surface clean. "Tony," he said, addressing the catcher, "if you're throwing at this kid, I'm gonna run the both of youse . . . and see to it that you get fined. Got it?"

"Hey, blue, it wasn't me. Nobody called it. Just a slip, that's all." Tony didn't sound very convincing.

All the while, Barry was standing in the box, ready to hit, staring at Buzz Adams and mouthing the words *kush mir tuchis*.

The shouting died down and Buzz went back to the mound, ready for the next pitch. He went into his windup, kicked his leg high, and again uncoiled toward the plate. The ball flew straight and hard toward Barry's left shoulder, the seams rotating tightly, biting the air for traction, finally breaking sharply down and toward the inside corner. The crack of the bat told the whole story, that and the fact that the outfielders barely moved before the ball disappeared beyond the left-center field fence. Barry rounded the bases, touching them all, and was greeted at the plate by his teammates, shaking his hand and pounding his back.

Sarge saw it all, from the second the pitch left Buzz's hand, watched Barry coil with that sweet smooth motion, watched the short glide and plant of the left foot, watched as the left shoulder stayed closed and firm, watched as the swing released in the lovely fluid motion that was Barry Goldstein's snowflake. And then the sound, that beautiful sound when the ball meets the sweet spot on a Louisville Slugger.

Now Barry was coming down the steps and into the dugout, being greeted by more happy teammates. As he approached, Sarge reached out his hand. Barry ignored it and threw his arms around the old man's neck.

"Thanks, Sarge. For everything." He moved on down the dugout, leaving Sarge speechless—but very proud.

As it turned out, it was the only run the Solons scored. They lost three to one, and Buzz Adams earned his fourth straight victory.

None of that mattered to Sarge Martin. He'd seen everything he needed to see.

Joe Barty's saloon was just down Broadway from the ballpark. It was a popular hangout for the baseball crowd, fans and players alike. The walls were lined with pictures dating back to the early days of the local franchise. Sarge scanned the framed pictures for guys that he knew, stopping to smile at more than a few of the yellowing images. He slid into a booth near the rear of the bar and sat facing the door, waiting for his guest to arrive. It was quiet tonight because it was getaway day: both teams would be leaving town, the Solons for an extended road trip and the Oaks heading back to the Bay Area. Sarge called to the bartender for a pitcher of beer and a couple of glasses just as the door swung open and Buzz Adams walked in. Sarge waved to him and he headed toward the booth.

"Buzz! Great game today! That new pitch is gonna take you back to the bigs." Sarge reached out his hand and Buzz shook it firmly.

"Thanks, Sarge. I think your guy Barry had the only two solid hits all day."

The young bartender brought the beer and the glasses and placed them on the table between them. "Here you go, Mr. Martin . . . hey, great game today, Mr. Adams." He turned and walked away.

"How 'bout that? Out there," Buzz said, motioning toward the street, "we're just a couple of mugs. But at Joe Barty's, it's Mr. Martin and Mr. Adams. Is this a great game or what?" Both men laughed out loud.

"Listen, Buzz, thanks for what you did today. I really appreciate it. I owe you one."

"Well, tell you what, Sarge, it's the first time in my career that a coach asked me to throw at one of his own players." He laughed again and shook his head.

"I knew somebody would come high and tight to him sooner or later, Buzz. I had to see how he'd react. I wanted it to be somebody I trusted, somebody who knows what he's doing. Thanks again."

"Don't mention it. And, hey, did you see what he did to my slutter? I thought sure he'd jelly-leg after I buzzed him. But he hung right in there. And hit the snot out of it, I might add. Frickin' outfielders didn't even move!"

Sarge liked Buzz Adams; he always had. He was a real pro, and a great guy to share a beer and a few laughs with. They told war stories and drained the pitcher. Sarge started to order a refill but Buzz begged off.

They slid out of the booth and were on their way to the door when the bartender called out to them. "Phone call, Mr. Martin." Buzz waved and continued out the door while Sarge went to the corner of the bar where the young man had placed the phone.

"Hello."

"Sarge, it's Terry Hines. You weren't in your room, so I figured you'd be at Barty's. Listen, I got several things to hit you with."

He could picture Terry, in his office at the stadium back east, the only light still burning in the entire place. He glanced at his watch and saw that it was near midnight back there. As usual, Terry was in a hurry, like his hair was on fire.

"Shoot, Terry."

"Okay, I spoke to Skip and he told me about the kid's game. I got Shankman down with a broken ankle and I need an outfielder. I'm thinking about bringing Barry up. Whataya think?"

Sarge paused, but only for a second, just long enough to let the grin break across his face. "Go for it, Terry. He's ready."

"Okay, and I also got this. We're making a change at hitting coach. The job is yours if you want it . . . Sarge? . . . Hello? . . . Are you still there?"

"Yes."

"What? I could barely hear you."

Sarge cleared his throat. "I said, 'yes.' I'll take the job."

"Okay, great. We're making all the arrangements now. I'll call you at the hotel tomorrow and fill you in. Congrats, Sarge. And welcome back to The Show." With that he hung up.

Sarge stood still for a few seconds, staring at the phone, until it became a blur as his eyes welled. He reached across the bar and grabbed a few cocktail napkins and dabbed his eyes quickly, hoping no one had noticed. He drew a mental picture of himself wearing a Sox uniform.

"Damn," he said, just under his breath. "I'm gonna have to drop a few pounds."

GAME OVER

T he capacity crowd was on its feet, waving white towels and roaring loud enough to shake the old stadium. Two outs, bottom of the ninth, two-and-two on the hitter, the tying run on second base, the winning run on first. Grady Masters rubbed up the new ball while he looked around to soak up the scene. He wanted to remember every moment, every detail. This is what he got paid the big bucks to do: be the closer, shut 'em down, seal the deal.

The left-handed hitter was putting up a fight, fouling off pitch after pitch after going down two strikes and no balls. Grady had pounded him in on the fists, over and over again. Now he was set up for the backdoor slider, on the outside corner at the knees. He looked at the ball, rotating it in his right hand, getting the feel of the seams. He toed the rubber and looked in for the sign. His catcher knew exactly what to call. Grady went into his stretch, looking back at the runner, now his kick gathering his weight over his back leg, then driving hard toward the plate. The ball started six inches outside, breaking sharply in the last few feet to catch the outside corner. Or did it?

The hitter took the pitch, frozen, expecting another one in on the hands. The umpire took one step back and cranked up his patented punch-out move, as though firing up a chain saw: "STEE-rike! You're outta here!"

And now Grady's teammates were charging the mound, spilling over the dugout railing, sprinting in from the field, and the celebration was on. They danced around the mound, pounding each other, jumping up and down in unison, until the group began to topple and it quickly turned into a dog pile. When they finally scrambled to their feet, half the crowd was gone, the rest streaming toward the exits. They were back in the playoffs for the first time in four years and it was sweet to clinch it here in the home of their arch rival.

They hurried into the dugout and down the steps that led to the clubhouse, whooping and shouting along the way. As Grady entered the room, someone pressed an ice-cold bottle of champagne into his hand, and before he could raise it to his lips, he was hit with the spray from a half dozen teammates, shaking their bottles and squirting the foamy liquid on anyone within reach.

Grady grabbed his cell phone from his locker and slipped away into the trainer's room. He knew it would be quiet there and he wanted to call Gwen and share this moment with her and the boys. He couldn't wait to hear their voices.

The lobby bar at the Century Plaza was crowded with teammates and friends, and they gave Grady a rousing cheer when he entered the room. He sat at the bar and ordered more champagne. He wasn't much for partying, but this was a special occasion. The champagne went down smoothly, more like soda pop than wine, and Grady could feel a buzz coming on. They had one more game in L.A. before heading home, but the skipper told him he'd have the day off. He sat on the bar stool and thought about all this team had been through, going back to spring training, going through the long season with all its ups and downs, the injuries, the fights, the trades that sent friends away and brought new faces to their clubhouse, and the mind-numbing travel that left you wondering where the hell you were. And the whole damn thing was worth it, just to sit here and savor a shot at the big prize: the World Series. No, he wasn't much for partying, but he was going to enjoy this one.

Dexter Purdy—first baseman, young, handsome, single, self-professed ladies man—strolled over to the bar and clapped Grady on the shoulder.

"Way to go, man. You did it again. Really shut that crowd up. Did you see how fast they left the park?" Dexter was laughing at the L.A. crowd, notorious for its laid back *yeah whatever* demeanor.

"Thanks, Dex. Great game! Great season! And it ain't over yet, buddy."

"Hey, Grady," Dexter leaned in, speaking softly now, "see the gal over there in my booth? The gorgeous brunette with the magnificent rack?"

"Where? Oh, yeah. Pretty girl."

"Pretty? Are you kiddin' me? She's to die for. And those pretty titties don't just grow like that. Those are store-bought, man. We're talkin' ten, twelve grand at least."

"Really? How can you tell?"

"Are you serious? You just lay her down and see if they still pop straight up. It's a dead giveaway. Complete defiance of gravity." Dexter was laughing, having a good time. "Anyway, she says she's a big fan. Wants to meet you. Come on over." Grady followed Dexter over to the booth where he made the introductions. "Lyla, Grady. Grady, Lyla. Lyla is a big fan, right darlin'?"

She was wearing dark slacks and a very becoming white blouse with a few buttons strategically undone. A single strand of white pearls hung around her neck and rested softly at the apex of her cleavage. It was hard for Grady not to stare. He concentrated on keeping his eyes up, focusing on her pretty face: dark hair, dark brown eyes, high cheekbones, rosebud lips, a nose that was nice but not perfect. *Exotic* was the word that ran around Grady's head.

"Nice to meet you, Grady Masters," she said. "Dex is right. I *am* a big fan of your work." She fixed him with a brilliant smile.

"Really? Were you there today?"

"Yeah, I never miss a game if I can help it."

His eyes drifted down again. "Very pretty," he said. "Are they real?"

"What do *you* think?" She said it with a little tilt of her head.

"Ah . . . I really don't know much about pearls."

"Oh . . . we're talking about my pearls? Actually, they *are* real."

Grady felt his face flush. He tried to change the subject. "So, you saw the game today?"

"Yes," she said. "And congratulations. It's great to see a man who can perform under pressure."

"Thanks."

"What was that last pitch you threw? The replays showed it just caught the outside edge."

Grady was impressed. She seemed to know something about the game. "It was a backdoor slider," he said, wondering if he'd have to explain the terminology.

"So, is that your signature move, sliding in the backdoor?"

"Are we still talkin' baseball?" he said with a laugh.

"Yeah, as a metaphor."

"A metaphor for what?"

She motioned for him to come closer and he leaned in so that her lips were next to his ear. "A metaphor for fucking," she said. He could feel her cheek against his as she smiled.

Grady stood in front of the bathroom mirror, his hands braced against the countertop, his head lowered, staring into the sink. He couldn't look at himself. He'd never wanted to be *that guy*, the one who fooled around on the road and took advantage of the groupies that were abundantly available in every city they visited. And in fact, through his nine-year career, he'd never been *that guy*, not until now. How could he justify it, even to himself? He could say that he was drunk last night, but that didn't explain this morning, after the wake-up call from the hotel operator, when he was stone cold sober. To make it worse, he couldn't remember her name. Was it Leah, or Leslie, or Maya? All he could think of was store-bought, but he couldn't just go in there and say, "Hey, Storebought, could you please leave now so that I can get back to my real life?"

He'd seen what happened to the guys who got caught, their families torn apart, battling their way through divorce court. Or, the wife would show up at the ballpark one day sporting a diamond the size of a jawbreaker. He'd always been determined to avoid either scenario.

"God oh God oh God," he mumbled to himself, offering up a desperate prayer, "please get me through this and I swear, never never ever ever again!"

Right on cue, God answered his prayer, though it wasn't the answer he was hoping for. He heard the phone ring in the other room. And then he heard her voice say, "Hello . . ." He opened the door quickly and stepped into the room. She was sitting up in bed, the morning sun splashed across her naked torso, holding the phone out to him.

"It's for you," she said, smiling sweetly. "I think it's your wife."

There was a loud knock at the door and Grady knew it was Dexter, a few minutes late as usual. "It's open, come on in," he called, slurring his words slightly from the effects of the two bloody Marys he'd consumed for breakfast.

Dexter let himself in, casing the apartment as he entered. The dining area was empty, except for a half-dozen boxes stacked against the wall. The living room held a new leather couch, a battered old coffee table, a floor lamp, and a very large flat-screen television, its pedestal resting on the floor. The walls were bare; not even a poster to break up the freshly painted white surfaces. Beyond a high counter, Dexter could see a week's accumulation of dishes in the kitchen sink.

"Hey, man, I love what you've done with the place."

"Screw you," Grady shot back. "I didn't expect to be here this long." They had lost in the first round of the playoffs and now the long, dull off-season was underway, the dullness turned painful by his recent separation. "Want a beer?"

"Nah, too early. Speaking of which, how's it going with Gwen? Is she about ready to take you back?"

"No. I am still the unforgiven, cheating, asshole of a husband."

"So what are you going to do, man?"

"I don't know, Dex. She won't believe me, that it was the first time, that it won't ever happen again. The fact that it happened at all, even once, is unforgivable to Gwen."

He started to go on, felt the lump in his throat and the tears in his eyes, and said nothing. He thought of his boys, six year-old twins, and what this was doing to them. They bounced between days so heavily booked with activities that they barely had time to think, to nights when their mother cried alone in her bedroom while they were left to stare at the television. And then there were the weekends with Dad, swimming in the pool at his apartment complex, going to movies or the zoo or wherever their hearts desired, and then trying to choke down his pathetic attempts at cooking. The net effect was that they were left dazed and confused by the two people they loved most in this world.

"Ya know what, buddy, let me talk to her," Dexter offered brightly. "At least I can convince her that you never came out with us guys, chasing around to bars, hooking up with the groupies. Maybe she'll listen to me. I think I'll have that beer now. What's on TV? Aren't the Bears playing today?"

Dexter made a beeline for the refrigerator while Grady headed to the bathroom to splash water in his face and regroup.

Grady drove carefully down the boulevard toward the entrance to the gated community. A police car passed in the opposite direction and his hand instinctively reached for the Smith & Wesson 38 Special sitting on the passenger seat. The cruiser passed by, paying little attention to Grady's Porsche. He pulled up to the gate, entered the security code and waited for the crossbar to lift. It was nearly 2:30 in the morning. He pulled up to the curb across from his house and stopped. There in his driveway was the jet black Cadillac Escalade with the custom license plate: PRDYBOY. He shut off the engine, picked up the revolver and left the vehicle, heading across the street to the front door. The lock clicked softly as he turned the key. He pushed the door open, glancing at the wall where the alarm keypad was installed. The alarm was not set. The front of the house was dark as he passed through, heading to the hallway that led to the bedrooms. He passed the bedroom his sons Greg and Geoff shared, the door ajar, the beds neatly made and undisturbed. As he continued down the hall toward the master bedroom, he could hear voices speaking softly, a woman and then a man. He opened the bedroom door slowly, reached for the light switch and flipped it on. The room flooded with light and Dexter and Gwen sprang apart, as though they'd been poked with a cattle prod, clutching the pretty floral print sheet up around their necks.

"Ohmygawd! Grady, what are you doing here?" Gwen's face was turning a bright red.

"Ah, geez, Grady! What the hell! You scared the crap outta me." Dexter wanted to run, but there was no easy exit.

And then they saw the gun in Grady's right hand. Now they were talking over one another, desperate to reason with a man pushed beyond reason.

"Oh, God, Grady! What are you doing? Please put that thing down. Please, baby, don't do something stupid. Please!"

"God sakes, Grady. Put that damn thing down. You don't want to hurt anybody here. This is crazy. It's crazy. Come on, man, you're not going to shoot me, for chrissakes."

Grady raised the gun and leveled it in the general direction of Dexter's head. His hand began to shake violently. He steadied his right hand with his left and pulled the trigger. The sharp pop slammed the room, like a firecracker in a metal box. The bullet tore a neat hole in the wall behind Dexter's head, missing him by at least a foot. Now the pleas from Dexter and Gwen took on a new tone, one of sheer terror.

"Oh God oh God oh God oh God. Please don't shoot don't shoot don't shoot me don't shoot me—"

"Baby, no no no, please don't to this don't do this . . . think of the boys, think of your sons, think of the boys, they need their father, they need you, they need you, please please please—"

Grady walked quickly around the bed and placed the barrel of the gun against the back of Dexter's head. He would not miss this time. Dexter sat on the side of the bed, his head down near his knees, pleading for his life. And suddenly Grady could hear Gwen's voice and her voice alone: ". . . your sons, your boys, your sons . . ." It seemed that an eternity had passed since he entered the room, but it couldn't have been more than a few minutes. He had not spoken a word. Grady opened his mouth and tried to speak, but no sound came from his lips. He cleared his throat and tried again.

"Game over, PRDYBOY . . . Get out . . . Now!"

Dexter bolted from the bed and began to gather his clothes from a chair at the side of the room. The last Grady saw of him was his bare ass hurrying out the door, arms overflowing with pants, shirt, shoes and underwear. Grady sat down on the bed, dropped the gun to the floor, and began to cry, his body racked with violent sobs. And then Gwen was there, her arms wrapped around him from behind, sobbing with him.

"Oh, baby, I'm sorry I'm sorry I'm sorry. I just wanted to hurt you, to get even. I love you I love you. Please say you love me please please please . . ." Grady turned to hold her in his arms, to say he loved her and beg for forgiveness, over and over again.

And so it went, deep into the morning hours.

It was a beautiful March day in Phoenix. She walked along the stadium concourse, picking her way through the crowd, turning heads all along the way. Her blonde hair was cut in a sassy bob, her oversized sunglasses perched on top of her head for the moment. A large straw handbag was thrown casually over her shoulder, its leather accents matching her sandals. She wore khaki shorts and a pretty blue tank top that fit her taught runner's body perfectly. Gwen Masters was a beautiful woman in the absolute prime of her life.

She walked up a short flight of steps and out into the sunshine, the manicured green field spread out in front of her. She loved spring training, that magic time of year when every team is in first place and hopes for the coming season soar without limits. She searched the field for Grady and her sons, Greg and Geoff, and found them playing catch in the outfield. The boys could be on the field with their father until it was nearly time for the game to begin. She made her way to the box seats reserved for the players' wives and significant others and was greeted there by a half dozen friends. Then Martha Kemper, the wife of the bullpen coach, grabbed her left hand.

"Oh, my God! When did you get the new ring set? How exquisite!" She held up Gwen's ring finger to let the diamond sparkle in the sunlight. "Look at that diamond! How many carats?"

"I think it's four and a half . . . maybe five."

Of course, she knew *exactly* how many carats, as well as cut, color, clarity, market price, insurance cost, and so on. A girl's best friend, indeed!

THE PROSPECT

J on and Brent cruised slowly through the parking lot, looking for an open space, finally settling for one at the far end, in front of the motel. Jon pulled the car in and killed the engine.

"Man, what a crowd," Brent said. "Jill must be dancing tonight."

The Bird of Paradise, adjacent to the motel along the frontage road, was the first bar in Vallejo to go topless and business was good. James Brady, the proprietor, was an old school chum, known as Diamond Jim to all his customers. Jim had no problem recruiting attractive dancers, but he'd hit the jackpot with Jill St. Paul. She was the one pulling in the crowds.

They walked into the bar and found that it was standing room only. Jim was behind the rail, moving quickly to keep up with the drink orders. It was nearly 9:00 PM and the show was about to begin. Jon pushed his way through the crowd and waved to Jim.

"Hey, Jon! What's happenin', man? What can I get you?"

"Gimme a couple of Buds. Hey, Jim, is Danny here tonight?"

"Yeah, he's in the back. He'll be out in a minute." Jim slid the long-necked bottles on the bar in front of Jon. "Want to start a tab?"

"Yeah, thanks." Jon could barely hear over the noise. He passed one of the beers to Brent. Danny emerged from the back room with several bottles in his large hands. Jon caught his eye and waved him over. "Danny, how's it goin'?"

"Busy as hell, man. What's up?"

"Just wanted to remind you about the game tomorrow in San Rafael. We're gonna meet at Wilson Park at around 9:00 AM and carpool from there. We're counting on you to pitch tomorrow, okay? There should be several scouts there, man. It's a good showcase."

"Okay, 9:00 AM, Wilson Park. You guys stickin' around for the show?"

"Oh yeah. I take it Jill is dancing tonight."

"You got that right." Danny moved away to help another customer.

Diamond Jim had his system down pat. There were shows at 9:00, 10:30 and midnight. For each show, there was a two-drink minimum, though he'd waive that for his friends. He had three dancers and each one would do a fifteen-minute set with a little break in between. That would fill up about an hour, giving the cocktail waitresses time to settle up tabs and turn the room over for the next show.

Jill would be the third and final dancer and she'd become a minor sensation around town, for obvious reasons. She had long blonde hair, light blue eyes, and she was very pretty. Add to that the fact that she possessed a near-perfect body, long and firm and full-breasted. Perfect bodies were easy to find in magazines like Playboy, with makeup artists, professional lighting, professional photographers and airbrush finishing. But Jill was real and she was the complete package. To Jon, she was absolutely stunning. He was always amazed at the reaction of the crowd. When the other girls danced, the guys would whistle and shout and make wise-ass remarks. But when Jill was on stage, there was a general hush that came over the room.

Jill and Danny had been together for a couple of months now, living in a house that Danny shared with two buddies. They made a great looking couple, though Jon wasn't sure what the attraction was, beyond the obvious. At least they could keep an eye on one another, working in the same place night after night.

Jim bounded onto the stage and announced the start of the 9:00 PM show. He cracked a few lame jokes and then introduced the first dancer, a girl named Debbie. A couple of guys left the bar to move down in front of the stage. Jon and Brent grabbed the empty bar stools and settled in for the show.

Each girl had a similar routine, wearing some sort of top and maybe a sexy bra, and then slowly stripping in time with the recorded music. Bottomless had not taken hold as yet. That would come later. For now, topless was the rage, spreading from North Beach in San Francisco to many of the cities in the Bay Area.

When Jill was introduced, she received a rousing ovation from the rowdy crowd. She came out of the back room and headed for the stage, waving to Jon and Brent as she passed. Her first song was "Light My Fire," and she went into a slow grind with the music. When she unbuttoned her shirt and slipped it off over her shoulders, Jon heard Brent mumble, "Sweet mother of God!" He looked around the suddenly quiet room and saw several guys set their drinks down and swallow hard.

Jim had installed spotlights that rimmed the stage to highlight the dancers. The low ceiling and the closeness of the lights made the stage a very hot place. Jill's body glistened with sweat as her third song ended. She reached for a white towel that she'd placed on a stool next to the stage and began to dry her torso. A guy sitting up front spoke to her and she handed him the towel. He stood up and proceeded dry her back. Then the music started again and she picked up the beat and began to dance.

Diamond Jim witnessed this scene and let loose a stream of expletives that turned every head in his direction. The song ended and Jill took a deep bow. She put her shirt on quickly and left the stage to a standing ovation. As she rounded the bar and headed for the back room, Jim grabbed her arm roughly and pulled her out of sight from the customers.

"What the hell are you trying to do, cost me my license?" He was yelling at her, furious that she'd let a patron touch her on stage. "You stupid bitch, don't you know they could bust me for that? How goddamn stupid can you be?"

"Jim, I'm sorry, I didn't know, I didn't think. I'm sorry."

Jim's tirade continued and Jon thought for a minute that he was going to hit her. He waited for the scream, not sure what he would do if it came. Her apology fell on deaf ears and Jim continued to call her every rotten word in his vocabulary. Now her voice was rising and Jon could tell she was losing her temper.

"Okay, asshole, you want to fire me? Go ahead, say it. You're not the only bar in town. There are plenty of other places that will be glad to have me. Go ahead, tough guy. Fire me!"

It was quiet then. Jim came out from the back room and started working the bar, his face pinched in anger. Jon looked at Danny and saw that he'd ignored the entire scene. After a minute or two, Jill came out from the back room. Jon got up to give her his stool and she thanked him as she sat down. Danny brought a drink and placed it on a coaster in front of her. Her face was flushed and her eyes were welling.

"Thanks for the support, Danny." She spit the words at him. "It's good to know you've got my back."

"Hey, kiddo, he's the boss. Know what I mean?" Tall, well built, good-looking, Danny could charm your sox off. He grinned at her and moved on down the bar.

"Shit, Jon," she said. "What am I doing here? I must be out of my friggin' mind. They treat me like a goddamn whore. I'm *not* a whore . . ." Jon thought she was going to cry.

"Hey, Jill, you know how Jim is. He doesn't mean anything by it. He'll cool off in a minute and be over here apologizing to you, just watch." Jon did his best to calm her down, but he could see it wasn't helping much. He tried to change the subject. "How about coming with us tomorrow to San Rafael? Should be a good game. Danny's going to pitch. Why don't you come along, get out of town for a day?"

"Thanks, but I gotta work tomorrow." She smiled at him. "You're a good guy, Jon. Thanks for asking."

Jon and Brent finished their drinks, said goodbye to Jill and Danny and headed for the parking lot.

"Holy shit," Brent said. "Did you hear all that? I thought he was gonna smack her. And Danny never made a move. Can you believe it?"

"No. No, I can't. But that's Danny."

More cars were entering the parking lot, moving slowly, looking for open spaces. They passed a group of guys heading for the bar, laughing and talking loud. It was a busy night at the Bird of Paradise.

Everybody was there, except for Danny. The guys milled around the parking lot at Wilson Park, drinking coffee, munching donuts, conversing in subdued Sunday morning voices. They checked their watches and glanced toward the entry road. Finally, at around 9:20, Jon took charge. Five guys would ride in Jack's van, another five in Mike's station wagon. Jon and Brent would go by Danny's house and see if he was there and if he was coming; they'd try to catch up and get there in time for the game. The little caravan pulled out of the lot, two vehicles heading for Sonoma Boulevard to connect with Highway 37, and Jon and Brent splitting off to head for Danny's place.

Jill answered the door wearing red flannel pajamas, sweat sox and an exasperated look. "Come on in. I'm trying to get him up. He got hammered last night and now all he wants to do is puke and sleep."

Jon walked quickly down the hall and into Danny's bedroom. He was sprawled across the bed in his underwear, his right arm thrown across his eyes, moaning softly.

"Danny, come on, man. We gotta go. This is a big day for you. There's gonna be a bunch of scouts there. Come on, man."

"Ah, fuck the scouts. Leave me alone."

"Come on, Dan. The guys are counting on you." Jon took hold of his wrists and pulled him upright on the bed.

Danny jumped off the bed and hurried down the hall to the bathroom. They could hear him retching with the dry heaves, sounding like he was about to die. A minute later, they heard water running in the sink, and then he staggered out into the hall.

"Okay," he said, smiling at them sheepishly, "let's play some ball!"

They loaded Danny into the backseat of Jon's car. Jill brought a duffle bag with all his gear. She also brought a pillow, which he promptly tucked under his head. They hit the road knowing they'd have to drive hard to make it to San Rafael in time for the game. Danny was sound asleep before they reached the Napa River Bridge. Jon glanced over his shoulder at Danny, snoring softly in the back seat, and shook his head. He'd known him since they played Little League ball together. Now in his early twenties, Danny was at a major crossroads in his life. He was a little old to be a prospect. Talented players his age had gone off to college on scholarships, or signed with a pro team by now. But Danny wasn't scouted in high school because he could never stay eligible for the team. There was always a failed class or his grade point average dipping below 2.0 to jump up and bite him in the ass. He gave junior college a try, but again found it hard to stay eligible. And yet, when you could get him in uniform and on the field it was pure magic. He was a natural. As a pitcher, he was un-hittable. As a hitter, he roped line drives to all fields. It was frustrating for his friends, the people who loved him, to see all that talent go to waste. If it was ever going to happen for Danny, now was the time.

They made good time to San Rafael. Danny woke up hungry, so they stopped at a little shop for a toasted bagel and a small container of orange juice. He wolfed it down in the car and then struggled into his uniform as they drove to the city park. The rest of the team was on the field loosening up when Jon pulled into the parking lot. They laced up their spikes and Danny strolled off to the bullpen to start his warm-up routine.

The Vallejo team went down 1-2-3 in the top of the first. Jon strapped on the catcher's gear and trotted out for the home half of the inning. As he approached the plate, he could see a half-dozen scouts grouped together in the grandstand, right behind home plate. There were several players worth watching in this game. Danny was just one of them.

Danny flashed good command of his pitches while warming up in the bullpen and he brought it with him to the mound. Jon settled back to enjoy himself, working with Danny's fastball, change-up, and curve to set up the hitters and keep them off balance. His fastball was in the low- to mid-nineties and Jon's left hand began to turn red and swell, in spite of the padded glove he wore inside the catcher's mitt. It was a good feeling. It occurred to Jon that catching a guy with this kind of stuff was about as good as it gets. Danny pitched seven strong shutout innings and gave up only three scratch hits. He also ripped a double and a single and drove in two runs, including the game-winner. It was a typical performance. Jon thought back to that morning when Danny was "driving the porcelain bus," hurling his guts out. He shook his head in amazement.

After the game, the guys gathered under a tree behind the dugout and brought out an ice chest full of cold beer and soft drinks. They sat around and swapped stories while Danny met with a couple of the scouts up in the grandstand. Finally, they loaded their gear and started the drive back to Vallejo. Jon and Brent sat waiting for Danny to finish his meeting. They saw him shake hands with each of the two men; he came strolling over toward them wearing a huge grin.

"So? What's the story?" Jon couldn't wait to hear.

"The Giants are gonna offer me a contract," he said.

They rushed to pound him on the back and offer congratulations.

Brent popped open the trunk and tossed the luggage inside. He would drive Danny to the San Francisco Airport for his flight to Arizona where he would join the Giants' Class-A affiliate. Brent and Jon stepped away to give Jill and Danny a moment to say goodbye. As the car pulled out of the driveway, Danny gave them a farewell wave, his patented grin fixed in place.

"Want to get some coffee, Jill?" Jon watched her dab her eyes with a tissue.

"Sure, why not."

They drove across town to Scotty's on Tennessee Street, known for the best donuts in town. The coffee was from a freshly brewed pot, delicious as usual. Jon bit into his glazed donut with gusto while Jill picked absent-mindedly at hers.

"Well, that's that," she said.

"Whataya mean? He'll be back, Jill. Hell, the A-ball season is over in August."

"He won't be coming back here, not for me."

"Don't be so sure."

"Why do I always fall for guys like Danny? Arrogant, self-centered, selfish bastards. I never ever learn." There was bitterness in her voice.

"Because they're charming, and they're fun, and they're pretty, and you always think you can fix whatever's broken." It sounded harsh when Jon said it, but he knew it was true.

She looked at him intently for a few seconds and then turned away. "Shit," she said softly. "You're right . . . Why can't I ever meet a guy like you?"

He started to say "you have," but he thought better of it, and the conversation drifted to other topics. They finished their coffee and donuts.

"Jon, can you give me a ride to The Bird? I have to work tonight."

"Sure, no problem."

They left the shop and made their way to his car. She sat next to him, looking away through the passenger-side window.

"You know, I'm leaving at the end of the month," she said. "Don't say anything to anyone, cause I haven't told Jim yet."

Jon felt his heart sink. "Where are you going?"

"My friend Carol is a dancer in San Francisco. She's gonna get me an audition. We can share rent, and the money's better there. She's from Vallejo. Maybe you know her—Carol Doda? Anyway, I need a change from this town, that's for sure." Jon pulled up in front of the Bird of Paradise. "Thanks, Jon. You're a good friend. I'm gonna miss you." She leaned over and kissed him on the cheek. "Remember, don't say anything yet, okay?" And with that she was gone.

Jon thought about going in to see her show. He wondered if she'd start with "Light My Fire." He could picture her beginning to move to the music, unbuttoning her shirt. He really wanted to see her dance. But they were friends, she'd confided in him, and somehow it just didn't feel right. He wanted to be more, more than just another "arrogant, self-centered, selfish bastard," gawking at her with a growing lump in his jeans.

"Screw it," he said. He pulled away from the curb and drove down the block, not really sure where he was going.

PEACE WITH HONOR

Martin sat in his wheelchair watching the images on the television screen: desperate men, women, and children scrambling up the staircase on the roof of the U.S. embassy in Saigon, attempting to board the helicopter, their last chance to escape. How many would make it? How many would be left behind, and what would happen to them? Martin wanted to scream, to throw something at the screen, but there was nothing within reach.

His physical therapist entered the room, come to take him for his daily regimen of learning to walk again. Allison was a nice woman and a fine professional: strong, knowledgeable, compassionate, dedicated. She looked at Martin's face, then at the television screen. She found the remote and turned it off. It was quiet then, for a moment.

"Look, that's not your concern. It's over. It's done. Listen to me—"

"Yeah."

"That's not your life anymore, Lieutenant. Are you listening?"

"Yeah."

"It's done with. Nothing more you can do. Okay?"

"Right."

"You did your job. You did the best you could. True?"

"Yeah."

"Now your job is to get well, to walk out of here. Got it?"

"Sure."

She took control of his chair and wheeled him through the door and into the hall. "All right then, let's get this show on the road. Got a tough day's work ahead."

Martin didn't answer. He knew she was right. This was his life now: to work, to learn, to get stronger every day, and as she said, to *walk* out of this damn VA hospital. Vietnam wasn't his problem anymore. The dead and the wounded weren't his problem either. How many dead? Was it fifty thousand? How many wounded? He couldn't remember. This place was full of them, kids mostly. Some would recover, live fairly normal lives. Some would not. Some would swallow a gun, or shoot poison in their veins. Some would drink themselves to death. And for what? Don't think about that. What was accomplished? Don't even go there. Why were we there? Just forget about it. You went where they sent you and you did your job. Let it go. It's not your life anymore, Martin. Now it's done and it's not part of you, not ever again.

None of it.

Not one friggin' goddamn bit.

CODY'S WAR

arol plopped down in the patio chair and looked out across the deserted swimming pool. The three-story apartment building wrapped around on all four sides, forming a large courtyard with the pool as its centerpiece. The sun was rising to her left over the east wing of the building and the sky was clear and blue above. It would be a sunny summer day in the North Bay, maybe low eighties with a little luck. On the small table next to her was a steaming cup of coffee, a plate holding a toasted bagel and a sliced golden nectarine, its sweet juice collecting in little pools. It was Sunday and Carol Crane had the perfect morning planned. The most effort she intended to expend was to remove the rubber band from the newspaper and get caught up on the news of the day. A grueling workweek that extended through Saturday was behind her and she'd earned the right to do nothing at all.

The morning air was cool, but Carol felt comfortable in her jeans and the navy blue sweatshirt with "Cal" scrawled across the front in gold script. She took a sip from her coffee mug and was about to pick up the bagel when she heard a knock at the front door. She wondered who it could be. She wasn't expecting anyone. Maybe it was the maintenance guy needing to check on something. She padded across the apartment in her stocking feet and peered through the peephole. Carol flinched slightly and then looked again. Standing in the hall outside her door was a man with wild, dirty black hair and a full Walt Whitman beard. The small patch of his face that was visible through all that hair was burned a dark brown by the sun. He looked as though he'd been living on the street for months, if not years.

"Who is it? What do you want?" She wondered how he'd gotten into the building, but she knew the answer: someone was always propping open one of the doors, bringing in groceries or moving furniture in and out. Security was a joke.

"Carol? Is that you? It's me . . . Cody."

"Oh my God!" She looked again and this time she recognized the eyes. She unhooked the safety chain and opened the door. "Cody? Oh my God. Is it really you?" She started to lunge for him, to wrap her arms around his neck.

"Whoa, hold on girl! I'm a little gamey." He backed away slightly. "I don't think you want a hug right now." And then he laughed that all-too-familiar laugh and she knew beyond a shadow of a doubt that it was Cody.

"Get in here, you dope." She grabbed the sleeve of his shirt and pulled him into the apartment where he dropped a large duffle and a sleeping bag. As this was happening, it all started to come back to her. How long had it been? Five years? Longer? She had to stop and think. If not for the sporadic cards that would arrive out of the blue at Christmas or on her birthday, she would have long since given him up for dead. She thought about how badly it had ended and for a fleeting moment, she could feel all the old pain boil up inside. But he was here and he was alive, and for now, that was all that mattered.

"Come on out to the patio with me. You can share my breakfast. Can I get you a cup of coffee?" Thank God for the patio and the fresh air. The odor that clung to him was overwhelming.

"I'd love some coffee." He moved toward the patio. "Nice place, Carol! How long have you been here?"

"Oh, couple of years." She didn't have to ask how he'd found her. She'd always been listed in the phone book.

She handed him a mug of coffee and took the chair across from him. For all the years of separation, the conversation came easily, punctuated by bursts of laughter. Cody could always make her laugh; make that *almost* always. They devoured the bagel and the nectarine as they brought each other up to date on the progress of their lives. She asked him where he'd been and he launched into a recitation of his travels, from Minneapolis, to Miami Beach, back to Minnesota, and then a long westward journey that took him through Iowa, Nebraska, Wyoming, Colorado, Nevada, and finally back home to Vallejo.

While she listened intently to his story, she thought of the day they met, when she'd taken her car to a local mechanic to find out why it was overheating. When she returned to hear the bad news, there was Cody Barrett in his coveralls, wiping the grease from his hands and fixing her with the most beautiful smile. The details, the estimated cost, everything about the poor overheated car went straight over her head. Luckily, it was all written down so she could read it later. When he finished, he smiled at her again and patted his chest with his right hand.

"I'm sorry," he said, "I hope you won't mind my saying this, but you are . . . the most . . . beautiful girl I've ever seen. Would you be offended if I asked you out . . . for coffee . . . or something?" All the while his face was turning a bright crimson color. It was irresistible. Carol said no, she didn't mind, and yes, coffee—or something—would be nice. From that day on, she believed in love at first sight.

Cody continued with his story and she asked how were things in Minneapolis and Miami and all those other places. It turned out that Minneapolis was too cold, and Miami was too muggy, Iowa too corny, and so on across the country.

"And how were you in those places?" She had to ask.

"Not good in most of them . . . in all of them, actually. But I'm better now, Carol. Swear to God, I've been sober for nearly a year."

This was good to hear, even if it was hard to accept immediately. She'd been thinking about the bottles of liquor sitting on the upper shelf of the cabinet in her kitchen and wondering if she should hide them, or maybe pour them down the drain. She'd worry about that later, when the time was right.

Their timing had been atrocious all those years ago. When they first started to talk about getting married, Cody wanted to wait until he could establish himself, maybe start a repair shop of his own, one that people could count on for honest estimates and quality work. Then he learned that his draft lottery number was moving toward the top of the list. He chose to enlist rather than be drafted and he was sure the Army would take advantage of his skills as a mechanic, maybe enhance his career with experience on heavy vehicles. The Army, in its wisdom, assigned him to a combat battalion and before he knew what hit him, he was on his way to a place called Da Nang. That was 1968, right after the Tet offensive, and the Army needed boots on the ground. Nearly a year later, he was within days of the end of his tour in Vietnam when he was hit by a sniper's bullet while on patrol. The bullet entered his left side just below his ribs and exited without hitting any vital organs, leaving him with a very interesting scar. You could say that he was lucky. Or not.

It was only the beginning of Cody Barrett's war. He came home broken and none of the doctors who saw him in the VA hospitals could fix him. For starters, he couldn't sleep. The truth was he was afraid to sleep. When he let himself sleep, the nightmares came. *Nightmare* is such a feeble word. It doesn't come close to describing the flashbacks and the sheer terror that would cause him to jump up in bed screaming, the bed sheets soaked in his sweat.

He couldn't talk to anyone, not the VA doctors, not even Carol. She remembered only one comment from Cody about the war. That was when William Calley went on trial for the massacre at My Lai. "Sure," he said, "let's heap it all on Calley's shoulders and crucify him for our sins." And that was it, other than the screaming testimony that came in the middle of the night.

Cody found a way to make it though the night, or at least most of it. It was called vodka. He'd buy the cheapest, foulest brand available, quantity over quality, knowing that the more he drank, the longer the night terrors would stay away.

And so their life together spiraled down into the darkest pit imaginable. He drank and couldn't hold a job. He drank and they fought. He hid bottles everywhere, drank on the sly, and fooled no one. He drank and could not function as a lover. Carol fought for him and tried to love him, but she was only human with only so much capacity for pain. Finally, she gave him an ultimatum: get help and give up the bottle, or get out.

Cody left a note that said he loved her, more than life itself, but he couldn't put her through any more of his personal hell. He had to leave and try to find himself somewhere else. He didn't promise to come back. He knew his promises would be worthless. And now, here he was, looking and smelling like a wild man, sitting on her patio on a bright summer morning. Carol hoped with all her heart that he was in recovery. But that same heart had been locked away for so long, safe from all emotional exposure, that she knew it would take more than a few promising words to convince her.

"Okay, Cody, here's what we're gonna do. You're gonna take a hot shower and maybe a long soak in the tub. In the meantime, I'll hit the laundry room and get your clothes washed. Do you have any clean clothes to put on?"

"Don't think so," he said, with an embarrassed grin.

She remembered a box out in her storage locker by the carport. After he'd been gone for several months, she'd packed his things and stored them away, out of sight. She was sure there were some clean clothes for him there. "I've got some of your old stuff. I'll get it while you're in the shower."

Carol went to the locker and found the box. She removed the lid and saw some of Cody's jazz albums on top of the clothes and a small leather case off to one side. She unzipped the case and opened it to see the familiar barber kit she'd purchased years ago. There were scissors, a couple of combs, and an electric trimmer with several attachments. She had been Cody's personal barber when they lived together. She turned the clippers in her hand and smiled at the thought of cutting his hair. Then she closed the case and zipped it quickly, put the lid on the box and hurried back to her apartment. There she opened the box again to pull out clean underwear, a pair of jeans, and a T-shirt.

She opened his duffle bag to sort his clothes for the wash. On the very top was a thick book. The title proclaimed *Tanakh—The Holy Scriptures*. A Jewish bible! What was he doing with this? She'd never known Cody to practice any sort of religion. Well, she thought, whatever works.

Cody poked his head out of the bathroom door, steam billowing out around him. "Did you find anything?"

"Yeah, try these." She handed him the clothes she'd found.

"Do you have a razor I can borrow?"

"Better than that," she said, handing him the leather case with the barber tools. "And there's a razor and blades in the upper right-hand drawer. Help yourself."

She finished sorting his clothes and as she headed off for the laundry room, she heard the clippers buzzing steadily in the bathroom.

Cody emerged from his shower a nearly new man, holding his dirty clothes gingerly. "What should I do with these?"

"Toss 'em on the patio. We'll burn 'em later." That made him laugh, but he knew she was only half kidding.

She looked at him across the room and smiled. The Whitman beard was gone and he was clean-shaven. The sunburn around his eyes and nose looked like a funny little mask, but that would fade in few days. He looked thin and he tugged at his old jeans to hike them up on his waist. His dark hair was long and shaggy and he'd combed it straight back revealing his face. He was older, the lines in his face a little deeper now, but it was her Cody standing there.

Carol had pulled a chair into the center of her small kitchen. There was a tablecloth and a clothespin resting on the counter. "Bring the leather case and the clippers," she said. She was going to fix that shaggy hair. Cutting someone's hair can be an intimate, sensual thing, and she loved doing it when they were together. Cody sat up straight in the chair. She fastened the tablecloth around him and went to work, taking her time, trimming carefully, the dark hair falling in little tufts on the kitchen floor.

"Tell me about the bible," she said. "Where did that come from?"

"A friend in Miami gave it to me. I've carried it around ever since. I read a little almost every night. Somehow it makes me feel . . . what's the right word? . . . peaceful."

"Really?"

"Yeah. Especially the Psalms. The language is beautiful. The best of them are like . . . beautiful, perfect short stories. Peaceful . . . that's the right word."

"Why Minneapolis, Cody? Why Miami? What made you choose those places?"

"I knew guys there, from the Army, guys that I could talk to. They're the only ones, Carol, the only ones that understand. Everyone else tries as hard as they can, but they don't know. They can't know. Even the doctors wind up looking at you like you're crazy, like you're a strange specimen under a microscope. You need to talk to someone who understands."

She knew he was right. She was one of those who tried but could never really get it, no matter how hard she tried or how much she loved him.

"So, what's next? Where to from here?" Carol continued to comb and cut with the scissors, her barber skills coming back quickly.

"I've got a job lined up in Richmond. I have to be there on Monday. An Army friend of mine has a shop there. It's a service station with three repair bays and he needs a mechanic. He's a good guy, Carol. I think it's gonna work out—this time."

She was nearly finished now. She turned on the clippers and trimmed carefully around his ears, then the curly little hairs that sprouted on his neck. Now she stepped back and surveyed her work. He'd never again be the boy she fell in love with, but some of the young Cody had emerged from under the unruly mop. Time now to sweep up the hair and check on the laundry.

Carol dropped the bedding on the couch—a pillow, a couple of sheets and a blanket. "There you go, big guy. It's all yours."

"Thanks for letting me stay, Carol. It beats the hell out of where I've been lately."

They'd spent the rest of that summer Sunday shopping for things he'd need in Richmond, browsing through the sales racks in the discount stores, looking for bargains. Carol was happy with the purchases, sure that they'd saved every penny possible.

Cody's resources were limited, at least until his first paycheck came through.

It had been a long day and they were both tired now. But Carol was more than tired. She couldn't help but think of their last nights together, five years ago. She wasn't sure what to expect, or how she would handle it if it got bad. They'd talked about many things, but not about what his nights were like now. Finally, she said good night, closed her bedroom door and crawled into bed. It wasn't long before she fell into a fitful sleep, waking several times and then dozing off again.

Carol's eyes snapped open. What was that sound? She glanced at the clock on the bedside table. It was just after 2:00 AM. She could see a light under the bedroom door and knew it was from the kitchen. Cody must be up, unable to sleep, maybe looking for a snack or something. What if he was looking in the cupboard where the bottles of liquor were stored? She tried to put that out of her mind. He said he hadn't had a drink in a year and she had to take him at his word. But what if he was reaching for the vodka? Could she just lay there and let him fall off the wagon? She heard the clink of a glass. Oh God, what was going on? She threw back the covers and sat up on the side of the bed, listening. Another clink. That was it: she headed for the door and opened it quickly. There was Cody, a glass of milk sitting on the kitchen counter, quietly placing the carton back in the fridge.

"Hey, sorry, did I wake you?" He gave her a sheepish grin.

"No, I . . ." What could she say? *I thought you were into the vodka and I was coming to slap it out of your hand.*

"Do you have any cookies?"

So that was it: milk and cookies. In that moment, she wanted to wipe the milk off his upper lip and bake a batch of cookies just for him, standing there in his T-shirt and boxers, looking like a hopeful little boy.

"What?" he said. "Why are you looking at me like that?"

"Come here, dummy," she said, holding out her hand.

She knew this was stupid, that it wouldn't fix anything, that it wouldn't bring back the lost years, but for now, she didn't care. The bedroom had always been a special place for them, before Cody went off to the war. It was as if he had the magic key to unlock every nerve ending in her body, some secret code that had been conveyed only to him. The bedroom had been magical for them—then. She took his hand and led him there now to make the magic live again.

Carol heard the front door close with a metallic click. She opened her eyes and looked at the clock. It was 5:00 AM on Monday morning and Cody had insisted that he'd take a cab to the bus depot so that she could sleep. She dozed off and on until the alarm went off at 6:30. The coffee maker would start automatically. She waited a few minutes, wide-awake now, and then headed for the kitchen.

She found her favorite mug and turned to place it on the counter. There was Cody's bible, a folded paper napkin closed between the pages. Carol opened it and found that the napkin marked Psalm 103; the following passage was highlighted:

> *Man, his days are those of grass;*
> *he blooms like a flower in the field;*
> *a wind passes by and it is no more;*
> *its own place no longer knows it.*

What was he telling her? That he was gone? Gone with the wind? She read the psalm from the beginning and was moved by the passages that spoke of God's compassion and His love. Whatever Cody had seen, whatever he had done, surely God forgave him. She closed the book and clutched it to her chest with both hands. This was his prized possession and he'd left it with her for safekeeping. It told her that he'd be back, that his war was finally ending. Cody Barrett was coming home.

ROUNDING THIRD

"Henry. Henry, wake up, darling."

"Hello?" He opened his eyes, blinking in the pale morning light. "Marie? Is that you?"

"Who else would it be, sweetheart? Do you have other women come to your bed here?" She was sitting on the edge of his bed, smiling at him playfully, wearing a white terrycloth robe, her hair wrapped in a white towel.

"Did you shower already, sweetie?" He knew the answer. She always came from her morning shower like this, smelling of Ivory soap, her robe drawn around her and tied at the waist, her hair smelling of that shampoo with the wonderful scent of tropical fruit.

"Yes, I did. And I thought about you. And I couldn't wait to come sit with you and . . ." She was smiling at him now.

"And what, darling? What is it?"

"This," she said and leaned down to kiss him full on the mouth, gently but with clear intent.

"Oh, my sweet, sweet angel. Do that again."

And she did, again and again, with that wonderful skill that comes from decades of practice. He cupped her face in his hands, breathless from her kisses, and looked into her lovely eyes. She was a beauty, a great beauty, and that beauty had never faded, not for Henry. From the time he first laid eyes on her, all those years ago, there had never been another woman in his life. He slid his hands inside the collar of her robe, intending to open it and gaze at her lovely body.

"Wait, Henry. Not here, darling." She closed her robe around her. "There are no locks on these doors. They'll walk in on us."

"What? No locks? I don't know—"

"We'll go home, Henry, to our room, to our own bed. And we'll make love there, no interruptions, no little intruders."

"But, Marie, wait—" She was standing up now, moving toward the door.

"Just give me a few minutes head start, darling. I'll be waiting for you. Don't make me wait too long." With that, she was gone.

Henry swung his legs over the side of the bed and sat up, waiting for his head to clear. He saw the slippers arranged neatly at the side of the bed, slipped his feet into them and headed for the door. He opened it and looked out into the wide, empty corridor, the linoleum floor polished to a high gloss reflecting the fluorescent lights from the ceiling. He saw a white-clad figure disappear around the corner at the end of the corridor. He hurried in that direction, wondering why Marie could not wait for him.

All along the hallway were doors to other rooms, securely closed, the occupants sound asleep on this early Sunday morning. He turned right at the end of the hall and found himself in an empty lobby, couches and chairs arranged neatly around the low tables. At the far end of the lobby were floor to ceiling windows with wide doors that opened to a covered portico and a driveway that led to the boulevard beyond. As he looked out toward the driveway, he saw that white figure turn to the right, heading east on the sidewalk along the boulevard.

Henry hurried out through the doors as they opened with loud swoosh. He had to try to catch up before Marie was completely out of sight. He turned right, just as she had, and made his way along the sidewalk. The sun was rising to the east and soon the glare caused him to shield his eyes with one hand, wishing he'd had time to find his sunglasses. Maybe it was the glare, or perhaps she was just too far ahead, but he could not see Marie's figure any longer. Still, he was sure she had come this way, and so he trudged on, determined not to disappoint her. The sun rose steadily in the morning sky and Henry realized that he was tiring, his pace slowing to a crawl. His feet began to hurt and he cursed himself for not putting on his walking shoes instead of the damned slippers. And still he went on, ignoring the pain, ignoring the occasional car that rushed by on the broad, four-lane street. The pain became intense, running from his feet up through his calves and into his knees. A short distance ahead, he saw a bench and a sign that said "Bus Stop." He made it to the bench and sat down hard, the pain in his legs throbbing, more than he could stand. He decided to rest here for a while, just until the pain subsided, and then continue on after Marie. Had she come this way? Did he miss a turn? Suddenly he was afraid and very tired. He leaned back against the bench and closed his eyes.

The police cruiser moved deliberately along Oak Boulevard, the officers scanning both sides of the street, searching for their target: an eighty-six year-old male Caucasian, about five feet ten, one hundred and sixty pounds, probably dressed in blue pajamas and house slippers.

"Look, up there at the bus stop, Jack. That's probably him." The officer named Jack quickly pulled over to the curb and stopped, switching on the emergency lights to warn other drivers away.

"Sir? . . . hello? . . . Mr. Logan? Time to wake up." The voice came to Henry from far away, growing closer, growing more intense. He opened his eyes to see a young man in a police uniform standing over him. "Sir, is your name Henry Logan?"

"Yes. Yes, it is."

"It's him, Jack. We got him. Call it in."

Henry heard the crackle of the radio and the strange voice responding to the officer's call, and he saw the colored light bar flashing in sequence on top of the car.

"Mr. Logan, come with me now. We're going to take you back to the home. Your son is there and he's really worried about you. Come on now." He placed a firm hand under Henry's left arm and

helped him to his feet. In a minute or so, Henry was secured in the
back seat of the patrol car.

"Oh geez, Marty!" It was the other officer speaking. "Did you
get a whiff of him? We'll never get that smell out of the car."

"Take it easy, Jack. It's a short ride. We'll take the car in and they
can clean it up. Mr. Logan, we're taking you back now. Your son is
waiting for you there."

"Thank you . . . thank you both." Henry could see that the
younger officer, the one called Marty, was more sympathetic to his
plight. It seemed strange, talking to them through the heavy wire
screen that separated the back seat from the front.

"Henry Logan," the young man said. "Sounds familiar. Say, are
you any relation to Hack Logan, the ballplayer?"

"That's me," Henry said. "Or . . . it used to be me."

"Damn, Jack, we've got baseball royalty in the car with us. This
is Hack Logan, the best ballplayer that ever came out of this town.
Had a fine career! Mr. Logan, it's a pleasure to meet you."

"Thank you, son."

"What teams did you play for, sir?"

"San Francisco . . . mostly San Francisco. And St. Louie."

"The Giants and Cards!"

"No . . . the Seals and the Browns." Then softly, to himself, "I
met my Marie in Frisco."

"Geez, Jack, isn't this something?"

"Yeah, we'll install a plaque back there: 'Hack Logan shit here.'"
Jack was in a foul mood.

As they turned into the driveway leading to the entrance of the
retirement home, the officers could see a balding, heavyset man
who looked to be in his fifties pacing nervously on the sidewalk.
With him were two very sheepish looking orderlies in their white
uniforms, one of them holding a wheelchair.

"Okay, Mr. Logan. You're home safe and sound."

It wasn't long before Henry was out of the patrol car, into the
wheelchair and on his way into the building with the two staff
members. A doctor had been called to examine him and make sure
there were no ill effects from his adventure. His son John stayed

behind to thank the officers for finding his father, and to take a card from Marty with a promise to have Henry sign some piece of memorabilia and send it along to the station house. With that, the officers were on their way, the windows of the cruiser rolled down in hopes of clearing the air.

Within the hour, Henry was bathed and powdered, buttoned into a fresh pair of pajamas, and safely tucked into his bed. The doctor's prescription had been for plenty of fluids and lots of rest. The staff quickly delivered a pitcher of water, freshly squeezed orange juice, and a steaming bowl of oatmeal. They were determined to smother Henry with attention. And head off any liabilities

John, who had delivered a stern lecture to the staff about keeping an eye on the residents, waved them out of the room and was prepared to deliver an equally stern lecture to his father.

"Dad, listen to me now . . . this can't happen again! Do you understand? You cannot wander off and go hiking up Oak Boulevard. Dad? Are you listening?"

Henry looked into his son's eyes and felt terrible. In a very short time, he'd seen John's emotions range from relief to elation, from dismay to anger, and then repeat the whole cycle. He hoped he could make him understand.

"Johnny," he said, "she came for me. Your mother came for me. She sat right here, on the edge of the bed."

"Dad, stop it now. You know Mom has been gone for more than nine years now. You can't do this—"

"Johnny," Henry said, wrapping his fingers around his son's wrist and tightening his grip, "can you feel this?"

"What?"

"My hand. Can you feel my hand?"

"Yeah, Dad, of course. I can feel your hand."

"That's how real it was, son. She sat right here . . . in her robe . . . with a towel wrapped around her hair. And she kissed me, Johnny."

John's eyes were welling now. "Dad, you've got to stop it! Mom is gone and that's that! You're just going to make yourself sad. Do you hear me, Dad?"

Henry could see that there was no way to win this debate. "Okay, Johnny," he said, patting his son's hand. "I'm fine now. You go on home. Go be with your family. I'm very tired now. I need to get some rest."

"Are you sure, Dad?"

"Yeah, Johnny, please go . . . go be with the kids . . . give them my love." And with that he closed his eyes. He could sense John standing there, waiting and watching him carefully. Finally, he felt a gentle kiss on his forehead and heard his son turn and head for the door.

Henry knew that John was wrong. None of this had made him sad. Not in the least. He took a deep breath and exhaled, glad to be in his bed, scrubbed and clean, his head resting on the pillow. He couldn't wait to drift off to sleep. Surely Marie would come for him again. He could almost taste her kisses.

THE LAST ADVENTURE

The gear was spread out across the driveway and the lawn, everything they would need for a weekend camping trip. Sleeping bags and duffle bags, a canvas tarp and cooking gear, a small box full of canned goods, an old wooden cooler to hold the eggs and bacon and to keep the beer cold, and of course the fishing tackle. All of it would have to be packed very carefully, because there wasn't an inch of extra room in Rich's 1961 Austin-Healy Sprite, especially when three guys piled into a cabin designed for two at the most. They debated over whether or not to bring the ragtop and its metal frame, and Nick hustled into the house to find the paper and check the weather report one more time. He returned with the news that there was a storm due, but it should stay well north, up toward the Oregon border. And so they ditched the top. If it rained, well then they'd just get wet.

It was not an easy chore, packing the beloved old Sprite, even though they'd done it many times before. There was no trunk lid, so the only way to pack was by pulling the seats forward and stuffing items one by one into the cramped space. Slowly but surely, everything found a place in the "boot." That, of course, included Brent's 22-caliber rifle—which he insisted no camp should be without—and finally, a hard rubber football with "GVRD" (Greater Vallejo Recreation District) stenciled in bold black letters. The ball was Nick's contribution. He refereed after-school touch football games for the GVRD and so had access to a bag full of balls. How can you hang out on a beach all weekend and not have a football to throw around? That was Nick's rationale.

At last everything was in and they were ready to go. They stuffed a pillow over the emergency brake lever so that one of them could sit there, wedged between the two seat backs with legs thrown over to the passenger's side. It was ridiculous and they knew it, but they'd gotten away with it before and they could do it one more time. They'd put a lot of hard miles on the "green bug," as it was affectionately known. Over one hundred thousand to be exact, and she was really showing the wear and tear. Rich was nearly ready to upgrade and he had his eye on an MGB. He definitely wouldn't abuse a new car the way they did the Sprite, but she was good for one more trip.

Their destination on this sunny weekend in early October was Timber Cove, up the rugged Sonoma Coast above Ft. Ross. Nick and Brent had been there several times and they were anxious to introduce Rich to one of their favorite spots. They were certain that there wasn't a prettier ocean cove anywhere in the world, a rather shaky assertion for a couple of guys who had scarcely been out of California. But there was no denying the beauty of the place.

You came upon it rather suddenly, just a few miles above the old Russian fort on Highway 1. The highway turned inland for a run across a high ridge, and then back toward the ocean, bending to embrace this beautiful little cove. There was a narrow, sandy beach and a creek that ran out of a redwood canyon at the north end of the cove, flowing directly into the surf in the rainy season, or ending in a shallow pool out of reach of the waves during the dry months. A huge rock sat at the north end of the beach, as though a giant hand had placed it there carefully. The fresh water of the stream washed around the base of this rock, and at high tide, you could climb up onto its crown and fish for perch out into the surf. At the north end of the cove, high above the rocks and the crashing waves, was an old incinerator left over from the logging days. The incinerator stood about seventy-five feet tall and looked like a giant, rusted wigwam with a wire mesh spark arrestor on top. Once upon a time, this had been the site of a bustling lumber mill.

The first time Nick and Brent had been there was when they were about ten or eleven years old. Brent's parents had taken them on a weekend trip and it was one they would never forget. They awoke the first morning to find a great minus tide, the ocean pulled back several hundred feet from the beach, exposing a long rocky spine that ran out into the dark blue water. They hiked and crawled way out on that spine to cast their lines into the pounding surf, and they caught more fish than they had ever seen—black and red snappers, sea trout and cabazon—gunny sacks full of fish. When the tide started to come in, they scrambled back to the beach and then continued fishing from a rocky point at the north end of the cove. And the fish just kept coming, two at a time on some casts. They wound up with a metal washtub full of fish, iced down for the trip home where they became the main course for a neighborhood barbeque. They'd been back several times, hoping for a repeat of that first trip, but it was not to be. It had been a once in a lifetime experience. And a great fish story! It was a story Rich had to listen to over and over until he agreed to give Timber Cove a try.

And so they hit the road out of town, over the Napa River and through the salt marshes along Highway 37, the volume cranked up full on the radio, singing "Rock Around the Clock" with Bill Haley, and "Little Darlin'" with the Diamonds, and "Johnny B. Goode" with Chuck Berry. Then a quick jog through the town of Petaluma, with Nick and Fats Domino singing a duet on "Blueberry Hill." Then out through the beautiful countryside lined with chicken and dairy farms, harmonizing with the Brothers Four and the Kingston Trio on "Greenfields" and "Tom Dooley."

"Hey, Nick . . ." Rich had a question for his brother. "What did you do with the money?"

"What money?"

"The money Mom gave you for singing lessons."

In truth, the question applied to all three of them. Just three rhythmically challenged white boys who couldn't carry a tune, but refused to let that discourage them in the least.

They made a quick stop at Bodega Bay to buy bait and ice at The Tides. Then it was on north through Jenner, where the road climbs the high cliffs overlooking the mouth of the Russian River. Finally they saw Ft. Ross in the distance and knew they were nearly there. Three hours crammed in the Sprite were more than enough.

It took several trips up and down the steep trail to get all their gear to the beach. They were pleased to find a perfect place to set up camp. The trunk of a great redwood tree had washed up on the beach in a storm and wound up high and dry about 50 feet from the high water line. It was a great place to stretch out the tarp and make a lean-to shelter.

Brent scooped out a fire pit in the sand, shaping it like a large light bulb. He stacked the socket end with rocks that he hauled from the hillside and then placed a wire rack across the stones. He set the heavy cast-iron skillet on top of the rack and declared it ready for cooking. It was a good camp.

It was nearing mid-day now. Rich brought out the cutting board and sliced cheddar cheese and dry salami to eat with crackers. They leaned back against the great redwood trunk and enjoyed their lunch, all the while admiring their handiwork. Then it was time to grab the fishing gear and head for that rocky point at the north end of the cove.

They huddled around the campfire, bundled up in their jackets, caps pulled down tightly, soaking up the warmth that radiated from the leaping flames. The night air was turning cold and damp, though the fog bank had stayed well offshore. Every few minutes, they'd toss a new hunk of wood on the fire from the large pile gathered from the hillside and the canyon. The stars hung thick across the night sky and Nick was amazed all over again at how many more there were to see when you were out away from civilization. The beer pulled from the ice in the old wooden cooler was very cold, so cold that it hurt your hand to hold the can. Rich passed around a pint bottle of whiskey and they each took a quick swig, then cooled the burn of the whiskey with the ice-cold beer.

It had been a good day in spite of the fact that the fishing was slow. When the wind came up strong in the afternoon, they packed in the fishing gear and headed back to camp. Brent and Rich headed back out with the rifle, looking for something to shoot. Nick stayed in camp to relax and read his dog-eared copy of *Cannery Row*, where Mack and the boys were about to embark on their epic frog hunt.

Around the fire now, the conversation turned to the important matters or life and love. Nick sat quietly, listening to his brother and Brent carry on. It was strange the way the three of them had come together as a unit in recent years. Before that, it had always been Nick and Brent with their friend Darin as the third musketeer. But Darin fell into a love affair with bowling and would eventually become one of the best bowlers in Vallejo. At least they always knew where to find him: down at the Miracle Bowl on Tennessee Street.

Rich was Nick's half brother, though he never thought of him in that way. When Nick's father died, Rich had stepped up to hold things together and look after Nick and their mother Lucille. He commuted to Vallejo most weekends from his home in Sacramento and Nick looked forward eagerly to his visits. Friday nights, after their dates or a school dance, Nick and his friends would gather back at the house for pizza and a game of cards that could last until 3:00 AM. Saturdays were given over to chores around the house and yard work, and Sundays were generally devoted to hours of tennis over at the high school courts. Lucille Shane always prepared a special Sunday dinner for her sons, and then came the saddest part of the week for Lucille and Nick, when Rich loaded up his car and headed back to Sacramento.

Of course, there were the weekends when they planned something special, like skiing in the Sierras, or camping and fishing at Lake Berryessa, or a trip to Stinson Beach to ogle the pretty girls. Through this time—Nick's high school years—the brothers grew closer than ever, with Rich somehow becoming a combination father, brother and best friend.

The conversation turned to Nick's wedding, the date now rapidly approaching. Rich, of course, would be Nick's best man, and Nick asked Brent and Darin to be groomsmen. Beyond that, they were amazed that Nick knew so little about the plans for his own wedding. He knew the date, the time and place, and he knew he had to rent a tux. After that, he was clueless. His fiancé and her mother were taking care of the rest of it, and Nick was eternally grateful.

Rich and Brent needled Nick a little about the impact marriage might have on his career as an outdoorsman. Through the dancing firelight, Brent saw Rich wink in his direction and then say, "So, Nick, I guess after you're married, you won't be able to come with us anymore."

It was quiet for several seconds while that statement sank in. Then Nick burst out with, "Hey, I can come with you guys!"

It was as though he had slowly come out of a trance, and it brought gales of laughter from Rich and Brent. The story was immediately filed away as a classic to be told over and over again. *Hey, I can come with you guys!* It became their favorite tag line. The pint bottle went around again and Rich led them in a discussion of *the best of the best.*

Rich: "Okay, here we go. Best beer?"

Brent: "Easy. Budweiser, the king of beers."

Nick: "No. It's Falstaff, the choicest product of the brewer's art." He was picturing Dizzy Dean and Buddy Blatner on *Major League Game of the Week.*

Rich: "Both wrong. It's Hamm's, the beer refreshing; from the land of sky blue waters." Rich always bought Hamm's because he liked the commercials. "New topic. All-time best ball team?"

Nick: "You mean besides the '27 Yankees?"

Rich: "It's got to be a team you saw play, either live or on TV."

Nick: "The 1954 Cleveland Indians. Al Rosen, Larry Doby, Bobby Avila, the Big Four—Lemon, Wynn, Garcia, and Bullet Bobby Feller."

Brent: "What did they ever win? How about my Yankee killers: the Milwaukee Braves. Warren Spahn, Lew Burdette, Eddie Mathews, Hammerin' Hank Aaron."

Rich: "Not bad. Correct answer is the Brooklyn Dodgers 'old gang.' Pee Wee, Robby, Campy, Newk, and The Duke.

Baseball history, my friends. Okay, all-time greatest player?"

Nick: "How 'bout George Herman Ruth?"

Brent: "I say Henry Louis Aaron."

Rich: "Don't forget Joseph Paul DiMaggio. And what about Jack Roosevelt Robinson?"

It was quiet for a few seconds.

Rich: Okay, we'll table that one. New subject. How about all-time best movie?"

Nick: "I got this one. It's *On the Waterfront*." He could see Brando picking up Eve Marie Saint's glove, putting it on his hand.

Brent: "All-time best? *Gone with the Wind*. No Question.

Rich: "Nice try, but it's *Casablanca*. In a class by itself. Okay, best movie line?"

Nick: "How about 'I coulda been a contenda.'" He gave it his best Brando impression.

Brent: "Gotta go with 'Frankly, my dear, I don't give a damn.'"

Rich: "Nope. It's 'You should see me serve the meatballs.' Jack Lemmon, *The Apartment*." He remembered Lemmon rinsing the spaghetti on his tennis racket.

And so it went, through politics and singers and bands and every topic Rich could muster. They let the fire burn low, until only a glowing bed of coals remained, and then it was time to spread their sleeping bags under the canvas and call it a night. Nick listened to the sound of the waves breaking on the sand with a steady rhythmic beat, every so often one louder than the rest. He counted to see if it was always the ninth wave that was louder, but he was asleep before he could find the pattern.

Nick woke to a cold, foggy morning and he was grateful for the tarp that kept them dry through the night. He stirred the coals in the fire pit and found that they were still alive. It was easy to get the fire blazing again. He shoveled hot coals under the wire rack along with some small pieces of wood, then went about scooping coffee into the basket of the small metal percolator. When the coffee was on the fire, he went to the cooler and pulled out a package of bacon and a carton of eggs. When Rich and Brent finally crawled out of their sleeping bags, the morning air was filled with the aroma of coffee and frying bacon. It would be a breakfast fit for kings.

With the breakfast mess cleaned up and the gear safely stowed away, they assessed the situation at the cove. The tide was out, too low for fishing from the north point. Brent and Rich decided to go shooting again and headed out for the south end of the beach. Nick stayed behind in camp. He kicked back again with *Cannery Row,* where frogs had become currency at Lee Chong's market. After a while, he looked up from the book and spied the hard rubber football sitting on the sand; an idea popped into his head and he grabbed the ball and trudged off toward the surf.

The waves were tall, six feet at least, driven by the storm passing to the north. Nick devised a game where he was the quarterback, calling plays, barking signals, then dropping back to pass, hitting one of his trusty receivers streaking downfield. He would fire the football into the face of a wave just before it broke and the ball would be washed back up onto the beach, ready for the next play. He barely had to get his feet wet. Now Nick had his team marching downfield, completing pass after pass: a quick out pattern to the right, then the same to the left sideline, then a short look-in to his tight end over the middle. Down the field they went, driving relentlessly. He dropped back to throw a deep slant to his wide receiver, but the ball sailed high over the wave and skipped out into the water beyond the surf line. Nick stood there with his shoulders slumped, watching the ball dance away into the waters of the cove. Then he heard shouts and laughter from the south end of the beach where Brent and Rich were watching and enjoying his dilemma.

"Shit!" he said out loud and sat down on the beach to plot his next move. *Old Man Johnson will be pissed, probably fire me,* he thought. Lyston Johnson was the long-time director of the GVRD and he was known as a stern taskmaster. If you checked out ten footballs for the season, you'd darn well better bring back ten footballs! Nick thought about it for a while and then made up his mind.

Nick removed his cap, emptied the contents of his pockets into the crown, and set it carefully on the sand, upside down. He headed down the beach, onto the wet sand and into the backwash of the surf. He picked out a wave and dove into the face just as it was about break onto the beach. Swimming hard, he came up on the other side of the breakers, gasping for air, shocked at how cold the water was. He sighted the ball bobbing in a trough between the waves and swam toward it. Nick had not counted on the undertow, but now he felt its steady pulsing hand pulling him down below the surface of the water. Never a strong swimmer, he realized now that he was tiring quickly. He turned over on his back, attempting to catch his breath and rest, but again there was that invisible hand pulling him under. Fear began to grip his mind and he realized he was in no man's land, too far from shore to turn back and yet still yards away from the ball. It occurred to Nick that he was going to die here in this beloved cove and he struggled to fight off the panic that tried to overtake him. He kicked hard and filled his lungs with air, then went below the surface and swam as hard as he could, breast stroking and kicking his legs in a powerful scissor motion. He burst to the surface again and felt something bump his head. It was the football. He grabbed it with both hands and tucked it under his chin. He rolled over onto his back, the ball keeping his head above the water, and rested for a few seconds. Then he turned his head toward shore and began to kick again, propelling his body back toward the beach. Finally, a breaker caught him and shoved him forward, dumping him like a water-soaked log onto the sand. He struggled to his feet, stumbled up the beach through the backwash and sat down hard on the sand next to his cap. He sat with his arms around his knees, staring out at the cove.

Rich came running briskly to the spot where Nick was sitting. "What the hell was that all about?" Nick could hear the alarm in his brother's voice.

"I had to get the ball . . . Old Man Johnson would kill me." Even as he said it, he knew how stupid it was.

Rich was quiet for a several seconds. "Yeah, that damn ball must be worth . . . what . . . ten, maybe twelve dollars at least." He waited again. "Are you okay?"

"I will be . . . in a minute."

"Well, come on and get some dry clothes on." Rich helped his brother to his feet and they headed back to camp.

Nick changed into dry jeans and a sweatshirt and then crawled into his sleeping bag. Slowly he felt the warmth return to his body. Outside the canvas shelter, Brent and Rich were preparing to head off to the point to fish one last time before it was time to leave for home. Nick said he would join them in a while. But first, he wanted to take a hike up the redwood canyon, something he made a point of doing on every trip to Timber Cove.

As Nick headed out of camp and into the canyon, he saw that the stream was very low, waiting for the fall rains to come. It was easy walking along the bank, picking out the tracks of all the creatures that used the creek as a lifeline—deer and raccoon, possum and skunk. The pattern of the stream was to tumble along over rocks and tree roots for fifty yards or so and then bend slightly to the left or right, never straying far from its east-west course. At each bend, there was a pile of logs and tree limbs and debris, washed down out of the canyon by storms from years past. The debris line reached far up the canyon wall and it was clear that when a great storm came, it would flush through this gorge with a mighty rush.

The light that filtered down through the trees gave a cathedral feeling to the canyon, as though it was a holy place. And so Nick was not surprised to round a bend and find God himself sitting on a log, cooling his feet in the crystal clear water. He sat down on the log and removed his shoes and sox to dangle his feet in the stream. Before he knew it, half an hour had passed. There was a lot to talk about. After all, it isn't every day that you look death in the face through eyes burning from cold salt water. As Nick dried his feet and prepared to leave, they agreed to talk more often in the future.

He headed downstream believing that something good had come of this day.

The hardest part of the weekend was hauling all the gear back up the cliff to the car. They weren't nearly as careful with their packing for the return trip, but they managed to get everything stuffed into the Sprite and settled in for the long drive home.

This trip went into their collective history to be called up and recounted again and again, especially Nick's cry of *Hey, I can come with you guys!* Nick observed that his family and friends were natural born storytellers, and the very best social gatherings were those that included new acquaintances, people who had never heard all the old tales. Those people were in for a treat as one by one, the classics were retold. But some stories are too personal to share, and so Nick never spoke of his adventure with the GVRD football, or his walk up the canyon.

Nick kept his date with the preacher, and then went to work for the Vallejo Street Department while he figured out his next move. Brent enlisted in the Air Force and headed off to Texas for basic training. Rich continued his career in state government while keeping a close eye on the homestead in Vallejo.

As they headed down Highway 1, too tired now to sing, they had no idea that this was their last trip together.

LEGACY

I t is amazing what you remember from your childhood, the scenes you can never erase from your memory. Nick could close his eyes and see his mother kneeling on the dining room floor, lacing up his father's work boots and tying them in neat double knots. His father's back hurt so bad that he couldn't bend down to tie them himself. Take a day off? Call in sick? That was out of the question.

"I'm a working man," his father would say.

That's all the explanation that was needed. He would drag himself off to catch the bus, that old beat-up lunch pail in hand. He was a boilermaker, a trade he learned in the Navy, and he was proud of the fact that he could work any two men into the ground. Nick would see him come home at night with his overalls covered in brick mud, and he knew he'd been crawling in and out of those tiny openings all day, replacing the fire brick in a boiler. He'd take off his dirty overalls out in the garage and make his way to the dining room table, and Nick's mom would help him take off his boots. Nick wanted to tell him to stop, that it was a young man's job and he should let a young man do it, but he knew what the answer would be.

"I'm a working man."

Nick could still hear his father's voice saying, "The only things a working man has going for him are his union and the Democratic Party." Cross a union picket line? Never! Vote for a Republican? You've got to be kidding! Once the bakery workers went on strike for two weeks and Nick's mom baked bread at home until the strike was over rather than buy non-union bread. He could still remember the smell of the fresh baked bread, and how it tasted warm from the oven with real butter.

Nick voted for Ronald Reagan once, but his hand shook as he punched the hole in the ballot with the little metal stylus. He'd take a sick day every now and then, but always with a sense of guilt, as though he'd let his father down in some fundamental way. More often than not, he'd shower and shave and go to work, no matter how rotten he felt.

Once he was faced with crossing a picket line. He stood on the corner in front of the office building for a long time and watched the pickets parading with their signs. Finally, he hurried past them and into the building, his eyes fixed on the pavement. Then he rushed to the first men's room he could find and threw up in the sink.

Funny, the things you carry with you from your childhood.

VALLEJO REVISITED

C an you go home again? With all due respect to Thomas Wolfe, sure you can. Just take the Georgia Street exit from I-80 and head east a few blocks.

The streets where you played touch football are very narrow and the houses that seemed roomy then look tiny now. The church your father helped build is still there at the corner of Georgia and Cedar. And across the street is the first school you attended with its formal rotunda that fronts the auditorium, the rotunda with Franklin Roosevelt's four freedoms emblazoned around the cornice: Freedom From Want, Freedom From Fear, Freedom Of Speech, Freedom Of Religion—just as you remembered. Some things never change.

Of course, there are many changes and they are obvious as you drive into Vallejo today, beginning with the major amusement park sprawled across the space once occupied by the Lake Chabot Golf Course. Upscale homes now dot the hills that surround the city, extending all the way to the water's edge at Glen Cove. Down from the hills and the gated communities, the flatlands appear to be somewhat long in the tooth, a little worse for wear. On the campus of Vallejo High, the stately two-story main building is gone, torn down over concerns about earthquake safety. In the downtown area, there is yet another attempt to rebuild and revitalize, and it looks like the effort has gained some traction. There is an attractive waterfront walk with a great view of the shipyard. And, the notorious Lower Georgia area is long gone, cleared out decades ago.

The biggest change, the one that will require generations to absorb, is the closing of the shipyard. The Navy decided in 1996 that Mare Island's usefulness had run its course. The decline had been underway for many years, but it's still hard to think of Vallejo and not think of the yard. Where will people work? How does a blue collar, lunch pail, Navy shipbuilding town transition to a bedroom community? How will kids know when it is time to head home without the five o'clock whistle? Now efforts are underway to "convert" the yard to private industry. Similar transitions around the country have met with mixed success. One can only hope that Mare Island will flourish in the private sector.

If you were born in the Naval Hospital at Mare Island and raised in this town, and your father and your uncle and your cousin worked there, as did the parents of most of your friends, then a walk along the waterfront can tug at your emotions. You look across the water and you are struck by the fact that it still looks like the great industrial complex it once was. It has that unmistakable profile, with the docks and the massive shops and cranes and smokestacks. But two things are clearly missing. First, there are no ships in sight on a cool fall evening, something unheard of in a history that reaches back to 1854. Second, and even more striking, is the dead quiet. Dead quiet where once there was the constant hum and clank and bang and hiss and rat-a-tat-tat that happens when you are in the business of turning steel into warships.

They say a memorial is planned for Mare Island and that is a good thing. People from all over should be able to come and learn about the history of the place. They should learn about the ships built there that helped win World War II, such as the destroyer USS *Ward*, or the battleship *California*. And what about the cruiser *Indianapolis*, repaired there before embarking on her final voyage, a mission that would change the course of history? And let's not forget the seventeen nuclear submarines that helped win the cold war, including the Polaris sub *Mariano G. Vallejo*, one of the famous "Forty-one for Freedom." It is a rich history and it should not be forgotten. As Casey Stengel liked to say: "You could look it up."

You *can* go home again, but only to visit. In the end, you feel like an outsider, one of those who left hoping for bigger and better things. And yet there is no changing the fact that this place is a part of you, probably a larger part than you realize. Someone once said, "You can take the boy out of Vallejo, but you can't take Vallejo out of the boy." She didn't mean it as a compliment, but that doesn't matter. It turns out she was right.

Acknowledgements

I have to thank the usual suspects who, for most of the past decade, have read, commented, corrected, cajoled, and encouraged these stories: first and foremost, my son **Matt Spooner**, part-time editor, head cheerleader, and curator of the Spooner archive; my trusted first readers **Tom Campbell** and **Carolyn Vecchio Brown**; **Carolyn** again for a stellar job as my *beta* reader; my sister-in-law **Linda Yassinger**, an avid reader; and of course, **Harry Diavatis** who published many of these stories in the *Monday Update*, his fine weekly newsletter.

Ten years ago, I confided to my best friend that I'd always wanted to be a writer. The response was, "So what's stopping you?" I realized I had no answer for that question. This collection of stories is the result.

A heart-felt *thank you* to all of the above for helping to make this book a reality.

Garrison Keillor once said, "You never finish writing anything. The day comes when the instructor takes it out of your hands to assign a grade and you console yourself by moving on to other things." I can picture Mrs. Nunn, my high school English teacher, glaring at me over her reading glasses and saying, "You are late, Mr. Spooner."

Oh well. Time to move on.